CARVE
A WITNESS TO
SHREDS

A Journals of Kate Cavanaugh Mystery

CATHIE JOHN

JOURNEYBOOK PRESS

Journals of Kate Cavanaugh:
CARVE A WITNESS TO SHREDS

JOURNEYBOOK PRESS
is an imprint of
CC Comics / CC Publishing
P.O. Box 542 Loveland, OH 45140-0542
(513) 248-4170
ccpub@worldnet.att.net

Logo designed by Steve Del Gardo

ISBN 0-9634183-6-X

First Edition 1999
10 9 8 7 6 5 4 3 2 1

Printed in the USA by

MORRIS PUBLISHING

3212 East Highway 30 • Kearney, NE 68847 • 1-800-650-7888

By Cathie John

JOURNALS OF KATE CAVANAUGH MYSTERIES:

ADD ONE DEAD CRITIC
BEAT A ROTTEN EGG TO THE PUNCH
CARVE A WITNESS TO SHREDS

AUTHORS' NOTE

Clairmont is an imaginary suburb comprising Indian Hill and parts of Clermont and Warren Counties on the northeast side of Cincinnati, Ohio.

The authors wish to thank:
Rick Combs, Chief Deputy Sheriff
of the Clermont County, Ohio Sheriff's office,
for his expert advice;
Jeff Hillard, Assistant Professor of English,
College of Mount St. Joseph, Cincinnati, Ohio
for his enthusiastic support and critical eye;
and Lorraine Gibbs
for her attention to detail.

. . . 'cause it's only the moment that lasts.

Bonnie Raitt

CARVE
A WITNESS TO
SHREDS

1

I'M AN OUTSIDER, but I don't look like one. Some people think I'm a rebel, but I've never been the in-your-face kind. No matter where my travels take me, I find most people have to compartmentalize the world in order to deal with it. They make it into a landscape of black and white, with a box for everyone and everyone in their box.

I hate being put in a box.

I feel this hatred so deep in my bones that I'm sure when I die the undertaker will have to battle my flailing arms and legs to shut me into my coffin.

Even so, I sometimes think I've put myself into one of

those suffocating little cubicles. Now that I have reached the mid-point in my life, I've been giving this some thought.

It seems a lot of people get a great sense of security from such neat, well-defined compartments. I suppose that's what they aspire to right from the beginning and then have no difficulty molding themselves, over the years, to fit. Then there are others who, upon reaching middle age, wake up one morning to the sudden realization, *This box is killing me.* They try to break out and the results are sometimes deadly.

Hell, I was almost murdered because of someone's mid-life crisis.

It all started that Monday morning when Charlotte Oakley visited me at Trail's End Farm.

Monday, August 16

2

"I WANT YOU to investigate Victor Lloyd."

I peered over my tea cup, not sure I'd heard Charlotte Oakley correctly. She perched in a tense posture on the edge of the overstuffed sofa in my sitting room. The grandfather clock in the foyer ticked softly.

"You want me to what?" I said, putting my cup back down on its saucer. Standing on the coffee table, next to the serving tray, was the antique brass elephant toy I'd brought back from India. He stared back at me. He'd been through a lot—one ear was missing and his wheels were kind of wonky—but his wide-eyed look seemed to say he was just as startled by Charlotte's request as I was.

Charlotte fingered her chunky, gold button earring and turned it back and forth. "I want to hire you to look into Victor Lloyd's background."

"You mean that developer? That Barnum and Bailey guy who's always doing some flamboyant stunt to announce his latest project?"

Charlotte tilted her head back, pushed her fingers into her streaked blond hair and swept it off her forehead. Each strand of hair seemed to know exactly where to land, like on those irritating models in the hair color ads.

With her chin still pointing at me, she said, "Yes. The same one you're reading about in *The Enquirer*—the one with all the big ideas for the Kentucky side of the river."

"Charlotte, I'm a caterer, not a—"

"I've heard rumors he's connected with gangsters." She pushed her words at me as though she'd trumped any reasons I could possibly have for refusing.

But I had other cards. "And what does this have to do with you?"

"It's my daughter Melissa. She's about to make the biggest mistake of her life. Last night she tells me she wants to marry Mr. Lloyd's son, Eric. You know we have to be careful who our children marry. It's not a simple matter of falling in love with someone. There are things to consider. Like reputation, character, background—"

That sounded like something my mother, Tink Cavanaugh, would say. Even though Charlotte was the same age as me, forty-three, she was talking in old Clairmont matriarch lingo. Kind of a Tink-in-training. I don't have kids of my own, but I understood where Charlotte's fears were coming from. At the same time, I felt sympathy for Melissa. After all, I knew first hand what it was like to be pressured by your mother into choosing the suitable box to cram yourself into. Come to think of it, that's probably one of the reasons I'm still single—I see marriage as a box.

I held my hand up to interrupt her. "I suggest you hire a

private investigator. I'm sure, if you ask around, someone can refer you to a reputable one."

Horrified, Charlotte almost choked on her tea. "I don't want anyone to know I need a private investigator." Her cup clattered in its saucer as she deposited it on the table in front of her. "And I don't want any seedy stranger in a rumpled trench coat slinking around with his camera knowing my family's business."

"You'd be hiring him or her—there are plenty of female investigators—to snoop into Victor Lloyd's background. Not yours."

"Snoop? Oh, that's a nasty word."

I said, "Sorry," got up and walked over to the little gaming table in the corner of the room where I kept decks of cards and pencils and paper.

"Anyway, they're professionals," I called back to Charlotte. "They wouldn't be able to stay in business if they weren't discreet and didn't adhere to a code of confidentiality. Keeping their mouths shut is part of the service."

I pulled a sheet of paper out of the drawer, jotted down a telephone number, and returned to stand in front of Charlotte. "This is my Uncle Cliff's office number. He's a lawyer and I'm sure he's had many occasions to use private investigators."

Charlotte stared up at me with a pained expression on her face. I realized two things. One, she didn't like the answer I was giving her. And two, her neck was craned at an uncomfortably severe angle, and if I didn't bring my six-foot-three-inch frame down to her level she was going to need a chiropractor.

I sat down and laid the piece of paper on the table in front of her.

Charlotte didn't touch it. "But just the idea of a stranger having personal knowledge—ooh—" She closed her mauve-tinted eyelids and shuddered. "It sends chills down my spine."

She leaned towards me, placing her delicate fingers with their mauve fingernails on my kitchen-beaten paws. "Besides,

13

I know I can trust you. And you did solve a couple of murders this past year. I'm just trying to insure my daughter's future happiness. I don't want to wake up one morning to find she's married to the mob."

"But I wasn't hired to solve those murders. I was pulled in by the circumstances. I mean, those were my friends who were accused of committing those crimes. Their lives were going to be destroyed. I had to help them."

Charlotte jerked her hand from mine and frowned slightly. She looked a little miffed. "Aren't I your friend?"

Uh oh.

"Why Kathleen Cavanaugh! I was practically your next door neighbor for eighteen years. We went all through school together. I've known you all my life—except for those few years you disappeared and never wrote to anybody. But still, I considered we were friends."

Damage control. "We are. But you're asking me to do something I don't think I have the training for."

"But you're already being called the Amazon Chili Heiress Detective and for years you've been catering all of Clairmont's important parties, listening to all the gossip and rumors—you know everything about everybody."

She leaned forward again. "More importantly, people trust you because you keep your mouth shut." Her heavy charm bracelet jangled as she tapped my knee. "I think you're eminently qualified to take on this job."

The reason I hear everything, know everything, and don't talk about it, is because I'm always just an observer at these parties and don't involve myself in the antics and intrigues of Clairmont blue blood society. Charlotte seemed to think that because I was born here and understood the rules, I was one of them. But I never was. Even as a kid, though I was included in the popular groups, I felt different from the others—partly because I physically towered over everybody, even the boys who called me Giraffe Face. But more than that, there was a rebellious voice inside me I couldn't shut up. It kept shouting, *This is not enough.*

Obviously, Charlotte had placed a big black mark beside Victor Lloyd's name because he was "not one of us."

I sighed. "I wouldn't know where to begin searching his background."

"Well, you could start by eavesdropping while you mingle at the party on his riverboat this Friday."

"How did you know I was invited?"

"Melissa told me. She said you, your mother, and your uncle," Charlotte looked down at the piece of paper on the table in front of her and picked it up. "Your Uncle Clifford would be representing Crown Chili. Melissa's . . . um . . . Eric Lloyd told her who was on the guest list. *She's* going to be there with *him*, of course." Charlotte slapped the innocent piece of paper back down on the table.

"Kate, Melissa's my baby. All of a sudden I'm being shut out of her life. She spends more time with that Lloyd family than she does with me and I don't even know who they are, what kind of people they come from. I've tried to get this Eric person to talk about his family tree, but he's been very evasive, mysterious. It's obviously something Eric doesn't want me to know about. The whole family makes me feel kind of edgy. They seem to be friendly and neighborly, acting like they're trying to be part of the community, but there's something phony about them—not like us.

"Ever since that family moved into Clairmont four years ago, people have been talking about them. So all I have to go on is rumor and whatever I've seen of them in public. The Lloyds have never invited me over or said more than a few words to me. If you've ever been to some function with them, you'd know Mrs. Lloyd, Tammy," she rolled her eyes, "is a drunk. So when Melissa told me she and Eric were talking about getting engaged officially, I—I just couldn't . . . it's too much . . . I'm at my wits' end."

Charlotte looked at me and nervously bit her lower lip. "But then, I had this brilliant idea: hire the most trustworthy person in Clairmont who also happens to be famous for digging up the truth. I will pay for your services you know.

15

Whatever the going rate is—whatever is fair."

"Charlotte, I have no idea—"

She stood up and tried to smooth the wrinkles from her linen dress. "At least think about it. Give it a few days. Call me tomorrow."

I walked her out through the foyer to the front door. "Charlotte, I'm not promising anything."

She turned to me before stepping outside. "Well, even if the answer's no, you could still do me an enormous favor when you attend that riverboat party. I'd appreciate it if you would at least keep an eye on my precious little girl."

"Okay, Charlotte. I'll get back to you as soon as I can." I leaned my head against the door jamb and watched her walk down the flagstone steps towards her car.

I was used to the people of Clairmont hiring me to help them celebrate their children's weddings—not prevent them from taking place. But over the past few months, an unhappiness had grabbed hold of me. I was getting tired of walking into my kitchen and trying to generate enthusiasm for that day's list of parties and the awaiting crowds of hungry mouths. Was it a case of career burnout? I don't know, but I couldn't even get psyched up for the big Casablanca theme party fast approaching on my catering schedule. When Charlotte first arrived that morning, I was steeling myself to drag out my book of menus and prices and cake designs.

At first, her plea for help caught me off guard. It had the surprising and unsettling effect of putting a finger on that very part of my life I was struggling with. I resisted what my gut was telling me. I know, in the past I said I had no intentions of changing my career from caterer to full-time private eye, no matter how many friends of mine became murder suspects. But as I'd sat listening to Charlotte, I'd realized my next meal might be my very own words. Not that I wished any ill will on Melissa Oakley or the Lloyds, but all of a sudden the idea of conducting an investigation appealed to me more than baking and decorating a wedding cake.

3

I WAVED GOODBYE TO Charlotte as she drove away in her latté-colored Jaguar convertible. So far, the morning had been pretty interesting, but I had to set aside any struggles over the pros and cons that Charlotte's request stirred up in me. Tony Zampella, my trusty assistant, was waiting for me in the commercial kitchen. It was time to go over the week's catering schedule.

I was ready for the work ahead, my long blond hair pulled back in a braid, and wearing my kitchen uniform of cotton drawstring pants, T-shirt, and leather clogs. Clomping through the foyer, I made a left down the small corridor and headed towards my commercial kitchen. Since my purchase of this old, white clapboard farm house I live in, it has gone through major renovations, including the addition of an entire wing. A full-sized commercial kitchen was installed so I could run my catering business and, just for fun, I added a personal gym which has kept me sane.

I entered the kitchen. In contrast to the cozy room where we ate our family meals—with its cheerful yellow walls, oak furniture, and pots of scented geraniums lining the sill of the bay window—the commercial kitchen was the kind of room you could hose down at the end of the day. All the counters, doors, and shelving were stainless steel. The tile floor was covered in places with black rubber mats. Aside from my little side-office, where I kept a computer and some of my cook books, the only non-washable items were the cork bulletin board and the telephone mounted on the wall.

At that time of the morning, the sun shone at an angle that hit the stainless steel counters and door to my walk-in refrigerator, threatening to blind anyone coming into the room. I grabbed an apron and went over to the windows to lower the blinds.

"Tony? You in here?" There was no answer. I went over to the door of the walk-in refrigerator and rattled its handle. "Hey, Tony. You in there?"

The door opened. Tony poked his head out and grinned, his face covered with its ever-present, two-day-old stubble. He was dressed in a new pair of baggy chef's pants printed with Day-Glo green and pink mushrooms. "Hey, Boss. 'Bout time you showed up.

"What're you doing?"

"Reorganizing. Oh, by the way," he quickly added, "better tell Robert the dishwasher's broken again."

"Okay. Be back in a few minutes. Nice pants."

I STEPPED THROUGH the back door of the kitchen, letting the screen door slam behind me. Immediately, the hot, sticky air that plagued the Cincinnati Tristate area every August engulfed me. I figured my handyman/dishwasher fixer, Robert Boone, was probably out in the work shed, and I followed the flagstone path around to the front of the house where it linked up with the laneway that encircled my front yard. The work shed was actually an old barn a couple hundred feet away from the house. I could hear the sounds of hammering coming from that direction, and as I started walking towards the barn, my thoughts returned to that morning's meeting with Charlotte Oakley.

I was uncertain about taking on Charlotte's request.

It was obvious Charlotte hoped there was something criminal in the Lloyd family background so she could wave it in front of Melissa's face and stop her from marrying Eric.

As everyone in Clairmont was ready to remind me, I did get involved in a couple of murder investigations, and I did manage to find out things that the police weren't able to discover. But I was pulled into those situations—I didn't set out to go snooping around in someone's life when, as far as I

18

could tell, they'd done nothing wrong and had no connection with me.

Mind you, I do like to peek under people's masks and see what's really there. Nasty or not, "snoop" might be the right word for it.

I could see why old guard Clairmonters were upset with the Lloyd family moving into their community. Sort of. There'd been complaints ever since they arrived four or five years ago. Victor Lloyd was a loud, overconfident man with a tacky sales pitch. To me, that behavior was a mask—just as the Clairmont blue bloods hid behind their attitudes of cool detachment. A Clairmonter is expected to look and act a certain way, regardless of what simmered underneath. There was something kind of tribal about all this. Charlotte Oakley might as well be saying to him, "You're strange! You're not wearing the proper mask. Go back to your own neck of the woods!"

Victor's neck of the woods used to be minor real estate developments—a strip mall here, an outlet mall there, some mid-priced housing. But then there was that project enabling Victor to make a big splash in the local real estate development scene. *That* was strange.

"Hi there, Kate." Robert Boone was waving at me from the open window of the barn. "Where you goin'?"

"To see you."

I stepped over my Welsh Terrier Boo-Kat, who was sleeping in the sun at the entrance to the barn, and walked inside. Robert stood at a work bench cluttered with rolls of chicken wire, lengths of two-by-four, and various pieces of mysterious hardware. He turned to look at me and pulled the headphone of a Walkman off one ear.

He said, "What's up?"

"Dishwasher's on the fritz again."

"Okay." Robert hung his hammer on the loop of his blue overalls. "Let me get my tool belt."

"No, it doesn't have to be right now. Just sometime in the next couple of hours." I looked at the contraption he was

19

putting together. "What's that?"

Robert's usually rounded shoulders straightened up and he puffed out his chest. "It's my ultra, deluxe, super-duper model critter catcher."

"Oh yeah? What kind of critter you aim to catch?"

"Well, you were busy early on this morning, so I didn't get a chance to tell you, but we got coyote problems."

"Coyote? How do you know?"

He pointed out the window. "I was walking way down over there at the far edge of the property. You know, along the creek. First, I see a rabbit carcass—guts eaten outta it."

My nose wrinkled at the thought.

"So I look around and, sure enough, I spot tracks. Coyote tracks. I know what they look like—seen 'em all the time around where I grew up."

"Oh great." I looked out at my dog snoring peacefully in the doorway. What would he do if he came face to face with a coyote? I had visions of snarling muzzles, huge fangs ripping at fur and muscle in a fight to the death. In the fifteen years I'd been living at Trail's End, this was the first time I had to deal with this kind of problem.

"So what exactly are you putting together, Robert?"

He shoved aside a pile of hinges and other bits of metal, and pointed at the old, yellowing page of an opened book on his work bench.

"See here?" With his finger he indicated a sketched plan for building a cage. "You put a hunk of raw meat inside at the back end. The critter walks in and slam! Gotcha!"

"Then what?"

He looked at me. "Gotta shoot it. Can't just let him go, he'll come right back."

My back muscles tightened. "Isn't there any other way? There must be some kind of county animal control person to take care of this."

"Yeah. I called him and he asked me if I had a gun. Said it was open season all year 'round on coyotes."

"So you could actually point a gun at a caged animal and

blow its brains out?"

Robert looked at me intently. "Kate, they're vicious stalkers. They go after pets," he nodded at mine, "and even though Boo-Kat's a tough little guy, he wouldn't win that fight."

I sighed and sat down on an old kitchen chair. "What a pile of poop." Until this invasion was stopped, I was going to have to make sure Boo-Kat didn't wander around the farm by himself. I'd have to keep him in sight all the time. He wasn't going to like that.

Robert laughed. I looked over in surprise. "What's so funny?"

He put his hand to the headphone covering one ear and listened for a few seconds. "Sorry, Kate," he said, finally. "Don't want to miss anything this guy says. He cracks me up."

"Did you find someone else on that station to listen to, now that Phoebe Jo's banned Dick Rottingham from the house?"

"Nope," Robert said, scratching his bony chin. "He's filling in for one of the other guys—doing a morning stint, plus his normal night time show for the next few weeks. Phoebe Jo is the sweetest thing, that's why I made her my wife, and you know I love her dearly, but sometimes . . ." He shook his head. "Too bad she heard him the night he had the strippers on. I thought it was funny, but she threw a fit and pulled the plug. I thought she was gonna toss the radio out the window."

"A lot of people agree with her. He *was* voted Cincinnati's Most Obnoxious Radio Personality."

"Well, sometimes Dick crosses the line." Robert pulled off his headphones and left them hanging around his neck. "But he doesn't just do stupid stuff. He interviews important people in the news."

Robert leaned towards the old portable radio on the back shelf of the work bench and flicked it on. "Take a listen."

The old radio crackled as he tried to get it to stay on the

station. Finally, a squawky, high-pitched voice broke through the fuzzy airwaves.

"*Dick Rottingham here. You know we like to bring fascinating people into the studio. People you want to hear from. Well, we got us a big one today. Been making headlines all week. A man with plans to pump excitement into the riverfront. A great American. Mister Victor Lloyd.*"

Surprised, I sat forward in my chair. Now this was interesting.

"*Happy to be here, Dick.*" Even through the poor radio reception Victor Lloyd's voice was forceful and confident.

"*Boy, you're hot this week, Victor. Everybody's talking about you. Six months ago, you announced plans for a two-pronged riverfront development on the Kentucky side of the Ohio River. You had financial backing, everything. Suddenly, Bang! Plans fall apart! The condos go belly-up! What happened?*"

"*As you know, Dick, these things never go the way you lay them out on paper. But that's half the fun. You switch some things around, drop others, and inject some new ideas.*"

"*You got to inject some new money, I guess. It's an expensive game you play.*"

"*Yeah, but you always have alternative moves. For instance, now is not the time for Phase One: Luxury Landing at Newport riverfront condominiums. But that doesn't mean it can't happen later on.*"

"*Well . . . I guess to play that game you gotta have your hands in a lot of deep pockets.*"

"*Yeah, it's a gamble, but this new plan I have is going to benefit everybody. It's exciting.*"

"*That's why we got you here, old boy. I want an exclusive. What's next?*"

"*I'm continuing with Phase Two—*"

"*Yeah, that's the big mystery, Victor. Nobody knows what Phase Two is. C'mon, spill the beans.*"

"*Well, Dick, I've invited all the top media people—of course that includes yourself—and the movers and shakers of* the *Cincinnati-Northern Kentucky business community to my riverboat party this Friday night. I'll be unveiling a model of the entertainment complex that will add flash and sparkle to the area's night life. Newport's a perfect spot for this."*

"Yeah, and Cincinnati City Council has been dragging its heels for years on the issue of how to develop the Ohio side of the river. You show 'em, Big Guy. I'm already excited about it and I don't even know the particulars."

"I'll just say this, Dick. We're going to bring Newport back to its glory days."

"Ohhh, you're aiming to step into a hot pile aren't you, Victor. There's a certain segment of the population here—great citizens, but a little tight around an intimate part of their anatomy—that wouldn't look upon Newport's hey day as particularly glorious."

I could guess what camp Charlotte Oakley was in on that issue, but I had no more than a vague understanding of Newport's past reputation. In my high school days, that's where some of the guys would go to see strip shows. But I didn't think that's what Victor and Dick were talking about.

I had to admit the idea of looking into Victor Lloyd's background was becoming more intriguing by the minute. Even if I didn't find anything scandalous, Melissa's marriage to Eric Lloyd was going to shake up her mother and the old order in Clairmont. There is a little devil inside of me who would find that amusing. But more importantly, there's a big part of me that always wants to cut through the rumors and suspicion, and get to the truth. I can't stand to watch people mess up each other's lives and make important decisions based on information that is no more than back-stabbing gossip.

"You're listening to 707 W-O-W. The Big WOW!!"

I was going to tune out the commercial break and say something to Robert, but the music for the ad held my attention. It was an instrumental version of the *Battle Hymn of the Republic* played in the same style I'd heard on PBS Civil War documentaries. Over this musical background, a deep-voiced announcer began advising listeners of their constitutional right to free speech.

The announcer continued, *"And with that right comes freedom to choose what you do in the privacy of your own home. Any citizen over the age of eighteen is welcome to assert that right at The Eros Dynamic Shop, where the best in erotic paraphernalia and literature is available. Remember, you must be eighteen and older. Open everyday. Downtown Cincinnati. Don't forget, every Tuesday night is Ladies' Night. Twenty percent off all toys and gift items."*

I had to admit it was shocking to hear an ad like that over the Cincinnati airwaves. The existence of that store was a source of major controversy in the city. I looked at Robert to see his reaction, but his face was expressionless. He kept his eyes focused on the task of hammering chicken wire around the frame of the coyote cage.

"You're tuned to The Big WOW! Dick Rottingham, here. We're back with Victor Lloyd, the Entrepreneur Extraordinaire who is going to bring Newport, Kentucky back to her glory days. Tell our listeners how you're going to do that."

"I'll just say this. People won't have to go all the way to Las Vegas to see a high-quality, flashy show with big name entertainers."

"This is amazing! This is exciting! This is the kind of vision that is needed around this town! Before we go to the phone lines—all of which are blinking their impatient lights at me—I want to know one very important piece of information about the acts you'll be booking. Will there be strippers? Big breasted women with huge headdresses and tassels?"

I could almost see the drool dribbling out of the radio's speaker. Over the past twenty years, Las Vegas has worked hard to change its image from being a mob-run, adult entertainment mecca to a Disneyfied destination full of awe-inspiring circus acts and mind-boggling magic shows. But like Dick Rottingham, I still envisioned girlie shows and snappy, well-dressed gangsters whenever I heard the name Las Vegas. I didn't know if Charlotte had any previous knowledge of Victor's plans for Phase Two, but her fears were sure to be reinforced once she heard reports of this morning's program. I was certain Charlotte was not a Dick Rottingham fan and would not have heard it firsthand.

My image of snappy, well-dressed gangsters comes from all those old black and white movies I watch—James Cagney and Humphrey Bogart shooting up speakeasies, throwing bodies out of fast-moving cars. Then there's the Marlon Brando-Godfather type able to build enormous, illegal business empires because he has the local politicians and police in his hip pocket.

Come to think of it, movies weren't the only source of my understanding of mob behavior. I'd witnessed it firsthand in Providence, the rough and tumble Rhode Island city where I went to culinary school. Turns out it was the Mafia headquarters for all of New England.

It seemed like every week, some suspicious fire would break out in a warehouse or abandoned building. It was obviously the work of professional arsonists. They even burned down the historic train station half-way through its multi-million dollar renovation. The motive for all those fires was to either collect the insurance money or to clear the land for someone else's pet project.

When I moved back home to Ohio, I left my cynicism behind, never considering those sorts of underworld shenanigans happened around good, clean Cincinnati.

But now that I thought of it, Charlotte's suspicions were fueling mine. One of my favorite restaurants used to sit on a huge plot of land. I didn't know its owners were having trouble with the landlord over extending their lease. One morning, I woke up to read in *The Enquirer* that it had burned to the ground in the middle of the night. It was that mishap that enabled Victor Lloyd to make his big splash erecting *Le Galleria*, a shopping heaven for the rich and trendy.

Did Mr. Entrepreneur Extraordinaire have anything to do with turning that restaurant into toast?

* * * * * * * * * *

"TONY? I'M BACK."

No answer.

I heard a thud coming from inside the walk-in and was about to go and see what he was up to, when my attention was caught by a half-page newspaper clipping pinned to the bulletin board.

"What's that?" I walked across the kitchen to check it out. Half of the clipping was taken up by a color photo of a grinning Clairmont Ranger in his Smokey Bear hat posed beside his trusty horse. The headline announced, *Clairmont Rangers Judged 'Best Dressed'*.

I looked back at the photo and studied the smug face of Matt Skinner. Then I read the subheading, *Snappy uniform exudes authority*. The article went on to say that the Clairmont Rangers had been honored as the "Best Dressed Police Department" in the country by a uniform manufacturer.

I ripped the sheet of newsprint off the board and crumpled it into a ball. "Nothing but a catalog boy," I said and hurled it into the recycling bin.

I'd encountered Ranger Skinner a few times over the past nine months. There were days I thought he liked me, followed by weeks when it seemed everything I did irritated him to death. I'll admit I indulged in some fantasies about him and even thought there was a real possibility of something romantic happening between us. But when I saw him the last time with another woman, who was a totally different type from me, I had to face the fact that whatever sparks I thought I saw between us were probably nothing more than static electricity.

Worse than that was the fact Skinner couldn't admit I'd done a damn good job in solving two murder cases and, instead, told me to keep my nose out of his business. But I wasn't the type to stand by and do nothing when I could see he was going after the wrong guy. And, dammit, no man was going to tell me directly or by inference to *just stay in the kitchen*.

I stomped over to the walk-in and yanked open the door. Tony was standing on the top of a small stepladder, his sleeves rolled up over his muscular arms. He slid a case of mayonnaise jars effortlessly along the length of the top shelf. Boxes of butter, plastic tubs of Moroccan and Greek olives, blocks of cream cheese, and other miscellaneous perishables had been pulled off the shelves and stacked on the floor.

"Okay, Tony, what's the point? Was I supposed to admire that newspaper photo you pinned up, or throw darts at it?"

Tony turned and looked over his shoulder at me. "You've been in a real funk, lately. I thought gazing at that sexy face might jump start your battery."

I stepped inside and shut the door behind me. "Pay attention, I'm only going to say this once. Forget about him. Now, what are you doing up there?"

Tony climbed down from the stepladder and started gathering up blocks of butter. "Well, I looked on the board and there was no job sheet for today."

"Oh," I slapped my forehead, "I forgot to print it off the computer."

"I had to find something to do while you were busy drinking tea and yakking away in your sitting room."

"You make it sound like I was goofing off," I said, hand on hip. "It was a meeting. I was working."

"Okay, okay. Like I was saying, I wanted to make myself useful, so I started out there. Scrubbed down the stove, polished all the stainless steel, and then poked my head in here to see what needed to be done. That's when I got the brilliant idea to reorganize, make sense of this place."

I looked around at the steel shelving packed with food items in various stages of preparation. "It doesn't make sense?"

Tony shook his head. "Every time I need an ingredient, I come in here and freeze my buns off trying to find it, so I'm rearranging everything according to their food group. Let me show ya. Over there I have—"

This is dumb. Tony was capable of running the whole show by himself, and I'd set things up in a way that wasted his time, talent, and all that energy. I used to have the energy and enthusiasm he has. But lately, it wasn't there. The fact I'd forgotten to print out the job sheet was just another one in a recent string of minor slip-ups that was a warning to me that I was losing interest in my own business. *Danger! Danger!* 'Round the World Catering was getting busier all the time, but none of it challenged me anymore. I'd always figured Tony would eventually take on the day-to-day operations and I would supervise. Maybe now was the time to hire an assistant to help *him*. I didn't want Tony to feel unchallenged and go off looking for something else. He'd be snapped up in a minute. I didn't want to lose him.

One of the things Dad taught me was to always have a five year plan. I'd reached the goal of the last plan I drew up—running a successful catering business. But then, for some reason, I stopped making plans. Now, the only thing I could see in my future was coming into this kitchen doing the same old thing day after day, or sitting on the board of Crown Chili, my family's little empire of fifty-two chili parlors. It's not that I wasn't proud of what my Dad and his father had accomplished with that simple chili recipe, it just wasn't *my* accomplishment. If I wasn't careful, I was going to wake up one morning smack-dab in the middle of a full-blown, mid-life crisis. Now I could see how important Dad's advice was.

I can't be like my friend Cherry Jublanski, who's very happy to jump on her Harley and take off down the highway with no destination in sight. Nor am I like my other friend, Jasmine Woods, who never seems to learn from her mistakes and keeps running on the same loop over and over again. I wasn't really surprised when Jaz called and told me she met another guy and wouldn't be coming back to stay with me like we'd planned during her traumatic visit a few months ago.

"Hey, Boss? You still on planet Earth?"

I don't know how long I was gone, but the floor of the walk-in had been cleared and all the items were back on the shelves, supposedly in their new and improved order.

Tony was waving his hands in front of my face. "So what was the big meeting about? We got another wedding like you thought?"

"No. There's no job. Turns out it was a personal matter, but that's okay, we don't need any more work."

I pushed open the heavy walk-in door. "Let me write out what needs to be done today."

"It's a happy day for me," Tony said as we made our way over to the desk in one corner of the kitchen.

"Oh, yeah? Why's that?" I grabbed a sheet of paper and began writing.

"I remember Mrs. Schinkelberg called Friday, so I know we're gonna do one of those lowfat cocktail party jobs you had the great wisdom to add to our repertoire. I get to carve teeny-tiny boats outta cucumbers, fill them with plastic cheese, and try to stuff snow peas with God-knows-what without breaking them. I don't understand why they're so popular. Stuff doesn't taste like anything. You ever read the ingredients lists? The stuff's toxic!"

I rolled up the lowfat menu and swatted him on the head with it. "That's enough! Here! Get to work! Make their mouths water!"

Tony looked at his assignment, his tongue planted firmly in his cheek. Holding the menu out at arm's length, he cleared his throat and in a warbly, high-pitched voice said, "Tuna Watercress Pinwheels. Lettuce Shrimp Rolls. Banana Strawberry Kebabs with Mango Honey Dip. Yummy."

Behind Tony's joking, it was obvious he couldn't get excited about the job. I realized I'd better take the first step on my new five year plan. "Next week we're doing that Casablanca theme party. How would you like to be in charge?"

Tony did an impression of playing Statues. Actually, he reminded me of those goofy-looking male store mannequins as he stared up at me, his grin frozen in place.

It was my turn to ask, "Hello? Who's left planet Earth now?"

29

He blinked and shook his head. "What's the matter, Boss? You sick? You going away?"

"Just want to give you a chance to run the show for one night." I wasn't ready to reveal my master plan to him. Not yet.

Tony yipped with excitement, jumped in the air, and gave me a hug. He almost kissed me, changed his mind at the last split second and pulled away. I thought it was an over-reaction myself, but then Tony's one of those excitable Mediterranean types. At least I got the impression my plan had a chance of succeeding.

Tony's words came at me in a rush. "I won't let you down, Boss. You won't be sorry." He spun on his heels and started off to his work station to prepare his lowfat menu. He stopped halfway across the kitchen. "Uh, Kate? You're going to give me the recipes, right? Or do you want me to go through your travel diaries and pick them out myself."

Not on your life, I thought. "*I'll* give you the recipes."

Just then, the telephone rang. I answered it on the third ring, "'Round the World Catering. Kate speaking."

"Kathleen—" It was Mother. "I'm calling a meeting. We have to discuss this Victor Lloyd business!"

Tuesday, August 17

4

"I DON'T WANT TO GO. I'm against the whole idea." Mother paced up and down in front of the floor-to-ceiling windows in the board room of the downtown Cincinnati offices of Clifford T. Vasherhann, Attorney-at-Law.

Uncle Cliff and I sat in leather chairs at the highly polished mahogany table and watched her make a little trail of spike-heel holes in the eggplant-purple carpeting. It was a meeting of the board of directors of Crown Chili, and all three of us were present.

I had struggled to find something to wear that morning that was both business-like and flimsy. I wasn't used to being in the middle of all that steel and concrete, and the temperature was going to reach the mid-nineties. Naturally, the air conditioning in Uncle Cliff's office was turned up to arctic so there I sat, shivering, with his jacket wrapped around my bare shoulders.

"And I don't think we should even be associated with Victor Lloyd." Mother stopped and glared at us. "I just don't trust that distasteful man."

My uncle leaned back against his chair, snapped one of his red paisley suspenders, and swiveled from side to side. "There's no harm in going to hear what he has to say, Tink. At least we can do that."

"Little Brother, dear, you don't understand. I don't even want to be *seen* boarding his rattletrap riverboat."

I sat forward and leaned my elbows on the table. "It's hardly a rattletrap, Mother. He's just finished spending hundreds of thousands of dollars to refurbish that paddle wheeler. Supposedly, it's quite glamorous inside."

"I don't care what it looks like."

Uncle Cliff groaned and looked up at the ceiling. He twisted the uncooperative tips of his newly-grown moustache, trying to train them into handlebars. "Everybody else with any stature in this business community is going to be there. You don't want Crown Chili to be left behind."

Mother *hmphed*. "Crown Chili stands for honest, wholesome family values and we do not belong in some sleazy adult entertainment center."

"Mother, it was Dick Rottingham who talked about strippers. Victor Lloyd said it was going to be top-name entertainment."

"Las Vegas style," Mother quickly interjected.

"You have an outdated notion of what Las Vegas style means," I said.

Uncle Cliff waved his hand. "There's no sense sitting here and arguing about what Victor may or may not do. I say we go to the party and find out."

Mother clamped her lips tight.

Uncle Cliff continued. "Things are hopping in Northern Kentucky. Newport's built that huge aquarium and has plans for a 3-D Imax theater. And, of course, there's that Millennium Monument World Peace Bell—the largest free-swinging ding-dong on the face of the earth. Look, if we ignore what could turn out to be one of the more successful developments in the area, we might as well lie down and let the competition roll over us. I can tell you there are several ambitious chili franchises who are not giving wholesome, family values two seconds of thought. They're just looking at the bottom line."

Uncle Cliff frowned at Mother. "Tink, we've been stalled at fifty-two parlors for years. We've got to think about growing, or Crown Chili's territory could start shrinking."

Mother turned, crossed her arms in her I-don't-care-what-you-say-I'm-right posture, and looked out the window. I doubted the sweeping view of downtown Cincinnati and the Ohio River registered in her brain at that moment.

I gave Uncle Cliff's leg a playful kick. "I thought this was going to be a lunch meeting. Where's the food?"

"Oh, yeah. You're always thinking about food, aren't you, K.C?" He swung around to the phone behind him, punched an intercom button, and shouted into the speaker, "Where's Jeff? I sent him down to the food court to get us some chili. Did he get lost?"

"Uncle Cliff? You're giving us Crown Chili for lunch? I thought a man with your style would have served us some trendy North African takeout from Café Maroc."

He shot me a look of mock indignation over his shoulder. "Shame on you, K.C. You should be eating your own family's product once in a while just to make sure it's good enough to have your name on it."

"That's just my point, Clifford, dear." Mother's words bounced back at us off the window she was still staring out of. "We need to be concerned with what we attach our name to."

"Which is why you are going with me and K.C. to Victor's party Friday night."

33

I walked over to Mother and stood beside her. The top of her head with its helmet of stiff, silvery hair barely reached my shoulder.

"Mother, just going to the party doesn't commit us to anything. There are lots of others going who probably feel the same way you do about Victor Lloyd. Like it or not, he's going to have a major impact on the region. We also need to see firsthand how the other business leaders react to his plans."

She didn't respond. I stayed quiet and looked out the window. It was a magnificent view if you ignored the construction upheaval along Fort Washington Way, the major artery through downtown Cincinnati that had been almost completely shut down for repairs.

I let my gaze travel across and upriver towards Newport, Kentucky. I watched a barge round the bend and chug past Victor Lloyd's docked riverboat.

"Mother? What's this about Newport's glory days? Dick Rottingham mentioned something about that in the interview, yesterday."

She gave me a sideways glance. "No one *I* know thinks those days were glorious."

"Ha!" Uncle Cliff slapped the table. "You're so naive, Tink. They just kept their mouths shut."

"About what?" Now I was really curious.

Mother straightened the scarf she had around her neck and pinned to one shoulder of her tailored gray business suit. "You were just a baby back then and wouldn't remember what it was like, but in the fifties, Newport was a lawless, sinful town. Gambling casinos were everywhere. In fact, it had been like that for a long time. I think it started back in the 1920s. Slot machines were in almost every drugstore, grocery store, and candy shop."

"You could even lose your shirt at the dry cleaners," Uncle Cliff added.

I laughed.

Mother looked at me, one eyebrow raised. "He's not

kidding. That really happened. But the worst of it was the other dirty, illegal activities that go along with that kind of lifestyle."

Uncle Cliff said, "Tink, every city has its share of brothels."

"But it was so *blatant*. And on top of that," she jabbed her finger at Newport, "the mayor, city manager, police chief—almost *every*body in that town was taking bribes from the casino operators. Their hands were so deep into the cookie jar, they were virtually part-owners themselves!"

Wednesday, August 18
6:30 AM

5

A MORNING MEDITATIVE RAMBLE along the wooded banks of the creek that ran through the back edge of my property is normally an enjoyable way to start my day. But now that Robert had spotted the coyote and declared war, Boo-Kat and I were struggling with the accompanying restrictions. He pulled incessantly on the six-foot leather leash that connected him to my wrist. I couldn't let him out of my sight to wander the farm alone, and he kept giving me pained looks that said, *What the hell's going on?*

Added to that frustration was the obvious fact he was picking up the enticing new smells of the invader, and was desperately trying to free himself so he could tear off into the woods after it.

As we walked, I imagined the cold, soulless eyes of a stalker peering out from behind every bush and tree, just waiting for the chance to sink its teeth into my furry little pet and drag it away to some bone-strewn lair.

Sometimes my own imagination spooks me. I felt extremely uncomfortable and decided to head for a trail that would take me back to the farmhouse, and cut short my usual route.

Tramping through some brush, my thoughts turned to what I'd learned yesterday from Mother and Uncle Cliff about Newport's "glory days".

Mother ranted on about the twenty-four-hour-a-day availability of hookers. There were houses of prostitution catering to daytime clientele and houses that opened up only for the night trade. Uncle Cliff entertained me with tales of 1920s Newport when gangsters strolled down the streets carrying machine guns in plan view and people went for a deadly dunk in the Ohio River wearing a "Newport nightgown" made of concrete.

In the forties and fifties, the Cleveland mob helped make Newport the Midwesterner's Las Vegas by running high-class operations and booking top drawer entertainers. Frank Sinatra and Pearl Bailey appeared in the dining rooms of casinos like The Oasis. And every now and then, feuds broke out between rival gangsters, ending in blood baths.

I guess from a business point of view, I could understand Mother's concern about sleazy operations coming back into the area. Cincinnati had kicked out all the porn shops and strip shows from its downtown. Now the city was a target for people like the owner of the Eros Dynamic Shop, who had found a way around that earlier court order and moved back in to challenge the community's standards.

In the radio interview, Victor Lloyd had said he was bringing Las Vegas to Newport. Surely, he didn't mean in the old style with gangsters and strippers. But with Dick

Rottingham talking about "glory days" and Charlotte Oakley's rumors of underworld connections, I had to admit the scenario was getting darker. But, so far, that's all it was—talk and rumors. I guess I'd have to wait until Friday's riverboat party to hear for myself what he had planned. Guess I was going to accept Charlotte's offer, too. It was just getting too damned interesting.

A pile of cut branches caught my attention. I could see a glint of metal through the leaves and, as we got closer, I recognized Robert's ultra *dee-luxe* critter catcher.

"No!" I yanked Boo-Kat away from the opening.

He snarled and dug his little paws into the ground, refusing to turn away from the irresistible smell of the rotting meat Robert had placed in the cage.

I gave the leash another quick yank. Boo-Kat's head snapped around. His eyes had a crazed, unfocused look—hard black pupils bulging out of balls of white. His upper lip curled back, baring his fangs, showing me pink and black gums.

"Bad dog! Down! Stay!" I couldn't let him get away with that. I had to immediately assert my dominance as Alpha Dog. I growled. Really.

Boo-Kat's snarling lessened, until he finally lowered himself onto his belly and assumed a quiet, submissive position. Though back now to being my furry little pet, Boo-Kat had given me a glimpse of the aggressive predator that only his prey saw when he was on solo patrol around the farm. It was disconcerting to think that in his eyes, during that uncontrolled moment, *I* might have been his prey.

But why was I surprised? I'd learned the hard way that all creatures, great and small—human or animal—have a hidden predatory side.

Friday, August 20
5:30 PM

6

"AFTER ALL HIS TALK, that insufferable little brother of mine—*your* Uncle Cliff—poops out on us."

I fanned myself with the boarding tickets to Victor Lloyd's riverboat party and turned to look at Mother. She was just adding to the discomfort of the eighty-seven degree evening air with her temper at a constant boil.

"Mother, let it go. You started this when we left Clairmont forty minutes ago, and you nattered in my ear all the way down the 71 and across the river. I'm hot and irritated, but here we are and I'm determined to have a good time." I was also determined to find out as much as I could about our host.

Shortly after Wednesday morning's walk with Boo-Kat, I telephoned Charlotte and confirmed that I would take her on as a client. Relieved, she quickly offered to pay me whatever I asked for. I faxed her a list of my favorite local charities and told her, when I came up with my final bill, to donate that amount to one of them.

I was starting to feel excited about the mission I'd accepted as we joined the line of a dozen or so people still waiting to board the *Queen of Newport*. It was a grand stern-wheeler, newly painted—all spanking white with fire engine red railings and paddle wheel. All three decks, their railings draped with red, white, and blue bunting, were loaded with a couple of hundred people already drinking and schmoozing. Flags lined the open top deck. Two black smokestacks with golden crowns belched out puffs of white steam.

As we moved along the line towards the gang plank, Mother brushed at the sleeve of her navy blue blazer and patted needlessly at her stiff, silver hairdo, which not even a tornado could muss up. The blazer was a double breasted, gold braided, gold buttoned number that she wore with a white, knife-pleated skirt and blue and white high-heeled shoes whenever she went on board a boat of any kind. I like to call it her Cap'n Crunch outfit.

I could never understand how Mother could wear so many layers of clothing and look so cold. As for me, I'm hormonally challenged thanks to the chemotherapy given to me when I had breast cancer almost seven years ago and the estrogen-blocking drugs I've had to take ever since. It doesn't matter what I wear, I'm always uncomfortable—either overheated or freezing to death. Of course, my attire was one of the topics of Mother's earlier rantings. But I didn't see anything wrong with the gauzy, sleeveless cotton dress I was wearing. It covered my knees and had a white cotton paisley print embroidered strategically over the areas you didn't want people to see through.

Mother said I looked too sexy. "And the kind of men

42

hanging around with Victor Lloyd will probably think you're just *asking* for trouble."

I can't win.

"I still can't believe it, Kathleen. Clifford was so insistent that we all come here, even though he knew how much I didn't want to. I don't understand him. How could he abandon us at the last minute?"

The line was barely moving. There were at least a dozen people ahead of us waiting to be allowed on board.

I said, "Oh, stop it. It was an emergency and you know it. How would *you* like to be arrested and brought in for questioning by the police, only to be told by your lawyer, 'Sorry, I can't help you. I promised to take my sister and niece to a party.'"

Mother pursed her lips, craned her neck and turned her attention to the front of the line. "Oh, look, darling. There's Ted Mueller."

I looked over the line of heads in front of me and directly into the eyes of the six-foot-two local football hero-turned-developer. Ted smiled and winked at me. Thirty years ago, after his pro career as a quarterback was cut short, Ted "The Head" Mueller discovered the real estate business was the perfect new arena in which to show off his talents. He took his almost psychic ability to read football defenses and call the right plays and created Touchdown Enterprises. *The Wall Street Journal* marveled at Ted's ability to make legal end runs around the objections of residents to get his projects okayed by the political powers-that-be.

Mother continued. "I guess Ted's got to keep track of the competition." She looked at me out of the corner of her eye. "You know he's got his own plans for an entertainment complex on the Cincinnati side of the river."

"Yeah, I know. But they might just stay on Ted's drawing board if Victor gets his built first."

I imagined it must have been infuriating for him to watch Victor get a foothold in Newport while Cincinnati's political leaders squabbled over how to develop its riverfront. I looked across the river at Cincinnati's stalled skyline and could almost see the dust settling on her buildings.

A loud blast from the *Queen of Newport's* whistle made both Mother and me jump. It was followed by a few more syncopated blasts—some kind of riverboat language. The steam calliope broke into a chorus of *Waitin' For The Robert E. Lee,* its chirpy melody adding to the festive atmosphere.

The line moved forward. A few more stragglers came running up and got behind us. I was close enough to see Victor Lloyd and his wife Tammy greet each guest as they boarded. Victor had a pencil-thin moustache and was dressed up to look like a riverboat gambler in a gray cutaway jacket, black ribbon tie, and white panama hat. Standing beside him, cooling herself with a large lacy fan, was his always smiling but slightly bleary-eyed wife, Tammy. She must have been hotter than I was, because she was wearing ten yards of royal blue hoop-skirted taffeta. They looked like Rhett Butler and a bleached blond Scarlet.

Just then, my back went up. Alan Casey, a local photographer, was posing each group of guests with the Lloyds and taking their picture. It wasn't the idea of my picture being taken that made me react like that. It was Alan. The last time I had any dealings with him, I was throwing him out of a client's house and saying, "I'll never hire you again."

I rarely have problems with people I hire to help me with my catering jobs. Most people don't need to be told they shouldn't wander around the private areas of someone's house. So, when I found Alan in the upstairs master bedroom of one of Mother's best friends, snooping in her closet, I saw red and fired him on the spot. God knows I'm not a prude, and I don't care if he gets his jollies fondling some poor old lady's bathrobe, but the jerk had specifically been told to stay on the main floor of the house. He didn't, so he's off my list. I haven't gone out of my way to black ball him, but whenever I'm asked, I say, "Don't use him."

My thoughts were interrupted by the irritated voice of the man standing in front of me.

"You mean you can't fit *one* more person on that big boat?"

I looked down to see who was having the problem. He was a "suit", one of those gray insurance salesman types. Somewhat short and dumpy, he was visibly straining to appear taller and more intimidating to the little red headed sailor girl who was taking boarding passes and checking off names on her clipboard.

Sailor Girl wasn't budging. "I've been given specific instructions not to allow anyone on board whose name is not on my list. Everyone has to have a boarding pass."

The Gray Man shoved two tickets at her. "Here! These are for my wife and I. This is my daughter. She's just come home on an unexpected furlough. See? She didn't have time to change out of her uniform, so there certainly wasn't enough time to arrange for an additional boarding pass."

I looked. The daughter was standing at attention in her khaki Marine uniform. She wore her black hair military style—blunt cut, just hitting the sharp edge of her jaw. Her hat, its shiny black visor pulled down, shaded her eyes so they were half hidden. Ms. Marine appeared fit enough to handle a half dozen little Sailor Girls in a cat fight with one hand tied behind her back.

Sailor Girl shook her head. "I'm sorry, Mr. Sims—"

"I can't accept that," Mr. Sims replied. "This is utterly ridiculous! I—I—" He coughed violently a couple of times.

The Wife, as unremarkable in appearance as her husband, placed a hand on his arm. "Donald, let's go home."

"No!" Donald loosened his tie as he coughed again. Fist to mouth, he hung his head, stared down at the ground and swallowed a few times.

The Marine twisted her head around to look at her father. Almost immediately, she shot a look at Sailor Girl.

I could only see the back of the Marine's head, but it must've been a hell of a look—Sailor Girl withered in its glare and backed away, clutching her clipboard to her chest. "I—I'll go ask Mr. Lloyd."

45

This was getting painful to watch. I figured I could save everyone a lot of angst by stepping in.

"Wait," I said to Sailor Girl, "we're the Cavanaughs. One of our party couldn't make it today, so we'd be happy to give up our extra spot."

Mother immediately chimed in. "Yes. Yes, indeed."

Sailor Girl looked at me, down at her list, then back to all five of us. "I—I have to . . . I'll be right back."

She made her way around the other party waiting to go on board, and quickly crossed the gangplank. I couldn't hear what she said to Victor Lloyd, but he looked down towards us, squinted, then, recognizing the Sims Family, Mother, and me, touched the brim of his panama hat in a one-fingered salute.

Sailor Girl came back down the gangplank, nodding her head. "Okay. Please wait until the party in front of you has been greeted and photographed before you go on board."

Donald Sims turned around and held his hand out towards me. His gray complexion was still a little mottled with patches of red. "Thank you, it's most generous of you. I'm Donald Sims. This is my wife Gloria and my daughter Janie."

Gloria Sims focused her attention on Mother. "It's been a very stressful day, and we thank you for your help."

Janie lifted her chin up at me, revealing her visor-shaded eyes. I was surprised to see they were a soft gray and friendly. But I wasn't surprised by her powerful grip when she shook my hand. "Thank you, Ma'am." Very military.

Sailor Girl shepherded the Sims up the gangplank.

"What a nice family," Mother said.

I grunted so she knew I was paying attention to her, but I was more interested in watching the little dance the Sims and Lloyds did up on deck with Alan Casey unsuccessfully trying to control the choreography. It appeared Victor didn't want to stand beside Donald. Janie was finally used as a buffer between those two. They all smiled through gritted teeth, the picture was quickly taken, and then it was our turn.

Mother and I pasted on our matching Cavanaugh smiles and proceeded up the gangplank.

Victor doffed his panama and greeted us with a sweeping bow. "Welcome aboard. It's a great honor to finally meet y'all." He looked up at me. "Why those fuzzy newspaper photos don't do you justice."

That wasn't much of a stretch—I'd always believed since childhood every camera lens was focused to make me look like the Wicked Witch.

"Isn't she striking, Tammy?" Victor turned to his wife, whose head was nodding from side to side.

Tammy smiled, happy in her own little world. Up close, this Scarlet was no Dixie Peach—she had the hard look of a used up dance hall girl. Then I realized her whole body was listing from side to side. But the Ohio River was calm and everyone else was standing solidly in place. I figured her hoop skirt was probably the only thing keeping her from hitting the deck.

"Mrs. Cavanaugh," Victor said, looking directly at Mother, "I've long admired the way you run Crown Chili. It's no secret I want you to be part of my team as we bring excitement back to Newport."

I saw the major vein in Mother's neck begin to throb, so I grabbed her arm and squeezed it. She kept her smile aimed at Victor and gave my hand a little pat—her way of saying, *I know, I know*—and replied, "My daughter and I have a great interest in making sure certain standards are kept up."

"My thoughts exactly! By the end of this evening, you'll be just as excited as I am." Victor swept his hat towards the muddy waters of the Ohio. "There's a second golden age for Newport just coming down that river." He held that pose a little longer than was natural, then looked over his shoulder. "Where's that damn photographer?"

I guess Alan Casey was supposed to be documenting the entire evening. Instead, like he'd done the last time I hired him, Alan had gone wandering. I spotted him just inside the enclosed lower deck trying to chat up Janie, who had pulled the visor of her hat further down over her eyes and was strolling away as though he wasn't there.

47

Victor shouted, "Casey! Get over here . . . please."

Alan avoided looking at me as he directed us to our places around Tammy. They'd probably found out early on it was best not to move her. We smiled. Alan snapped.

Victor reached over to a table piled high with small, colorfully wrapped boxes and picked up two of them. Handing one to Mother and one to me, he said, "Enjoy yourselves. I guarantee this evening will be full of surprises."

We headed towards the crowd of people mingling around the open bar. Mother held her wrapped gift gingerly, as though it was Pandora's box stuffed with every evil in creation. She stretched up and muttered in my ear, "I don't feel good about this."

7

I THOUGHT ABOUT MOTHER'S REACTION. Usually, I have gut reactions to the situations I'm in, but at that moment I wasn't feeling anything one way or the other.

I held my wrapped box up to my ear, shook it, and heard a muffled jingling. I asked, "What do you think's inside?"

"I'm afraid to find out." Mother held the box in front of her and wrinkled her nose at it. "Something will probably jump out at me."

"Go on, Mom. Open yours first."

"Oh, Kathleen, stop playing with me. If you're so anxious to find out what's inside, unwrap your own. I'm sure they're all the same."

I tore off the yellow paper and opened the flap of the green cardboard box. "Money!"

"Huh?" That got Mother's interest.

She came up close and watched me pull out a small, crystal bowl with a net pouch full of silver and gold coins stuffed inside. I held up the bowl and turned it around. On one side, etched into the crystal was a picture of a riverboat. On the other side it said, "Queen of Newport."

There was a little note tied around the pouch. I read aloud, "Join in the fun. Try your luck at the games. Guest with the most chips at the end of tonight's cruise wins dinner for a party of ten at the opening night of Victor Lloyd's soon-to-be-built fabulous new entertainment experience."

Mother's chin went up. She looked like she'd just smelled a dead skunk. Holding her gift out in front of her and turning, she stepped deliberately over to a corner table, placed it down, and came back.

Linking her arm in mine, she said, "I think I would like a glass of wine."

We started weaving through the crowd towards the bar, which was situated halfway down the first deck and to one side. To get there we passed several gaming tables already surrounded by huddles of guests eagerly playing roulette, some kind of dice game, and blackjack.

The bar was an impressive length of intricately carved mahogany and brass railings. A bartender with a walrus moustache and wearing suspenders and a boater hat manned his post in front of a giant mirror etched with a swirling design of lilies and palm leaves. The entire tableau looked like it had been transported intact from a first-class 1880's riverboat—or, more likely, from Victor Lloyd's fantasy.

"Mother, I have a feeling you might change your mind about what Mr. Lloyd is doing. This is quite impressive, don't you think?"

She ignored me. Instead, looking in the opposite direction, she pulled her arm out from mine and turned to greet Gloria and Janie Sims.

"Hello again," Mother said.

Gloria Sims smiled back shyly. "Oh, hi. Thank you again for being so kind."

I noticed Janie the Marine had taken off her hat and was carrying it tucked under her left arm. We exchanged a friendly nod.

Gloria, picking at the wrapping of her unopened gift, said, "This is all a bit overwhelming for me. All these important people. I feel kind of lost."

I could almost hear the gears shift as Mother slipped into her gracious hostess mode. "Well, I'm sure you're just as important as anyone here. After all, you were invited."

"Yes . . . well . . ." Gloria reached up to her throat and pulled nervously at the skin of her neck. "Donald was the one invited. He's here somewhere. I guess he's still a little worked up over what happened."

I said, "It didn't appear to be a problem with Victor Lloyd. The little sailor taking tickets didn't have the authority to make those decisions. But she could've handled it better."

Gloria bit her lip. "That's not the only reason Donald's upset. There have been a few things happening lately and he's a little high-strung."

I noticed Janie shoot her mother a look—a nonverbal *shut up*.

Gloria didn't see it. She was looking towards the front of the boat where a Dixieland jazz band had just launched into *When The Saints Go Marching In*.

"When Donald gets that way," Gloria continued, raising her voice slightly, "he usually goes for a walk, says it calms him down. He's strolling around on the upper deck right now. I sure hope it helps him feel better, 'cause I've been very worried about him lately. He seems to get upset so easily. I'm sorry, it was kind of embarrassing back there. It's been a very bad day—" Janie gave her mother a quick tap on her arm.

Gloria shut up.

At that moment, the deck beneath our feet began to vibrate and all talking stopped. The *Queen of Newport* started to rumble. Her whistle blew a couple of sharp blasts, followed by two long ones, as if to say to the river traffic, *Out of my way, I'm coming.*

Someone shouted, "We're off!"

50

Chattering excitedly, guests started moving toward the staircase leading to the upper decks. The band broke into a Scott Joplin rag.

"We'd better go find Dad," Janie said to Gloria. "See you later," she added, waving to us.

I ordered two glasses of white wine and handed one to Mother. "Shall we go up top?"

IT WAS A PERFECT evening for a riverboat ride. The sun was still a few hours away from setting, and there was just enough breeze to ruffle the *Queen's* flags. We chugged downriver, past the restaurants lining the Kentucky side. Their balconies were jammed with people sitting at umbrellaed tables, enjoying the end of a hot summer day. They waved and saluted us with their happy hour drinks. I felt relaxed and contented, but it was time to get to work.

Being tall definitely has its advantages—cuts down on the time it takes to find someone in a crowd. Though with Victor Lloyd, I heard him before I saw him.

"Biggest damn fish I ever caught."

I looked across the crowd and saw Victor surrounded by a small huddle of polite listeners. His arms were stretched out in a visual aid to his brag. I saw Alan Casey immortalize the moment with his camera. The performance came to an end. Victor moved on, trailed by Alan and his camera, to a couple standing by themselves. He slapped the man on the back and flashed his wide, confident grin at the woman. "Having a good time? Great." Victor didn't wait for an answer.

I followed them around, watching Victor work the crowd. Sometimes he stopped to talk, flagging who he considered important. Most of the time he just smiled and offered a quick greeting, but in a way that said for those few seconds that guest was Victor's best pal.

The hour I spent stalking him offered no surprises—his behavior was just reinforcing the clichéd image I had of him.

51

Of course, that made me more curious as to who he really was underneath that mask.

Maybe Charlotte was being a bit hysterical. I hadn't heard any of those rumors linking Victor to the underworld, and I wasn't sure what I'd see following him around on his riverboat that would tell me one way or the other. There were no neon signs flashing over the heads of those he spoke to announcing them as Bad Guy or Good Guy. He was just behaving like any normal businessman networking at a social function.

I watched Victor descend the stairs leading to the middle deck and started to follow, intending to continue my surveillance, boring as it was. On second thought, I figured I'd better check on Mother. A sense of responsibility for talking her into coming here nagged at me. The last I saw of her, she'd found some Clairmont business cronies and it looked like she was starting to have a good time. But that could change in a heartbeat with some misunderstood comment. Mother's a Libra and her scales at times seesaw wildly.

I turned in the direction I'd last seen her.

"Kate! Hi!"

"Oh. Hi, Melissa."

Charlotte Oakley's "precious little girl" was standing in front of me. Blond, blue-eyed, and smiling radiantly as any newly-engaged young woman usually is, she pulled on the arm of the good looking guy beside her.

Melissa said, "I want you to meet my fiance, Eric Lloyd."

I shook the offered hand of Victor's chip off the old block and expressed the obligatory congratulations. Suddenly, I felt like that wicked witch in my newspaper photos. I'd been sent on a secret mission by the Evil Queen Mother to find some reason to pry apart this wide-eyed princess and her Prince Charming. I pictured my hand, still clasped in Eric's, turn into a gnarly, clawed appendage and my nose grow into a warty beak. I was afraid to open my mouth lest a bat fly out as I cackled.

Melissa chirped on, "We are so in love, Kate. I can't wait to announce our engagement. It's not official yet, but I wanted to let you know because you just have to cater our wedding. No one else will do."

I thanked her and looked at Eric, who was gazing with puppy eyes at Melissa.

He must have felt my witchy eye on him, because he turned to me. "My dad says you're the greatest—you give amazing parties. And your catering our reception would make Melissa very happy. That's all I care about. I'd do anything to make her happy."

"And I would do anything for you," Melissa cooed.

The bat inside my mouth gagged from the sugar overdose and my brain searched for a suitable exit line.

Melissa's wide eyes got even wider. She screeched, "Look who's here! Come on, Eric, you must simply meet one of my best friends!"

Melissa grabbed her Prince Charming and pushed past me.

Off the hook, I smiled and said, "See ya," to the backs of their heads.

NOT FINDING MOTHER AFTER a quick search on the top deck, I moved down to the middle deck. Aha. Food. This was where I wanted to be. My stomach grumbled in agreement.

I scanned the length of banquet tables in the middle of the deck. From where I stood, the spread seemed a little sparse. I noticed a tray of fruit tarts that looked like they came from some run-of-the-mill bakery chain. Down at the far end was a separate round table encircled by a curtain of red satin. Regardless of my stomach's complaining, I had to first answer that annoying little voice in my head that's always asking, *What's over there?*

I swept past the banquet tables without a second glance at the offerings and stopped in front of Curtain Number One. I wanted to reach out and lift the bottom edge of the drapery to see what was behind it, but that wouldn't have been good manners. Obviously, it was meant as a surprise to be unveiled

53

later on. I stretched up on tiptoe, but even at my height I couldn't peek over the top edge. Well, I could wait like everyone else. Had to.

The smell of fried chicken lured me back to the buffet tables. Picking up a plate, I studied what lay before me. It was pretty basic stuff—platters of greasy southern fried and barbecued chicken, bowls of mayonaise-laden salads, baskets of Wonder Bread rolls, and those fruit tarts glistening with a thick, gummy glaze.

Tony and I would've done a much better job.

"They got any chicken wings here?"

The high-pitched nasally voice that seemed to come out of thin air made me jump. I was so intent on finding a piece of chicken that wasn't dripping in grease, I hadn't noticed the freckle-faced man in the straw hat come up beside me. He looked like a slightly deranged Howdy Doody marionette, broken loose of his strings.

He reached over my arm and grabbed a couple of wings with his fingers. "I just *love* barbecue—hey," he said, his eyes following a path up my chest to my face, "I know you. I've seen you on TV and in *The Enquirer*. You're Kate Cavanaugh."

Howdy Doody extended his right hand after quickly wiping it with a paper napkin. "Dick Rottingham, here." His fingertips had tiny bits of napkin stuck to them. I bravely shook hands.

I said, "Oh, yes. I know you, too."

"Nice party. Having a good time?"

I didn't get a chance to respond.

Dick's head anticipated my answer to his question with a couple of rapid nods. "Good. Good. Vic's a class act all the way."

He looked up at me, his words escaping his broad mouth like they were fired out of an automatic pistol. "But you're a class act, too, Ms. Amazon Chili Heiress Detective. I've been thinking about inviting you to come on my radio talk show for a long time, so now that we've been thrown together like this, how about it?"

"How about what?"

"Coming on as a guest some night—we can talk about capturing criminal masterminds 'n stuff and eat chicken wings. You know I have my own riverfront restaurant sports bar—Dickie's in Newport." He waved in the general direction of Kentucky. "We do the best chicken wings. In fact, why don't you come on my special Labor Day Weekend radio show that I'm broadcasting live from Dickie's right after the Rozzi fireworks?"

Oh, brother. More publicity. That's the last thing I wanted. "Thanks, but sorry, I don't want to draw attention to myself."

Dick looked a little stunned. "You don't want publicity?" He scratched the back of his ear. "My brain doesn't understand that. But hell, suit yourself. You can still come and watch the fireworks from Dickie's deck. Bring your family."

Well, Mother surely wouldn't want to come, but Robert Boone would get a big kick out of it. And the Rozzis are world famous for their spectacular fireworks displays. Every Labor Day Weekend five hundred thousand people line both the Cincinnati and Northern Kentucky sides of the river to watch the official End of Summer Celebration. Of course, we'd have to find a way past Phoebe Jo's objections.

I said, "Thanks. Can I get back to you in a couple of—"

Dick whipped a card out of his wallet faster than I could finish my sentence. "You can always reach me at any one of these numbers."

As I slipped the card into my purse, I changed topics, tilting my head in the direction of the mystery table. "By the way, do you have any idea what's behind that curtain?"

A broad grin stretched across Dick's face. "Oh, you don't want to know. Victor's got a little man back there, pulling levers and pushing buttons."

I laughed.

Dick continued, "Seriously. You watch. Victor Lloyd's going to do big things. He's the one who can change the image of the whole area. Wait and see—the guy's a real wizard."

My smile froze. I felt like I was living out one of my crazy dreams—some kind of weird, mixed-up fairy tale filled with deranged Howdy Doodys, Evil Queen Mothers, Wicked Witches, and Wizards. I looked up from my plate of unappetizing food and stared at the red satin curtain, my stomach twisting into a knot.

The dream wasn't over—Pandora's Box was still waiting to be opened.

8

I FINALLY DID MEET up with Mother. She'd come down to the middle deck in search of food and found me sitting by myself at one of the tables, picking away at my Wonder Bread roll and nibbling on a barbecued drumstick. I got some pleasure from her observation that 'Round the World Catering would never have put together "such a sad buffet." After dinner, we went up to the top deck to watch the sunset.

Leaning on the railing, we watched the sun dip into the muddy Ohio and disappear behind a thickly wooded bend in the river as the *Queen of Newport* made a wide turn and headed back upstream towards the city. It was a peaceful moment, shattered by the blast of a trumpet call over the riverboat's sound system.

Victor Lloyd's voice boomed, "Ahoy, mates. Y'all please come to the middle deck. We are about to have the unveiling."

This was what we'd all come to see, so I wanted to make sure I had a good view. I hustled Mother down the stairs and, focusing on the red satin curtain as my goal, maneuvered our way through the crowd as though I was on a basketball court trying to get into position for a good shot. Guess at times I can be a little aggressive, but we did wind up standing right in front of the curtained table next to Alan Casey, who had his camera poised.

Some people in the crowd were jostling around, trying to get as close as they could. Others hung back, pretending indifference. I couldn't believe everyone wasn't anxious to find out what was behind Curtain Number One. From somewhere behind me I heard Howdy Doody shout, "Hey Kate! Sit down, you're blocking the view." That pushed a button—I was back at Clairmont High dealing with fifteen-year-old jerks. I turned and gave Dick Rottingham what I thought was a withering look. He just winked and waved at me.

The phony gas lamps lining the walls dimmed and the crowd's chattering subsided. A spotlight hit the red satin curtain. One of the jazz band's trumpeters blasted a fanfare as Victor Lloyd stepped into the light.

"Ladies and gentlemen, this is the moment you've all been waiting for. I believe this project will help reawaken the energy that once made Northern Kentucky one of the hot spots of America." The red satin curtain automatically began to rise, revealing its secret. "I proudly present to you—The Oasis!"

Everyone on board gasped. Some with excitement. Some, like Mother, in horror.

We all stared at the model of a white stucco building with a domed top. It had a sort of biblical Middle Eastern look to it, except for the giant green and yellow neon palm tree that was planted in front. Smaller pink and green neon palm trees surrounded the exterior of the building which hugged a blue-painted line representing the Ohio River. A cute little *Queen of Newport* was docked in front, waiting for dozens of miniature plastic people to stroll from the entrance of The Oasis across a promenade and come aboard.

Victor went to the side of the table and pushed a button which split the model down the middle. It opened and fanned out so we could see the interior.

The guests started to push from behind like little kids wanting to press their noses up against a store's Christmas window.

Victor waved his arms. "Wait, wait, wait. You'll all get your chance to see. Just form a line and walk around it."

Mother was mumbling something to herself.

"What's the matter?" I said, turning to look at her.

"The old Oasis was a horrible place. Full of criminals."

"Oh, for crying out loud. No it wasn't," I replied. "Cindy Schmitz had her first wedding reception there just before it closed."

Mother clamped her mouth shut. She knew this was neither the time nor the place to get into one of our debates. Besides, we were being forced into line and had to start shuffling along as Victor directed traffic.

The model showed off its chandeliered foyer, a huge main dining room with a dance floor and stage for an orchestra, a triple-tiered cabaret room with its own stage, and several smaller dining rooms with names like Starlight, Sahara, and Caravan. A Smokers Clubroom, complete with fireplace and miniature leather armchairs, offered safe haven to tobacco-dependent customers. Facing out over the river was an enclosed patio dining area that looked like it could be opened during warm weather. In the back of all this was a kitchen big enough to swallow my 'Round the World cooking area ten times over. More tiny, plastic people strolled outside in the extensive gardens and down a walkway towards a small chapel. It was very similar to the layout of the original Oasis, except everything was bigger and showier.

I said to Victor, "You're building this by the river? The old Oasis was up on a hill, further south."

"Too far from where all the action is. The riverfront is the place to be."

"What's with this giant neon palm tree? Did you just stick it on the model for fun?"

Victor shook his head. "Nope. Everything there is to

scale. It'll stand one hundred and seventy-five feet straight up in the air, welcoming everybody coming down the interstates. It will light up the night sky and you'll see it for miles around. Why, this'll be the first thing all those millions of people flying in to the Cincinnati-Northern Kentucky International Airport will see."

Dick Rottingham popped up beside me. "That's exciting!"

Mother cringed and started to move away.

Dick pumped Victor's hand. "I love it. The Oasis will help make Northern Kentucky a national destination spot like Branson, Missouri. Only a helluva lot more sophisticated."

Victor made a sweeping flourish with his hand over the incarnation of his vision. "The Oasis will have top name adult entertainment—singers, comics, musical reviews. Even its own chorus line of dancers."

"I can see it all now," Dick motor-mouthed on, "The Oasis Harem Dancers—a dozen leggy beauties doing the Dance of the Seven Veils; high-kicking, hip-grinding, big breasted—"

I let Mother pull me away from those two guys. She picked up her nattering where she'd left off earlier. "It's just awful, Kathleen. I don't want any part of it."

"Except for those gaudy palm trees, it looks kind of exciting to me. I don't know what your problem is."

"You're too young to remember, but just hearing the name The Oasis brings up all sorts of memories. The Mafia ran that nightclub in the 1950s. Every kind of criminal activity you could imagine was going on and nobody did anything about it. Why, hoodlums were even murdering each other on the street over who would control that horrid place."

"Well, that might have been true then, but I don't see where Victor Lloyd is going to get into anything illegal. He's just bringing back the style of that time. It's big now. Everybody's back into drinking their martinis, smoking cigars, and listening to Tony Bennett. I'll bet Victor's going to be real successful with this."

Mother wagged her finger at me. "You watch. He's just going to build a hangout that'll attract all kinds of lowlife."

I was tired of Mother The Wet Blanket, but after seeing the scope of Victor's project questions began prickling my brain. Who were his backers? After the failure of his condominium project, where did he get the money to buy the land and draw up the architectural plans? It was obvious this riverboat party was intended to entice more investors to the project, but someone had enough faith in Victor's plans to get him this far.

Maybe there was something to Charlotte's suspicions.

9

I FIGURED I'D LEARN a few things about Victor if I hung around the gaming tables he'd set up. After all, that's where I'd expect to find those who were sympathetic to his vision, and they might be willing to talk about how they knew him. Liquor had been flowing all night, and probably loosening a few tongues, so I headed for the casino area on the first deck. Mother ran in the opposite direction. Maybe to hook up with her business cronies to start a petition drive against our host.

I found out gamblers were still gamblers even when they were playing with funny money.

The intensity of the players was palpable, though there was plenty of laughter and cheering as cards were dealt, dice were flung, and roulette wheels spun 'round and around. You'd think we were on a floating casino across the state line in Indiana waters where gambling has been legal for the past few years.

Not being too familiar with the various games, I just watched until I understood the rules—or at least enough of them so that when I lost, and the dealer raked in all my chips, I'd know why. I found myself attracted to the roulette table. There was something hypnotic about the sound of the ball whooshing around the rim of the spinning wheel, then falling onto the wheel itself and bouncing around with a series of *clicketyclicks* until it finally settled into a numbered slot.

"Give the lady some room."

I smiled back at the well-dressed, elderly gentleman, who was holding out his hand towards me. He said, "Come and play," and stepped aside a few inches.

Moving into the space he'd made for me, I looked around, realizing just then I was the only woman at the table. I greeted the two players I already knew—a couple of Clairmont businessmen. And nodded at the others.

My new friend was tanned, silver-haired, and stood about five inches shorter than me. Though he had workman hands—large but with short, stubby fingers—the nails were manicured and he wore a heavy gold signet ring on his pinkie. The starched cuffs of his white shirt were linked together with matching chunks of gold. His full head of hair looked as though he had a standing biweekly appointment with a personal barber. He smelled good, too.

Standing next to him, on his other side, was a very large, very expressionless man with a hawk nose that had been broken in several places. He also was wearing an expensive suit, but he didn't appear to be playing. He just stood there, his eyes watching. Not the game, but everything else. For some reason, I felt the two were attached by an invisible cord.

My new friend said, "Do you need any chips?"

"No, still have all of mine." I pulled them out of my shoulder bag and studied the numbers on the table. Guess I was holding things up. He leaned closer and suggested quietly, "Red-19."

I obeyed and quickly placed a chip on the spot he indicated.

The dealer spun the wheel.

The ball sounded its *clicketyclicks*.

I felt butterflies in my stomach.

I held my breath.

The *clicketyclicks* stopped.

"You won!"

I could see how people got hooked on this game.

We played a few more rounds and, between my gambling partner and me, we amassed a phony fortune. Piles of chips grew like little skyscraper towers in front of us—his the more impressive skyline. It was fascinating to watch him. He carried himself with grace and confidence. Every move he made was decisive, elegant. I had to find out who he was.

"Sammy," he said to his large companion, "would you get me a brandy and something for Miss Cavanaugh?" He turned to me. "What would you like?"

My thoughts are usually written all over my face, so he answered my question without my having to verbalize it. "I already know who you are because I read the newspapers."

"Oh. A brandy, please." One of these days, I'll get it through my thick head that everybody knows who I am and I'll stop being surprised.

"How about a formal introduction?" I extended my hand. "I'm Kate Cavanaugh."

He shook my hand with a firm, warm grasp. "Peppino Giuliani. My friends call me Peepo."

Cute. "How do you know Victor Lloyd?"

"I'm Victor's uncle—he's my sister's son."

Now I really was surprised. And I made no attempt to hide it. I felt as though Charlotte Oakley was standing beside me jabbing my ribs with her elbow saying, *See? See? I told you.*

Sammy came back with our drinks, handed them to us, and once again took up his post alongside Mr. Giuliani. Peepo.

It was getting more crowded at the roulette table. Someone bumped my arm and my brandy sloshed back and forth in its snifter.

Peepo's silvery-grey eyebrows pulled together in a frown. "Bah. This isn't the way to enjoy a brandy. Shall we go sit down? Over there by the bar."

He held my drink as I swept my chips into my purse. I noticed, as we walked away, Sammy gathering up his boss's winnings.

We sat down at the one unoccupied table by the bar. Sammy found a perch nearby and watched the crowd. Peepo was focused on me. I wasn't sure why he invited me to have a drink with him, but I was glad he did. It looked like my opportunity to find out more about Victor. However, the conversation would require careful steering—I doubted liquor ever loosened Peepo's tongue. Sipping my brandy, I returned his gaze and waited.

"So," he said, "what do you think of the project?"

"I think it could be very successful."

Peepo nodded as though I'd given him the correct answer. "Are you enjoying the party?"

"Very much. I have to laugh though. Victor's always got such a flashy presentation. Nobody else around here has his style—we're a pretty conservative bunch. Guess that's why he gets so much media attention."

Peepo swirled the brandy in his snifter. He watched it, didn't look up at me. "And that's a bad thing?"

"I don't know. But it sure makes him stand out from the crowd. Where's he from?"

Peepo laughed to himself. "Victor's a native. He was born right here in Northern Kentucky."

"But I'd never heard of him until four or five years ago. We're a relatively small business community—someone like him wouldn't go unnoticed."

Peepo hesitated, lingering over his sip of brandy. After a moment, he said, "His family moved out West when he was a teenager."

"Hey, Victor—" The loud voice coming from behind us caught our attention.

Peepo and I turned and watch Ted Mueller greet our host who was approaching the bar. Just then the jazz band launched into a new set.

Ted shouted over the music, "So, when legalized gambling comes to Kentucky look who's in front of the line ready and waiting to pick people's pockets." Guess he wanted everyone to hear what he had to say. He continued in a loud voice,

"Add a few slot machines to The Oasis and you've got instant casino."

"All I want to do is provide an exciting place for people to come and be entertained," replied Victor. "If that means fine dining and a great show, I'll do that." His words sounded a little slurred, and I wondered if he'd had too much to drink.

"Knowing you," Ted shouted louder, "you probably got lobbyists in your pocket working overtime."

"If gambling ever became legal and people wanted it, then great—I'll provide that, too." Victor's voice was now matching Ted's in volume. "No matter what, I'm here to stay. I know you don't like it, but you don't hafta worry, I'll stay on my own side of the river."

"And drag Northern Kentucky back into the sewer where it used to be."

Victor stood as straight as he could and braced himself against the bar. "What's wrong with providing entertainment for adults? If you want family stuff, go to King's Island."

Peepo was visibly disgusted by the public display of bad manners. He quickly rose to his feet and marched over to the two crowing roosters.

It appeared the old gentleman used humor to quiet them down. I couldn't hear what he said—only saw his facial expressions. Ted shrugged in response to Peepo's intervention, and walked away. Peepo immediately turned to Victor. I half-expected him to grab his nephew by the ear and take him behind the nearest woodshed for a good whipping.

Sammy was also in my line of vision and I saw him reach into his jacket's breast pocket and pull out a cel phone, flip it open and speak into it. He listened to the caller, said a few words in response, and approached his boss, waiting for an opening before interrupting.

Peepo took the call and quickly terminated it. He came back to our table and said, "Please excuse me, Miss Cavanaugh. Seems there are times a businessman like myself is forced to work after hours. I must return this call, but perhaps we can speak again, later. It's been a pleasure." And off he went to look for a quieter spot, followed by Sammy, his giant hawk-nosed shadow.

I sure hoped we were going to speak again later. That man had information I wanted. I was starting to get up from the table when Victor sauntered over.

"Wait, Kate. Please don't go away. I was hoping to get a chance to talk to you."

Dutifully, I sat back down. "You've got my undivided attention."

Victor planted himself in the chair across from me. Other than his black ribbon tie being askew and visible patches of sweat at his temples, he didn't look too ruffled by Ted's accusations.

"Kate, your family runs a first-rate business operation that I've long admired."

"Well, thank you."

"Everybody knows Crown Chili is a Cincinnati institution, so I want your company to be part of this."

"You mean The Oasis?"

"No, no. The Oasis is just one part of my plan. Ted Mueller thinks I'm anti-family, but I'm not. That's why I bought and refurbished the Queen of Newport—to run daytime cruises for families." Victor leaned forward, his eyes wide. "The way I see it, kids are bored stiff just sitting on a boat going up and down the river. So we're going to give them some entertainment. We're going to do *mystery* cruises. Great idea, huh?" His eyebrows jumped up and down in excitement.

"Well, I don't speak for Crown Ch—"

"Now wait." Anticipating a negative comment, Victor quickly held up his hand. "Just listen. There will be actors dressed up like Tom Sawyer, Huckleberry Finn—that kind of thing. Then there'll be someone dressed up like Mark Twain who'll tell the kids a story while they eat their Crown Chili three-ways or Coneys, whatever. Maybe it's a spooky, scary kind of story and something happens. The kids have to solve it. So they run around the boat looking for clues. We can call it The Crown Chili Mystery Cruise." I mentally backed away.

"Now that you're this ace detective and getting all this publicity, half the job of promotion is already done."

Shaking my head slowly, I said, "You're a very creative man, Mr. Lloyd, but I'm not going to let you turn me into Crown Chili's version of Ronald McDonald." What comes next? Amazon Chili Heiress Detective action figures?

"No, no. Don't worry, don't worry." He looked reassuringly into my eyes, then resumed his pre-planned patter. "And then in the evening, the boat will be available for private parties, fancier affairs that your 'Round the World Catering might want to handle. God knows, you could do a helluva lot better job than the mediocre one done by the caterer Tammy hired. And with your eyes closed."

He was right about that last comment. But I felt insulted that I wasn't asked to run the higher profile restaurants in The Oasis.

"There's a fire!"

Alarmed, Victor jumped out of his chair. I jerked my head towards the voice. The man didn't shout loud enough to panic the entire deck, but people in the vicinity of the bar were preparing to run when someone else added, "It's only a plastic straw burning in an ash tray."

Donald Sims was there with his bottle of mineral water which he promptly used to douse the flame.

Victor sat back down. "See what I mean about this caterer? They're supposed to be taking care of this party, keeping things tidy and running smoothly." He indicated the ashtray on our table. "Another disaster waiting to happen."

I'd already noticed the plastic straw twisted into a bow nestled in amongst the cigarette butts and, in fact, had seen another one tied exactly the same way in an ashtray up on the middle deck. Someone had a nervous habit.

"Vic!" Tammy Lloyd was stomping towards us, her hoop skirt swinging and swaying like a huge blue taffeta bell. "I want to talk to you, you sonofabitch!" Guests milling around the bar moved aside, startled by her clanging.

Tammy planted herself in front of our table, hands on

hips. "Now you're hitting on this blond bimbo?" She aimed her mouth at me. "Don't you know this asshole'll jump on anyone wearing a skirt? He even tried to pick up a transvestite last year in Vegas."

Bimbo? I've been called a lot of things in my life, but "blond bimbo?" What the hell was her problem—besides the fact she'd replaced all her bodily fluids with Jack Daniels?

Victor angrily shoved away from the table and jumped out of his seat, looking as though he wanted to stuff Tammy in a bag. He quickly hustled her out the exit leading to the staircase.

Ah, the married life—nothing like airing out your dirty laundry in public.

What time was it? I automatically looked down at my wrist, forgetting I hadn't worn a watch. Sure felt like it was time go home, but I couldn't. That's the trouble with partying on a boat—you're trapped. I decided to go up top for some air. Maybe even find Peepo and continue our conversation.

THERE WERE ONLY a few people on the top deck, nobody I knew. I moved away from them, halfway down towards the stern. The air was cooler, fresher than below, and I leaned on the railing and breathed in slowly and deeply. It was pitch dark. Somewhere up ahead in the distance was Cincinnati, a core of lights hidden now behind the bends in the river. I'd had enough of this quaint Mark Twainish rollin' down the river and wanted to push a button to rev up the paddle wheel and go scooting across the water to home.

I looked up at the sky, searching for the Big Dipper, the only constellation I recognized.

It's funny, just a couple of days ago the whole idea of working in a kitchen was not on my Top Ten List of favorite things to do. In fact, it was in danger of being crossed off the list entirely. Yet here I was, disappointed by Victor's business proposal. Why didn't he ask me to run his first-class kitchen at The Oasis? I'm perfect for the job. Who could he get with more qualifications than me in this city?

As I started going through the list of the other possible candidates, I stopped myself. What did I care? How about going down the list of complaints I'd made about the business the last few months? Picky, unreasonable clients. Suppliers who keep delivering the wrong items. Hot, stuffy kitchens. Sore feet. Now *there* was a list that could go on and on.

I realized this wasn't just a list of petty complaints. Maybe I was depressed. I felt something switch over in my brain and saw that I was facing a real issue, something that had to be confronted and dealt with before it was too late. To ignore my feelings would eventually throw me into a serious crisis. When I was a teenager, it seemed like I was having an emotional crisis every few months and Dad would talk me through them.

At that moment, I wished he was there. I had no one else to talk to. If I went to Mother, she'd just say, "Find a husband, Kathleen, then give me some grandchildren. We'll all be happy."

But it's not that simple—I don't fit into that box.

If Dad was here, he'd ask, "Where's your five year plan?"

And I'd say, "I forgot to make one."

And he'd say—

I heard a man shout.

10

I *THOUGHT* I HEARD a man shout. I couldn't be sure over the noise of the churning paddle wheel, so I walked to the stern end of the deck where I thought it had come from.

But then the shout, "Man overboard!" came up at me from two decks below, right under where I stood.

I looked down and caught a glimpse of the top of Alan Casey's head as he turned from the railing and ran inside. Squinting, I tried to make out the form of a swimmer in the water. It was too dark.

Then I saw something caught on one of the bright red paddles as the giant wheel churned up towards me. As the object came closer, I could see what it was.

A body.

My first thought was: Oh for crying out loud. There's another hour or so left before the boat docks, so Victor Lloyd's starting his mystery cruises early and this is a dummy victim riding on *The Ferris Wheel of Death*.

But in a split second, that thought turned to horror as the paddle reached the top of its arc and the grizzly reality passed in front of my eyes before being plunged back down into the murky water. It was a real body. A badly mauled body. Victor Lloyd's badly mauled body. Or so I thought—couldn't really tell, the face was so mangled. But the body was wearing Victor's riverboat gambler's costume and this was no special effect.

I heard a commotion break out on the first deck, but I turned and ran past several startled guests to the wheelhouse at the bow, yelling, "Stop! Stop the boat!"

I yanked the door open and saw the Captain shouting into his intercom. He turned to me. "I can't talk now, Ma'am. I've got an emergency."

He obviously didn't need me to tell him what was happening, and I stepped back as he shut the door and continued shouting his orders into the mike. I heard the riverboat's giant paddle wheel slow to a stop.

Taking the stairs by the wheelhouse two at a time, I headed for the lower deck to find out what had happened. Yeah, I know, Victor was dead—but the question was how? Did he fall overboard or did someone push him? When I got to the first deck, it was obvious my questions would have to wait. Everybody on board had already made it down by way of the other stairs. They were jamming the casino area, trying to push forward to get a look at the gruesome scene.

There was a buzz of excited talk. Some people were shouting, some were crying. Suddenly, there was a loud screeching wail. It was a female voice and seemed to come from very near the paddle wheel. I looked over the heads of the crowd. Eric Lloyd, arm around his mother Tammy, was trying to pull her away from Victor's bent body, which hung in an unnatural manner from a giant red paddle.

Peepo Giuliani shouted, "Get her out of here."

One of the crew members addressed the crowd in a loud voice. "Please go back to the upper decks. There's been an accident and the police have been called. We'll be underway shortly."

The guests continued their anxious chattering as we funneled into a line to go back up the narrow staircase. Nobody seemed to know how it had happened. There were lots of questions, and weird rumors had started already. I overheard a woman say, "Did you see his body? Someone said he was split right down the middle."

"Kathleen! Kathleen!"

I looked over my shoulder, saw Mother, and squeezed back through the crowd to join her. She grabbed my arm and clung to it.

I said, "Do you know how it happened?"

She pressed her lips together and shook her head. We shuffled along and up the stairs before I said anything else. When we reached the top of the stairs I asked, "You okay, Mom?" All I got was a nod.

I looked around for a place to sit and found an empty chair at one of the tables. "Mother, I want to talk to some people. Is it alright if I just leave you here for a little while?"

"Where are you going?"

"Don't worry, I'm not going to jump ship and swim ashore. I'll check back with you in ten minutes."

She nodded, but it was obvious she was very upset. No grouchy nattering, no derogatory comments, no "Victor got what he deserved."

I didn't believe that Victor fell overboard. He had looked a little unsteady when he was confronting Ted Mueller at the bar, but our conversation after that proved he was in control of his motor skills. Certainly, some of the guests were enemies of his and Charlotte was sure to ask me who I thought did him in. Victor's mysterious death was just going to reinforce her belief that he was linked to some kind of underworld activity. I had been hired for the evening to find out whatever I could about Victor's background. Just because he was dead didn't mean my commitment was finished. That also didn't mean Melissa's plans to marry Eric were canceled. I still had a job to do—to find out what was truth and what was rumor. Better get to it.

I wanted to find Peepo. It occurred to me that, since he was a family member, he'd probably be down below by Victor's body, waiting for the police. Along with Tammy and Eric Lloyd. Maybe even Charlotte's baby. Figured I better keep my eyes opened for Melissa as I wandered through the crowd. I did see the Sims family. Donald was sitting at one of the tables, coughing and loosening his tie, his face blotchy. Gloria and Janie stood behind him, both wearing the same worried expression.

Ted the Head was at the buffet table, alone, piling chicken wings on to a plate. He looked calm and content, like nothing had happened. Nobody else had an appetite for the food, including me, but I pretended to be stricken with a sudden urge for one of the gummy fruit tarts and joined him at the buffet table.

I said, "This is horrible. Do you have any idea how Victor fell overboard?"

Ted shrugged his massive shoulders. "Dunno. He was pretty drunk."

"I spoke to Victor after the two of you faced-off at the bar. His words were a little slurry, but he wasn't as drunk as Tammy, and she was walking around okay."

"Who knows? Maybe he jumped."

"Why would he do that? This was a big night for him. I

71

don't buy it."

Ted chomped on a chicken wing. I watched his teeth pulverize the hunk of meat as he spoke. "Then someone did us all a favor and pushed him."

"Interesting. Any ideas who?"

"Yeah, lots of people wanted to get rid of that big piece of turd, but I don't want to mention names because I might get someone into trouble—the fines for polluting the Ohio River are pretty steep." He turned and lumbered off. "See you around."

That sure wasn't the most earth-shattering revelation. I could put my own dear Mother on that suspect list—except she doesn't have the arm strength. I looked over to where she sat to see if she was still okay. She wasn't. Dick Rottingham was right at her elbow, talking to her. I quickly strode over to her table and halted, mouth open, ready to say something to rescue her when, unexpectedly, she looked into Dick's face and smiled at him. A real smile, not the pasted-on Cavanaugh grin. What was this?

"Mother? Hi. Is everything okay here?"

She turned to me. "I'm fine, dear."

Dick's eyes shifted from Mother to me. "Where've you been? Your mom's been sitting here all by herself, traumatized by this tragic event. I could see it on her face as I walked by. I thought, Dick, you better stop and do the Christian thing and talk to that poor woman. Give her a chance to use these big shoulders of mine to cry on if need be. After all, I've had experience in dealing with the aftermath of crises like this evening's."

Mother looked at me, undoubtedly noting the shock I was trying to cover up. "This has been such a difficult evening, but I feel much better thanks to Mr. Rottingham."

Unlike your cruel, uncaring daughter who selfishly left you all alone for ten whole minutes. Bad girl.

Dick said, "Kate, you know that invitation to view the fireworks from my deck includes your mother."

"Oh?" She looked at me. "What invitation is this? You

didn't say anything."

Yeah right, Mother. A half hour ago you'd rather drown than be saved by Sir Rottingham the Rescuer. "A lot has happened since my conversation with Dick. We can talk about it later."

I turned to him. "Did you see Victor acting strange or drunk just before he died?"

"Last I saw, he was having a not-so-romantic tête-a-tête with his charming Tammy outside on the lower deck. In other words, a full-blown domestic dispute. He called her a drunk and she called him a mother—" and Dick proceeded to recite the longest list of four-letter words I'd ever heard strung together as an adjective describing Victor's mating habits. "Then she walloped him with her evening purse and walked away."

Mother's body stiffened and, without moving in her chair, she gave the impression of pulling away from Dick. Aside from the bright red spots on her cheeks, no one would see a difference in her, but I saw her mask slip back into place.

At the same time, Dick started pointing at something behind me. I turned and practically jumped out of my skin.

Sammy was standing right behind me. "Sorry, Miss Cavanaugh. I didn't mean to frighten you," he said in a very soft, raspy voice. Could have been his tie was too tight—his thick, muscular neck bulged out over his collar. I also noticed he wasn't wearing his suit jacket and the entire front of both his shirt and pants was soaked. "Mr. Giuliani wishes to speak with you."

"Oh?"

"He's down below with the rest of the family."

I looked back at Mother and Dick, raising my eyebrows. "Well. Wonder what this is all about. Guess I better go find out."

Sammy led the way, nodding at a crew member who stood at the foot of the stairs, talking into his walkie-talkie. The casino area had been cleared of all guests, who obviously no longer cared whether or not they had the most chips at the end of the evening. It was like a ghost town saloon where an unspeakable horror had just occurred, wiping everyone off the face of the earth—some right in the middle of their winning streaks, as indicated by the huge piles of chips at a few spots on the gaming tables.

I heard a woman sobbing to my left. I looked over my shoulder and saw Tammy, Eric, and Melissa seated at a table by the bar. Tammy was crying into a big wad of tissue, her hoop skirt bowed out in front of her revealing a white ruffled petticoat.

At first, I was a little surprised at the intensity of Tammy's grief, given the angry outburst I'd witnessed earlier between her and Victor. But then, what did I know? I'd never been that passionate about anyone in my life.

I saw Alan Casey talking to Peepo and a second crew member at the rear of the casino area. A few yards away, a man I didn't know was bending over Victor's body which had been laid out on the deck. Water was puddling around the body and a third crew member was mopping up the wet trail that showed where they'd brought him in.

As I followed Sammy up to where Peepo and Alan were having their conversation, I heard Peepo say, "Make sure nothing happens to that roll of film. I want the police to see how Victor looked before Sammy and those sailors took him off the wheel."

Alan fidgeted with his camera. "Are you sure the police won't be angry with you for moving the body?"

"So? I wasn't going to leave him hanging like some dead fish on a line. They should be grateful I thought of getting those shots of him."

Peepo turned away from Alan as we approached. His eyes had a hardness I hadn't seen in them when we first met. "Miss Cavanaugh, thank you for coming. Please, let's sit over here." He indicated the tables back by the bar, took my arm and quickly led me away, as if attempting to shield me from the sight of Victor's body. He had no way of knowing I had already witnessed his nephew's mashed-in face.

We passed Eric, Melissa, and Tammy, who was calming

down and beginning to get control of her tear ducts. Peepo and I sat down at a table at the opposite end of the bar from them.

I said, "What can I do for you?"

"Help me piece together what happened tonight." He pointed to the man who had been bending over Victor's body. "One of our guests turns out to be a doctor, but unfortunately he was not able to help Victor. Now this photographer," he waved at Alan, "says he was outside on the deck taking a breather from his strenuous job of documenting the evening's activities, when he saw Victor lean over the railing by the paddle wheel, lose his balance, and fall into the water." There was a hint of disgust at the corners of his mouth. "For the police, it'll be simple. An accident. Case closed. But it's not so simple." Peepo's eyes hardened even more as he looked past me and towards his dead nephew. "Not for me."

"It doesn't feel right to me either," I said. "Victor seemed to have been drinking, but you saw him as late in the evening as I did. I have a difficult time believing Alan's story."

"Tell me, Miss Cavanaugh. Did you talk with Victor after I left you to make my phone call?"

I'd had enough of this Miss Cavanaugh stuff. "Call me, Kate—and yes, I did talk to Victor. We were having a very lucid conversation about business ventures, when his wife came storming up to the table, accused Victor of philandering and called me a 'blond bimbo.'" I couldn't keep the outrage out of my voice.

Peepo looked at me, incredulous. "I've met a lot of bimbos in my life. Believe me, Kate, you're not—" He shook his head and waved the thought away. "What happened next?"

"Victor didn't say anything, but he looked angry, grabbed Tammy and took her outside. That's the last time I saw them, but you may want to talk to Dick Rottingham because he says he saw what happened next."

"Thank you, I will. But just tell me your understanding of what he saw."

I repeated Dick's report of their argument and the way it ended with Tammy's slugging Victor with her purse.

Peepo looked over at Tammy. "Then I will talk to her next."

I don't know why I was coming to her defense, but I said, "She still looks a little distraught. Can't it wait?"

"No."

He got up from his chair. I really wanted to grab his arm, pull him back down and say, "Who do you think you are?" But he was the type of man who was obviously used to taking over situations and people surrendering all control to him. Then I found myself stepping back and playing detective, and included him as a suspect in my investigation. Maybe this was all just an act to cover up some dirty business between him and Victor. I watched.

He said something to Tammy.

She looked up at him with watery eyes and honked into her wad of tissues.

He said something about Dick Rottingham.

She shook her head and Eric jumped and shouted, "Leave my mother alone. You have no right to ask that question."

Melissa sat in her seat staring at them like a frightened little doe.

A stream of fresh tears burst from Tammy's eyes.

Peepo didn't push it—he waved his hands, which in body language said, "Oh, screw it."

Just then, the crew member with the walkie-talkie shouted, "The police are here."

Peepo moved over to stand with the doctor and Alan by Victor's body. Three uniformed Kentucky State Police officers entered by way of the door at the other end of the deck and walked past where I sat. I watched as they went through their routine—examining the body, asking questions, and taking notes. Alan was confident and cooperative, handing over the roll of film he took out of his camera. Peepo was glum and almost silent, just giving monotone answers. He did not convey his suspicions about any alternative scenarios regarding Victor's death, which seemed to be reduced by the police to a clerical task consisting of noting it as an accident and filling out the proper paperwork. Pretty cut and dried.

One of the crew members produced a boarding list when it was requested by the policeman in charge, "Just in case the autopsy shows something questionable and there's a need to talk with the other guests." But that was shrugged off as something the police weren't anticipating they'd have to do.

Looked like Peepo was right about the police. Guess he was keeping his cards close to his chest and was going to play his own game. By his own rules.

The instruction was given to the wheelhouse to return to full power and head for home. I felt the rumbling under my feet increase and heard the giant wheel make its slushing sound as it started pushing through the water.

In my mind I pictured Victor falling over the railing into the muddy river and trying to swim away from the relentless pull of those red paddles. I pictured Alan seeing this and shouting, "Man overboard." Where was he standing? I know when I looked down from the upper deck I could see the top of his head. So Alan was on the same side of the boat as me. There wasn't a lot of room down there by the paddle wheel. Victor must've been on the other side of the wheel; otherwise, Alan would have been standing right next to him and could have kept him from falling over.

Of course, Alan could have pushed Victor overboard. I had enough time between hearing that first shout and Alan's "Man overboard!" to walk half the length of the boat to the stern end where the incident took place. Did Alan just stand there and watch Victor's body get sucked in under the churning water before raising the alarm? If that was the case, we had a murder weapon that couldn't be dusted for prints.

I wanted to march up to Alan and ask him outright, but we were not on speaking terms to begin with. I decided to ask Peepo, who said, "They were on opposite sides. Victor was alone and didn't know Alan was there. At least that's the creep's story."

We were on the same page about Alan, but I don't know if we were on the same trail. I decided not to ask him any more questions. If I was going to consider Peepo a suspect, I'd better start keeping my own cards face down.

FINALLY, BY MIDNIGHT, Mother and I were back in her white Mercedes traveling up the I-71 towards Clairmont. She'd recovered and was chattering nonstop about all that had happened.

"Well, Kathleen, if you want to know what I think, it's got something to do with the fact Victor Lloyd is a gambler. Anyone involved in that kind of activity is going to be associating with violent people. He probably owed money all over the place and tried to run away. But the past always catches up with you."

I couldn't argue with that. I checked the rearview mirror before passing a truck, and wondered briefly if there was anything in my own strange past coming up behind me.

I looked at Mother out of the corner of my eye. "So tell me, Miss Marple, who killed him?"

"I have no idea."

"Look, we don't know anything about Victor Lloyd's past, but I'd say there are plenty of people right here and now that would probably like to get rid of him. People you know, Mother."

"Like who?"

"Ted Mueller," automatically tripped out of my mouth.

She clicked her tongue. "Oh, don't be silly. He's not a violent person."

"Are you kidding? Ted the Head, Mister Football? Even after a couple of decades of soft living, he's still huge and strong enough to toss almost anybody overboard." I told her about the confrontation that took place earlier in the evening between him and Victor.

"Kathleen, you get that wild imagination from your father." She pointed straight ahead. "Watch out! You're getting too close to that car in front of us."

I gunned the engine and went around it.

Having no answers to my question, Mother shifted to a topic where all she had to do was express her opinions. "And there's Charlotte Oakley's poor daughter Melissa sitting in the middle of all this. Charlotte's already mortified about the possibility of her daughter marrying into that family, I don't know how she'll cope when this so-called accident is front page news tomorrow morning. And it will be on all the TV and radio stations. That foul-mouthed Rottingham man will surely talk on and on about it. Poor Charlotte should just lock Melissa in her bedroom until Eric finds someone else to marry. Maybe the Lloyd family will leave town."

I let Mother run off at the mouth and occupied myself with my own thoughts. I agreed about Victor being a gambler, but with real estate—not poker chips. And what about Peepo? Was Victor really his nephew? Or was that a cover for a different kind of "family" connection? Maybe this "accident" was the result of an underworld family squabble and Peepo got in the last word. If so, why was Alan covering for him? Maybe I do have a wild imagination. But I still didn't believe Victor was drunk enough to fall to his death.

Then there was that other family squabble. Tammy was so pissed off, she might have sneaked up on Victor and slugged him on the back of the head with a bottle of booze, launching him into the river. His head was so mangled and covered with swollen bumps from the churning paddle wheel, you'd never know. But if that happened, why would Alan lie for her? The guy's a sleazy character and I could imagine him doing all sorts of things for money. Or sex. Did he have the hots for Tammy? Yuck! My imagination was really getting out of control.

Back to Mother's idea. Gambling probably did him in. Nobody knew what Victor's plans were until the model was unveiled. He was betting The Oasis was a sure thing. That might be enough to frighten someone into action, hoping Victor's death would cancel the project.

In any case, as to the question would Newport ever relive its glory days under the glare of that towering neon palm tree—all bets were off.

Saturday, August 21

11

MY PEACEFUL COUNTRY KITCHEN was filled with *SPLATS!*
KA-BOOMS! and the accordion sounds of collapsible bodies
springing back to life. It was our new Saturday morning
routine. Robert, Phoebe Jo, and their fourteen-year-old
daughter, Julie Ann, sat with me around the oak kitchen table,
eating banana pancakes and watching Bugs Bunny outwit
Yosemite Sam on the Cartoon Network.

In a weird example of deja vu, Yosemite Sam, playing a
riverboat gambler, fell into his own paddle wheel trap for Bugs
and got the Mother of All Spankings.

If only life could imitate art, Victor Lloyd would have

been able to unwind his bent body from the giant paddles, straighten himself out by blowing into his thumb, and still be around to plant his neon palm trees.

"See that last chase scene?" Julie Ann pointed at the frantic cartoon action on the TV, her elbow almost knocking her glass of orange juice off the kitchen table. Robert calmly slid the glass over to a safer area away from Julie Ann's gangly arms.

"Yeah, that was pretty goofy," I said.

"Do you know how many drawings it took to do that?"

I returned her wide-eyed intense stare. "A hundred?"

Julie Ann rolled her eyes to the ceiling. "You haven't *a clue*, Katie."

Phoebe Jo looked up from under the table, where she had darted to retrieve a piece of pancake before Boo-Kat could pounce on it. "Julie Ann Boone! Mind your manners. Don't ask someone a question and then make fun of their answer."

I said, "No offense taken. Two hundred drawings?"

Julie Ann sighed loudly. "There are twenty-four drawings a second for every character on the screen. So we have Yosemite Sam chasing Bugs Bunny—that's forty-eight drawings a second. Now, how long do you think that chase went on for?"

Robert licked the maple syrup off his fork. "About long enough for me to eat one pancake. But at the rate I chew . . . let's see . . . that could be one second per chew—"

"Okay, okay!" Julie Ann instinctively pushed at the bridge of her eyeglasses, more of a nervous habit than a necessary gesture since getting her new trendy tortoiseshell specs. "Let's say it was sixty seconds long. Sixty times forty-eight . . . that makes two thousand, eight hundred and eighty drawings! And it took two animators a month to draw that by hand! With the new program I just got for my computer I can do that in two days! Someday, I'm going to do my own feature film!"

I said, with exaggerated hurt in my voice, "Last month you told us you wanted to be a caterer. You were going to help me in the kitchen."

"Changes every month, Kate," Robert said, winking at me. "I'm just glad she got off that idea of learning how to ride a Harley and trailing around the country after your friend Cherry Jublanski."

I smiled to myself. Julie Ann was a lot like me when I was fourteen and full of ideas and dreams of adventures that I hoped would one day take me out of my ordinary existence. So far, it's been very interesting to watch her develop her outside-the-box thinking abilities.

The phone rang. Phoebe Jo jumped up from her chair and stepped quickly across the kitchen to answer it. "Cavanaugh residence."

She frowned as she listened to the caller. "Well, Mrs. Oakley, I'm not sure if she's up yet—she had a late night. Let me check."

Phoebe Jo turned to me and raised her eyebrows in a silent question.

I nodded and whispered on my way past her, "I'll take it in the library."

I went down the hall and turned left into a room with built-in mahogany bookcases on two of its walls. A small sofa, holding a collection of pillows made from Indian saris, sat at one end of the room. At the other end was a mahogany desk. I padded across the Tibetan carpet, plopped into my big executive chair behind the desk, and picked up the receiver.

"Hi, Charlotte."

"Kate, I'm sorry for getting you up, but I couldn't contain myself any longer. I've been awake all night. That girl's driving me crazy. First, I was worried sick about where Melissa was and then, when she got home and told me what had happened, I started worrying about her throwing the rest of her life away. You can't tell me nothing sinister's going on in that Lloyd Family now."

"Charlotte—"

"It's front page news in *The Enquirer* and it's on TV, radio—everywhere!"

It was part of my religion not to look at any news before

noon on Saturdays. "I haven't seen or heard anything yet. How are they reporting it?"

"Well, they say it's an accident and that someone saw Victor Lloyd falling overboard. But I don't believe that for a minute, not with Melissa telling me about this Oasis business. And my daughter still wants to marry his son—the girl has no sense! She was up all night crying because she was afraid it was going to disrupt their wedding plans! Kate, I'm beside myself. Did you find out *anything* last night?"

She wanted instant answers that would confirm her suspicions, but I really had nothing concrete to tell her. And I wasn't going to let her know about my own suspicions. That would just scare the pants off her. But I had to say something.

I took a breath. "Charlotte. I'm on a trail, but I don't know where it's going to lead. If anywhere. Sit tight, be patient, and give me time."

"Time? I don't have time. Melissa's badgering me to announce her engagement in *Clairmont Living*. We got into a huge fight last night and she threatened to elope with that Eric Lloyd who probably put that irresponsible idea into her head."

I pulled the phone away from my ear, pinched the bridge of my nose, and began counting backwards from ten. I could hear Charlotte screeching, "Kate? You there?"

Two . . . One . . . Zero. "Yes. I'm going to make phone calls and start talking to people this afternoon."

"Okay. Then what?" From her tone of voice, it sounded like she was expecting me to lay out a party plan, no different than if she'd hired me to do a catering job for one of her mystery dinners. It wasn't that simple. In this case, there wasn't a card with the answers on the back that I could whip out at the end of the evening and read out whodunit to the befuddled guests.

On second thought, Charlotte probably didn't care whether or not Victor was murdered, or who his killer was. She just wanted me to explain, from start to finish, how I was going to wrap up the Lloyd Family with evidence of criminal

84

behavior so she could present it to her precious little girl and say, "See? Mommy told you Eric comes from bad seed."

It was going to frustrate the hell out of her, but all I could be was matter of fact. "Then what? Well, then I make more calls and talk to more people and keep doing that until there's nothing more to find out. I write up my report and give the information to you to do with as you wish.",

"*Melissa!* Sorry, Kate, can't talk anymore. Melissa just walked out the back door. I have to catch her and find out where she's going."

"Bye," I said, as the phone clicked in my ear.

Holding in the button on the receiver, I sat and contemplated what to do next. I'd been thinking of paying a visit to Eleanor Sloane, one of Mother's bridge partners, and Clairmont's unofficial clearing house of information. A big Texas Gal, whose wealth came from her daddy's oil fields, Eleanor was pretty savvy when it came to Cincinnati's wheelings and dealings, and was an important player in the local investment scene. In fact, I had expected to see her at Victor's riverboat party—she must have been invited—so I wondered why she wasn't there. Maybe she stayed away intentionally. In any case, ever since she kicked her husband out last Christmas, we'd become pals. If there was any behind the scenes talk about Victor, she would share it with me.

I punched in Eleanor's number. I was going to ask her if we could meet that afternoon, but all I got was her answering machine. I left a message for her to call me. I clicked off and went back to the kitchen.

Phoebe Jo had already cleared away the breakfast plates. Seeing me, she went to the oven and pulled out a plate piled high with the remaining pancakes.

"I knew you didn't have enough breakfast, Miss Kate," she said, setting the plate down in front of me as I slid into my chair. "And don't forget to take your vitamin E. I read in one of my magazines it increases your thinking power."

Phoebe Jo plunked the vitamin bottle down in front of me. "Your brain'll need this if you're gonna figure out who killed that poor Mr. Lloyd—oops, sorry, I forgot. Not supposed to talk about that before lunch."

If I took all the little bits of advice Phoebe Jo handed out, I'd have pills lined up the length of the table. But I go along with anything that promises to help my brain work better. I'm sure pancakes were good for that too, so I dug in.

Julie Ann and Robert were mesmerized by a Road Runner cartoon. I watched Wile E. Coyote unroll a huge coil of wire connected to some explosive gadget he'd just finished screwing together, and hide behind a rock where he hooked up the other end of the wire to a giant dynamite plunger. The Coyote waited for his prey to come *beep-beeping* across the desert landscape.

I said, "Getting any pointers, Robert?"

He turned to me with an exasperated expression. "If only my coyote was as dumb as this one."

"No luck, huh?"

"You would've heard me singing the Hallelujah Chorus if I had."

KA-BLAM! The plan backfired and we watched Coyote crumble into a heap of ashes.

"That's what I'll do," Robert said, "—hire the Rozzis to come over and blow him up for me."

"Oh. That reminds me." I sat forward in my chair. "We've all been invited to watch the Labor Day Weekend Rozzi fireworks from one of the prime viewing locations on the river."

All three Boones perked up.

And then I ruined the moment by answering Julie Ann's, "Who invited us?"

"Dick Rottingham," I said.

"Hey, Dad, isn't he that weird guy you're always listening to on the radio?"

Robert had an ear-to-ear grin on his face.

Phoebe Jo's nostrils flared and her lips were pinched. "Well, y'all know what I think of that man." To her, the very mention of Dick Rottingham's name had soiled the air in the kitchen. I'd seen the same expression on her face whenever Boo-Kat farted under the table.

"Aw, Mom," Julie Ann said, "does that mean we can't go?"

Phoebe Jo turned her back to us and began clattering dishes in the sink.

Robert winked at Julie Ann, and mouthed to me, "I'll talk to her."

The phone rang. Robert said, "Kinda busy around here, don't ya think?"

"I'll get it." Julie Ann pushed her chair back from the table, accidentally knocking into Boo-Kat's outstretched leg. He jumped up, tucked his tail between his legs and growled.

"Cut it out, Boo!" I said.

He ignored me and slunk out of the kitchen, retreating to the laundry room to curl up in a dark corner next to the dryer—one of his favorite moping spots.

"What's got into Boo-Kat?" Robert asked.

I shook my head. "I don't know. Maybe it's that coyote. Boo can smell it all around the farm and it's put him on edge. The sooner you get rid of that thing the better. I don't like this aggressive side of him."

Julie Ann was holding the phone to her ear and frowning. She cupped her hand over the mouthpiece. "Um, Katie, it's a funny-sounding man. He talks with a funny accent."

I reached out towards Julia Ann, indicating for her to bring the cordless phone over to me. "Hello? This is Kate Cavanaugh."

A gurgly, high-pitched voice with a singsongy East Indian accent said, "This is Baba Gee Bob. I am calling to you from India. We are live on the radio. Your name has been drawn as winner of the 45th Annual Bombay Cow Pie Lottery, and you've won a year of free yoga lessons."

I could hear a second person in the background mumbling something. "Who is this?"

Mr. Baba Gee Bob said, "Are you not excited? The cow pie with your name in it was picked from thousands of others."

"Oh, yeah? And how exactly did my name get in that cow pie?"

"Gracious me, you have a couple of very good friends who wish you every good fortune and wonderfulness."

"Who, exactly, are these thoughtful friends of mine. Tell me their names."

"Oh, no. Oh, no. I cannot do that. But I will tell you one is very big and wide, and the other is very small and skinny—like a Popsicle stick. And the big one is jolly. And the small one is very wise."

The voice was beginning to lose its Bombay accent and I could detect a trace of Brooklyn. A snapshot of two crazy guys on the beach popped into my head. It was hard to believe, but I said, excitedly, "Paco? Bobby and Paco? Is that you?"

12

"SORRY, PACO," I SAID, after he revealed they'd just landed and were at the airport. "Cincinnati doesn't have much public transportation to speak of—at least not what you're used to in Asia. But you don't have to take a bus or a cab—I'll pick you up. 'Course, you'll have to wait—it'll take me at least forty-five minutes to drive there. And I'm still in my jammies."

Paco replied, "Ah, we're used to Bombay time. Don't rush."

"Well, I'm anxious to see you two, so I'll spring for a limo. You'll be here in less than an hour."

I gave my old friend directions from the airport in Northern Kentucky to Trail's End and clicked off.

"Who's coming now?" Julie Ann asked. Her whole face

was lit up with excitement and she leaned towards me, gripping the edge of the kitchen table.

"Bobby and Paco."

Robert grinned. "Couple more of those pals from your good ol' days find you through the Internet?"

"Yeah. Klaus still has his web page. Thankfully, he screens people before handing out my address. But he knows I'd be excited to see these two guys again."

I'd become a regular visitor to Klaus' web page. When we were all living on the Goan beaches in India a couple of decades ago, Klaus kept us all informed and connected with his quirky little newspaper *The Goan Pig*. So it was natural he'd jump on the Information Highway with a cyberspace edition.

Phoebe Jo pulled off her apron as she hurried out of the kitchen. "I'll get two of the guest rooms ready."

I yelled out after her, "Don't fuss."

She yelled something back, but I couldn't hear what. She was already halfway up the stairs.

"Let her go, Kate," Robert said. "You know she loves it."

Julie Ann grabbed my arm and shook it. "So, who *are* these guys?"

"Bobby and Paco are two Jewish brothers from Brooklyn—Paco's the oldest. Hmmm . . . they'd be in their mid-fifties by now. Anyway, they've been living in Asia for close to thirty years and, as far as I knew, they had no desire to come back to the States, so I don't know why they're here now. The last news I had about them was that they were still roaming around between Bali, Kathmandu, and southern India, wheeling and dealing in jewelry and exotic artifacts. They're a lot of fun. I'm really looking forward to seeing them." God knows I needed some fun in my life.

The only thing I knew for sure at that moment was I needed to change out of my kimono and slap on my left boob.

* * * * * * * * * *

"HERE THEY COME!" Julie Ann shouted up the stairs. She'd taken it upon herself to set up a watch post under the huge oak tree on the front lawn and ran into the house as soon as she saw a car come up the road.

I finished buttoning up my ankle-length flowered skirt and went over to my bedroom's bay window. From there I could see the front yard with its long gravel lane. A white Buick sedan came crunching up the drive towards the house and I caught a glimpse of a big straw hat on the driver. I slipped into my sandals, shut the door behind me to keep Boo-Kat in the bedroom, and ran down the stairs.

As I stepped out the front door and started down the flagstone walk, Julie Ann directed the car to the parking area beside the house.

The front passenger door opened and a small bony head emerged. I laughed right out loud—I couldn't help myself. Except for his receding hairline, he looked exactly the same as the last time I saw him. The skinny man straightened up, turned and waved at me. His teeth were brilliant against the nut brown tan of his skin. He wore a casual white linen suit and purple T-shirt that was more appropriate for walking along the beach than down the streets of Cincinnati.

"Bobby!" I ran around the back of the car and greeted him with a hug. It felt like my arms could wrap around him twice, he was so small. Bobby squeezed me harder and held onto me longer than I expected him to. When I pulled away and looked down into his face—the years of sun had obviously done their damage—I could tell he was even a little choked up.

By this time, the driver had pulled himself out from behind the steering wheel and was standing next to the car, leaning his elbows on the roof and fanning himself with his hat. "Hey, hey! What am I—the chauffeur?"

"Hi, Paco! Oh, I'm so glad you're here. It's great to see you both." I hurried around to the other side of the car and hugged the older brother who, except for the same tanned complexion, was the physical opposite of the younger. Paco was big and soft and sweaty, and looked like he'd slept in his baggy blue cotton pants and white cotton shirt. The banded collar of his shirt was open and I could see some kind of leather choker with amber and silver beads. He still had his bushy beard, but it was now more gray than black.

"You didn't take a limo," I said, looking at the car and watching Bobby pull a long cardboard Delta Airlines box from the back seat.

"Nah!" Paco waved his hand. "Since you can't just hail rickshaws in this part of the world, figured we'd better rent a car to get around."

Bobby already had the trunk open and was yanking out heavy-looking pieces of luggage that made *thuds* when they hit the ground. "Kate, we may never make it out of Ohio alive with this maniac behind the wheel. He hasn't driven in the States since he was in his twenties and I can't get it through that thick skull of his that you have to drive on the *right* side of the line—not down the middle."

Paco waved him off. "Hey, with your navigating— 'It's up on the right! No, the left! No, turn right! Right!' What the hell else can I do?" He shrugged, his hands in a helpless gesture. "This is a great place you've got here, Kate. Looks just like Cherry and Jaz described it in their posts on Klaus' web page. Anyone else visit you?"

"Nope, and you're the first guys," Julie Ann said, obviously wanting to be included in the conversation. I introduced her to my two friends.

"Is she yours?" Bobby asked.

Surprised, I laughed and looked at Julie Ann, who stared up at me as if searching for some resemblance. "No," I said, "she belongs to the couple who live here on the farm with me."

"Well, you never know," Bobby replied. "It's been a long time. You kind of look the same."

I pulled on Julie Ann's single brown braid, a style she had copied from me. Julie Ann had grown to her full height of five-feet-nine and she had the same bony, gangly build I had, so the assumption was understandable.

"Need some help?" Robert came down the flagstone walk

and without waiting for an answer began gathering up their duffel bags and carry-ons. I introduced Robert and grabbed a suitcase. Each of us picked up what we could and formed a caravan, hauling what probably represented all of Bobby and Paco's earthly possessions towards the house.

We entered the foyer—the phone was ringing—and dumped the bags on the floor, except for Robert who continued on up the stairs with his load. Julie Ann tried to follow him, but she almost knocked one of the pictures of the Chili Kings, my ancestors, off the wall with the long cardboard airline box she was carrying. Backing away, she managed to wedge the other end of the box between two stair rails.

"Wait," Bobby said, "I'll take that." He helped Julie Ann free the box without smacking Grandpa Cavanaugh in the eye.

Bobby came back downstairs with the box and handed it to me. "This is for you, Kate. We brought it all the way from Bali."

"For me? Oh, boy, I was wondering what was in here." I ripped off the end, tipped it over, and caught the carved stick as it slid out. It was a solid five-foot length of richly grained wood, like a branch still with its knots and bends, but the top had been carved into a magnificently detailed elephant head.

"It's *beautiful.*" I held it out in front of me.

Bobby bowed and said, "The perfect accessory for the Amazon Warrior as she patrols the grounds of her kingdom."

Paco added, "And beats off all those wild fortune-hunting playboy suitors who keep trying to climb into her bed."

"Ha," I said. "Not as dangerous around here as you think."

Phoebe Jo called out from the kitchen, "Miss Kate, phone call. Eleanor Sloane."

I excused myself from my guests and took the call in the library.

". . . AND ALL I NEED is an hour of your time, Eleanor. Is this afternoon okay?"

"Sure. No problem, Kate." Eleanor paused for a moment.

"You don't believe it was an accident, do you?"

"No."

"Neither do I."

13

"BAMBOLEO, BAMBOLEA!" Paco, Bobby, and I sang along with a Gipsy Kings tune blasting from the CD player at a volume that was sure to cost us a five hundred dollar fine if we were caught by a Clairmont Ranger. Add to that another couple hundred for doing sixty in a thirty-five mile an hour zone, and the potential price tag for our exhilarating joy ride could be a little steep.

I was going to drive to Eleanor's by myself after lunch, but Bobby and Paco were in the mood for a little sight-seeing and had insisted on driving me there.

"We won't get in your way," Paco said. "We'll just sit outside and wait for you."

I'd let them assume I was visiting Eleanor to go over the details of a catering job. I was planning to fill them in on what was going on later that evening. Lunch had turned into a two hour nonstop conversation that left no time to get into the complicated story of Victor Lloyd. Not only were we catching up with one another but, as I remembered was always the case with Bobby and Paco, we got into one of those lengthy discussions that were half-comic, half-spiritual. That day's topics explored the Mysteries of Middle Age, the Meaning of Life, and the reason they were going to New Mexico.

Screech! My whole body lurched forward as Paco slammed on the brakes.

I said, "What the hell are you—?"

Paco swiveled around in his seat and looked over his shoulder, past me and out the rear window of the car. He put the car in reverse and stepped on the gas. The tires squealed as he backed up.

Bobby looked like he was going to smack his brother. "Now what?"

"You didn't see that?"

"What?"

I said, "Paco, you're going to get us killed." My body lurched again as he stepped on the brake.

"There it is!" Paco pointed out the window. "Get out your camera, Bobby. Take a picture."

I followed his point and when I saw what it was, I laughed. "Pull over and get out of the way of the traffic."

Paco twirled the steering wheel and we crunched onto the gravel of the shoulder. Bobby jumped out with his camera and took a picture of the dead raccoon in the middle of the road, which would normally not be worth stopping to look at. But the freshly painted yellow line running down the center of the road continued without a break across the furry back of this poor critter. Guess Clairmont's road maintenance crew was running behind schedule. No time to stop.

Paco shook his head. "I don't know, Kate, this is a weird place you're living in. It's got me on edge."

"You've lived in a lot weirder places."

"Yeah, well, I've been driving down this road and looking around and I'm thinking everything is so clean and understated. Not like where we just came from. Remember, Kate? Everything in Asia is gaudy and decorated to the hilt. And there's this chaotic energy everywhere you go. But here, even the road signs are subtle—they're these nice brown wooden plaques that blend into the landscape. Even the cars people drive around here, they're all gray and taupe and dark green. And you can't see the houses from the road, just these big stone gates. No people walking on the street. No sidewalks. No stores or street vendors. I'm driving along thinking this is scary. It's so sterile, so unreal. But then," Paco slapped his hands together and looked heavenward, "God bless him, some yo-yo leaves his mark! Individual self

94

expression! *I love it!*"

"Hold on a sec, Paco. I like driving around here. It's restful." I slapped his shoulder playfully. "You just have a warped personality that needs constant stimulation."

Bobby climbed back into the front seat. "I got a couple of good shots."

"Great," Paco said, "now we've got a start on the North American series."

Bobby looked at me and without my asking, answered, "We're documenting our travels with photos of bizarre behavior around the world."

Well, there was plenty of that going on around staid old Clairmont—if you knew where to look. Or who to ask.

I took one last look at the raccoon's body as we sped away and it brought to mind the sight of the mangled body of Victor Lloyd laid out on the deck of his riverboat. It wasn't a pretty thought, but I saw Victor as road kill in the rat race to riches. I hoped Eleanor Sloane would be able to help me find out whose path he was crossing when he got hit.

I told Paco, "Just up ahead there on the right is one of those big stone gates you love so much. Turn in there."

Having the guys wait for me in the car might seem like a really unfriendly thing to do to them, but I wanted Eleanor to be candid and able to talk seriously. If I brought Bobby and Paco inside with me, I was afraid she'd put on her Gay Divorcée act.

We drove down Eleanor's laneway which was shaded with pine trees and sycamores so thick you couldn't see the house until the driveway circled right in front of it. She'd bought the house with her own money after dumping her philandering husband, Patrick. It was an older home, a mini-mansion built of white painted brick with huge white pillars flanking the front entrance and second floor balconies that made it look like it belonged on a southern plantation. She was investing a small fortune in remodeling the interior and was living in a constant state of contractor chaos. Thankfully, there were no workmen's trucks parked outside. The front door was wide open—the space filled entirely by Eleanor's pink caftan-shrouded body.

I said, "Just park right here in the front, Paco."

He brought the car to a gravel-spraying stop. Bobby ejected the Gipsy Kings from the CD player and the sudden silence buzzed in my ears.

Eleanor swept gracefully down the steps towards us, her brilliant coral-painted lips already parted in a wide grin. She's a lovely woman, but it was sort of like being greeted by one of Fantasia's hippo ballerinas. "Why, Kate, you party animal," she said, padding her black curly hair with her pudgy fingers, "which one's for me?"

As Bobby and Paco exchanged startled glances, I thought, *So much for Clairmont's understated subtlety.*

I climbed out of the back seat, slammed the door behind me, and met up with Eleanor at the bottom of the steps. She gave me an absent-minded hug, but was already being pulled towards the car as if caught up in some magnetic field.

Eleanor bent down and peered into the front passenger window, her Navajo silver and turquoise earrings clanging like wind chimes. "You boys aren't leaving, are you?" She yanked the door open. "Come inside."

I should've known this would happen. As Paco and Bobby stepped out of the car, I introduced them to Eleanor. Each one gave her a gallant little bow of the head and a "pleased to meet you, ma'am" as they shook hands.

Eleanor herded us into the house. "I think the kitchen's the most comfy place to be right now. You can see the sitting room's not fit for sitting—it's being painted."

We walked past an enormous high-ceilinged room, it's furniture huddled together under drop sheets in the center. I peeked inside at the walls that were covered with strange splotches of yellowy-green paint, and said, "What're they doing? Dunking your cats in the paint and throwing them against the wall?"

Eleanor laughed. "Oh, Kate, what an awful sense of humor. You know it's not finished—everyone's having their walls spunge-painted these days. It looks god-awful until they get all the layers up. There's two more to go—then it'll be gorgeous." She turned to Bobby and Paco. "C'mon, I've got fresh coconut cake and a big pitcher of iced tea."

We followed Eleanor into her spanking white kitchen with all new green marble counters and glass-fronted cupboards.

"Have a seat," she said, shooing her two fat Persian cats off a couple of the wrought iron stools along one side of the center island. Drifts of white fur floated down to the floor after them.

Eleanor lifted the domed cover off a cake stand and began slicing huge chunks of coconut cake. She handed a plate to Bobby, who held up his hand and shook his head. "No, thank you. It looks great, but we just had a big lunch."

"I'll have some," Paco said, reaching for the plate.

"Me, too," I said.

"You'll be impressed, Kate." Eleanor licked a gob of frosting off her plump finger and smiled. "I grated the coconut fresh this morning."

As she poured tall tumblers of iced tea and stuck lemon slices on the rims, I decided not to be concerned with what Bobby and Paco heard and jumped right in with my first question. "I was expecting to see you at Victor Lloyd's party last night. Why didn't you go? You *were* invited, weren't you?"

"Oh, sure I was. Victor knew my pockets were jingling, but I was pissed off at him."

"Why?"

"Well, for one thing, he was an obnoxious bastard—the type of man who just had to be the star of the show and expected everybody else to be happy being a bit player."

"And did he want you to be one of those bit players?"

"Ha!" Eleanor picked a couple of shreds of coconut off her piece of cake and placed them daintily into her mouth. "Patrick and I—" Eleanor quickly turned to Paco and Bobby, "—my ex-husband who is not allowed to set foot in this house—" she looked back at me, "have been living in

Clairmont for about the same length of time as the Lloyds. We went to all the same functions and parties and acknowledged each other, but never became friends. As soon as I kicked Patrick out, Victor's knocking at my door. I thought he was trying to get into my bed, but I was flattering myself. He just wanted to get into my purse and figured he could sweet talk me into investing in his luxury condo project. Victor thought I was some dumb babe and I only used the business pages of *The Enquirer* to line my kitties' litter boxes."

Well, some people think that's all they're good for.

Eleanor picked up a knife and said, "More cake, Paco? What about you, Bobby? Change your mind?"

Bobby said, "No, thanks."

Paco accepted the slice she offered.

I kept the conversation on track, asking, "So what happened when you said you weren't interested in investing?"

"Never heard from him again. Until I got the invitation to what turned out to be his Oasis unveiling. Being invited didn't surprise me because Victor probably thought I'd be more interested in a nightclub. And I am—I think this area needs something to liven it up."

"Which brings up the rumors I've heard linking Victor to underworld types. What do you think?"

"Yeah, there were rumblings about that, so when Victor started sniffing around my door, I made a few phone calls to some business acquaintances of mine around here and in Texas. Turns out one of my Texas buddies had bumped into Victor. They were both checking out the potential for investing in casino operations in Indiana. All my friend knew was that Victor was from Las Vegas and that he was a jerk. Victor had all sorts of big ideas but he was just a small fry compared to the big corporations that were setting up there. So, Victor disappeared. That was about five years ago."

"Guess Cincinnati was the next stop on his route." And the last one.

Eleanor took the last bite of her cake and set the plate

down on the floor. The cats came streaking out of nowhere and attacked it with their tongues. She straightened back up, her face flushed from the aerobic workout. "As I told you on the phone, Kate, I don't think Victor's death was an accident. He rubbed people the wrong way, didn't make many friends here. Patrick and I moved into Clairmont at the same time as the Lloyds, but since Patrick's job with the Rodger's grocery chain automatically made us part of the corporate establishment, it was easy to find friends. But Victor was a maverick—not a team player, so he and his family were considered to be outside the loop. I've always felt kinda sorry for Tammy Lloyd—she didn't have a chance of being accepted. She drinks to dull the anger and disappointment that comes from living with someone like Victor Lloyd."

I asked, "Who do you think hated Victor enough to kill him?"

Out of the corner of my eye, I could see Bobby and Paco. Both were sitting very straight and alert on their stools—their faces showing identical expressions of total fascination.

Eleanor looked down at her iced tea and pulled the slice of lemon off the rim of the glass. "Hmm," she said, trying to dunk the ice cubes in her drink with the lemon. Giving up, she stuck it in her mouth and sucked it. I shuddered.

Eleanor said, "You're starting to sound like the Chili Heiress Detective. What are you up to?"

"Nothing," I lied, "just curious. I don't like questions running around in my head without any answers. The police don't seem to be suspicious. But on the phone you said you were thinking the same way I was. So, got any theories?"

Eleanor thought for a moment. "Okay, I'll play. The most obvious one is Ted Mueller. Was he on board last night?"

I nodded.

"There's been bad blood between those two for a while now. Victor beat Ted out of some big deal a few years back and Ted has always held a grudge because of that. And in the last year, he's watched Victor sail smoothly through all the red tape on the Kentucky side of the river, while the city and county officials on the Ohio side bicker about what to put where on their riverfront. Ted was stuck—couldn't get any of his own projects going.

"Now there's some Northern Kentucky business group running big ads in *The Enquirer* with the slogan, *Northern Kentucky: The Exciting Side of Cincinnati*—have you seen them, Kate? Ted must have been fuming. I figure he just had it up to here." Eleanor karate chopped one of her chins. "And so my guess is when Victor unveiled his Oasis project last night, he couldn't take it any longer and went crazy."

"And Ted's a big guy, so he'd be able to pick him up and toss him in the river like a football?"

Eleanor nodded. "Sure."

"But wait a minute, what about Alan Casey? Why would he lie?"

Eleanor stared back at me, as if her brain's electrical circuits had shorted out. Some emergency power source clicked in. She blinked and shook her head. "Oh gosh, I don't know. Even just watching those mysteries on TV, I get so confused I end up having to turn them off. Kate, you're not letting me talk to my other guests here."

She turned to Bobby and Paco. "How long are you boys staying? You know Kate will let you hang out as long as you want. And feed you good, too."

Bobby said, "We haven't got any definite plans, other than to wind up in New Mexico."

"And what's there?"

"Hopefully the start of a new life for us in this country."

Paco stood up and massaged the back of his right hip. "Asia's not as much fun as it used to be and it's gotten uncomfortable there."

Bobby added, "It's *always* been uncomfortable there." He nudged his brother with an elbow. "C'mon, tell her the truth. You're just getting too old and grumpy." He looked at Eleanor. "He's always complaining about his body.

Eleanor reached over and squeezed Paco's biceps. "I don't

100

know why—it looks fine to me."

Well, I'd certainly lost control of this conversation.

Eleanor switched her flirty look over to Bobby. "But you're *way* too thin—you need to eat more. Just stick around with Kate for a week or two and you'll be in good shape."

To me, she said, "You're bringing them to the Casablanca party next week? Aren't you, Kate?"

"Well, they're going gambling on the boats in Indiana—" I turned to Bobby. "When were you doing that?"

"Monday, but we'll be back by mid-week."

"Besides," I told Eleanor, "I'm the hired caterer. I can't just go adding my friends to the guest list."

"Oh, hang that!" Eleanor swatted the air. "I'll call Ruthie Yankovitch and tell her I'm bringing a couple of dates to her party and if she complains I'll tell her one of them doesn't eat very much." She winked at Bobby.

I think it was the first time I'd seen Bobby and Paco dominated by someone else's personality. In my memory, they'd always been the ones holding court and the rest of us were the audience. I'd never seen them just sit and watch for this length of time with those silly smiles pasted on their faces. But then, I guess this was the first time I was seeing them out of their own territory and they were looking to me for cues.

I said, "Well, guys, I can tell you that going on a date with Eleanor will be a lot of fun. It's up to you."

Both answered, "Sure!" at the same time.

Eleanor smiled. "That's great! Now I'm really looking forward to that party. I'm so glad you and the boys stopped by for a visit."

It felt like a good time to leave. The only new piece of information Eleanor had given me was that Victor Lloyd had come from Las Vegas and was definitely looking to get into the gambling business. Other than that, she just reinforced some of my own suspicions. But it didn't matter what road I went down, they all led back to Alan Casey.

And how the hell was I going to question him?

14

"YEAH, THAT'LL WORK." Bobby nodded. "I'll just tell this Alan guy you were taking us on a tour of this charming part of town. We were walking past his gallery and I noticed he was having a showing of photos of the Southwest."

Paco said, "We'll tell him we're photographers—well, you are, Bobby. No big lie. We're on our way to New Mexico, so we wanted to see his work."

After we left Eleanor's, I had directed Paco to drive to Montgomery, the town just west of Clairmont. On the way, I brought them up to speed with the story of Victor Lloyd and his demise. My explanation as to why I was involved in all this was like a shot of adrenalin to Paco.

"Hey, hey! Maybe this ain't gonna be such a boring place to visit after all."

Bobby looked at me and rolled his eyes back at Paco. "The guy needs more than constant stimulation—big brother's life has gotta be in danger before he says he's having a good time."

That explained Paco's New York cabby driving style.

We had arrived safely, though, and were sitting in the public parking lot behind the stretch of renovated clapboard and the newer "subtle" red brick stores that made up Old Montgomery, the center of town. Alan Casey's photography gallery was in one of those red brick buildings and we were going to pay him a visit.

I figured Alan would be really hesitant to speak to me—after all, our last conversation consisted of my telling him, "You're fired." But with the buffer of Paco and Bobby viewing his photos, Alan might want to put on a friendly show and be easier to engage in small talk.

I didn't have any definite questions to ask him. I just

wanted to get him into a conversation about what happened on the riverboat so that I could watch how he acted as he recounted his story—not quite hooking him up to a machine to measure his heart rate, but still a pretty reliable lie detector test. I don't usually brag, but it's hard to slip one past me.

"Okay, let's go, guys," I said, getting out of the car. I led the way across the parking lot, down a cobbled walkway between the buildings, and out to the sidewalk on Montgomery Road. We turned right. The gallery was two doors down. Just then, Alan Casey stepped out of his gallery, turned and inserted his key in the lock.

I shouted, "Alan, wait."

He turned, startled at first, then shocked when he saw who called him. But immediately, his chin shot out and his normally arrogant look returned to his face. Behind the tiny, black metal framed glasses were a pair of eyes so closely set together they almost touched. Aside from that, he was a nondescript type—medium height and build, with short brown hair. He was dressed casually in khaki chinos and a white T-shirt. Under his arm was a blue Express Mail envelope.

Alan didn't say anything, just waited—though he looked like he didn't even want to do that. All I got was a nod of the head as a greeting. Actually, he looked like he was about to snarl at me—hate rays were shooting out of those narrow slits of glass in front of his eyes. He definitely was recalling the last conversation we'd had.

Bobby said, "Hope you're not closing up. My brother and I wanted to see your Southwest photos. I'm a photographer, too. Name's Bobby." He extended his hand, leaving Alan no choice but to be civil and shake it.

Paco stuck his hand out. "I'm Paco. We're visiting Kate and we were driving by, saw your photos in the window and made her stop."

Alan frowned and his features converged in the center of his face like they were being sucked away from inside. Made me squirm.

He stepped back from us. "Um . . . you'll have to come

back Tuesday. I . . . uh, I have an important errand to run. And I'm not open Sunday or Monday."

Bobby said, "Well, that's disappointing. We're on our way to New Mexico and we'll only be here for a couple of days."

Paco pointed to his watch. "Just ten minutes."

Alan squinted up at me as if to say, *What the hell are you up to?* I smiled pleasantly. The guys were doing a good job. Didn't want to ruin it.

Alan looked at the envelope in his hand for a moment, then at his keys. He took a deep breath. "Okay. But only ten minutes."

He let us in. I don't really know why he did it. Maybe he was thinking that if he was nice to my friends, I might forgive him and go back to using him at my parties. I didn't promise or say a thing, except, "Thank you."

Even I was convinced Paco and Bobby were really interested in viewing Alan's photos. Actually, Alan was a good photographer and I found myself walking around the small stark gallery admiring his work but, at the same time, I launched into my planned small talk.

"Terrible what happened to Victor."

Alan grunted his response.

"It must have been awful to see him go overboard."

"Yeah." Alan wasn't very good at small talk.

"People say he might've been drunk. Did he look unsteady to you?"

He shrugged his shoulders. "I didn't even know he was there until I heard him shout. He was on the other side of the paddle wheel. I saw him go over and I called for help."

"Don't you think it was funny Victor was all by himself? I wonder what he was doing out there."

"I don't know." Alan was beginning to sound irritated, but he continued. "It was dark and noisy with that paddle wheel going. Didn't see anyone else around."

Guess I was boring him. He abandoned me and strode over to where Bobby and Paco were viewing his work. Bobby asked Alan a question about one of the photographs—probably just playing out his role, but then he got caught up in a stream of techno-talk that left Paco and me out of the conversation. Unfortunately, it ate up the remaining minutes.

As Alan led us around, pointing out each photograph and explaining what filters or lenses or settings he used, I tried to read the name and address on the envelope he was carrying. But the only thing I could make out was the first three digits of the zip code. It was local. As if he knew I was snooping, Alan nonchalantly put the envelope under his armpit, turning the addressed side away from me.

Alan checked his watch. "I gotta get going." He walked over to the door, held it open, and said, "Come back on Tuesday—I'll have more time then," forgetting or not caring that Bobby and Paco were not planning to be around. We shuffled out the door like dismissed schoolchildren.

After some quick thank-yous and good-byes on the sidewalk, Alan got into his BMW convertible parked in front of the gallery, and we headed back towards the public parking lot.

Bobby came up beside me and slipped his arm in mine. "Sorry, Kate," he said, "I didn't know that one little technical question was going to waste all your time."

"That's okay. Alan wasn't going to say more than he already had."

Paco was in front of us. He turned and said, "The guy's kind of a creep. Don't you think? Those funny little eyes? I don't trust him."

We reached the car and Bobby opened the rear door for me. Felt like I was on a date. I tried to fold myself into the back seat as gracefully as possible.

"Okay, Detective Kate," Paco said, gripping the steering wheel and looking at me in his rear view mirror, "where we going now?"

Bobby turned around in his seat—expectant, waiting for orders.

"Home," I announced.

Both brothers simultaneously flung their arms in the air in

exasperation and said, "Aw c'mon, Kate."

"I'm psyched!" Paco said. "You gotta have more people on your list to talk to."

"No, wait." Bobby waved his hand. "Kate's probably right—I'm sure she has a master plan. Timing is important. You don't just go storming around, asking a lot of personal questions. Right, Kate?"

"Right. But you're ahead of me. I haven't got my master plan figured out yet. Actually, all I'd planned to do this afternoon was talk to Eleanor. Alan was kind of a spontaneous thing, and apparently unproductive. At this point, I don't know what the next step is." I rubbed at my temple—my head was beginning to throb. "I think I'm suffering sugar shock from eating Eleanor's coconut cake."

Bobby slapped the dashboard a couple of times. "Home it is. Start 'er up, Paco."

Once I got us onto Route 126 I settled into a corner of the back seat and gazed out the window at the trees whooshing past. The dense foliage of their branches arched over the road before us like a green canopy. After a minute or two, I sensed Bobby turning in my direction. I looked at him.

"Feeling okay?" he asked.

I nodded.

Bobby said, "I know the acupressure points to relieve your headache. Soon as we get home, I'll take care of it for you."

"That would be nice."

"Kate, you're the type of person who's very strong, but easily thrown off balance if you don't keep to healthy routines. Eating that much sugar isn't good for you. I know you're aware of that 'cause I remember how you went to great lengths to eat right when we were in India."

Still looking at me, Bobby said, "Paco? Don't you remember how Kate always had it together when it came to food?" He turned to his brother. "Even in those dark little houses with dirt floors and no electricity, Kate would build a fire and cook up big pots of stew with god knows what in it. It always tasted great." He looked back at me. "Not surprising you made a profession out of that. You have this nurturing soul inside of you."

Paco tilted his head back towards me and said, "Yeah. Anyone who can throw stuff like miso and yak cheese into the stew and make it taste as good as Boeuf Bourguignonne, sure knows what she's doing."

I laughed, sat up quickly and pointed across Paco's shoulder. "Turn left up here at the light—that's Loveland-Madeira Road. Take it all the way to the end. I'll tell you where to turn when we get there."

To both I said, "You're right, I've always been like that." I sighed. "All of a sudden, there's a part of me that's dissatisfied. It's like I've accomplished what I wanted to with that and now I need something new to get excited about."

Paco said to the rear view mirror, "*I* could get excited about doing this murder investigation stuff."

Bobby added, "Yeah, Kate, maybe you can make a career out of playing private eye."

"Well . . ." I leaned my head against the side window. "They're already calling me the Amazon Chili Heiress Detective. But there's something about being labeled that makes my back go up. It's one thing to get pulled into these situations or find myself helping a friend out of a tight spot. That's kind of fun. But doing it every day as a career?" I shrugged my answer.

"You'd still be using your talents," Bobby said. "It's a constructive way to spend the day *and* contribute positive energy to the planet. Searching out the truth? Getting rid of the bad guys? I can see it—Kate Cavanaugh, Defender of the Good, bringing justice and order to the universe."

Paco turned around and looked directly at me, his eyes wide and dancing with excitement. "Now *that's* sexy."

"Paco!" I shouted.

He quickly jerked his head back to look at the road. "Goddamn!"

He'd let the car wander over the yellow line to the wrong side of the road and a Federal Express delivery van was heading straight for us.

Paco wrenched the steering wheel to the right.

The Fed Ex van swerved to the left. As it passed by, the angry driver cursed us with four-lettered blasts of his horn.

15

"RELAX, KATE, YOU'RE resisting me."

I was lying face down on the exercise mat on the floor of my gym. Bobby straddled my back and tried to loosen me up with soothing intonations while he pushed his thumbs forcefully up against the base of my cranium.

His fingers moved down to my rock hard neck and shoulder muscles. Though I knew I was in the hands of an expert, I couldn't loosen up. I was struggling with what to do next in my investigation. Paco and Bobby's enthusiasm for this possible new career was both supportive and pressure-inducing. Did I really have the ability to make the shift? Was this really the direction I wanted to go in? Trying to learn while on the job is the most intensive type of training there is, and flying by the seat of my pants can, at times, give me an incredible adrenaline rush, but also make every muscle in my body turn to stone.

Paco's stunt-driving didn't exactly help my condition.

Bobby's voice had a chant-like quality to it. "Relax your mind . . . let go . . . travel to a favorite place where it's warm and comfortable."

I tried to empty all thoughts out of my brain and start with a blank page. My mind took me to an endless white beach with palm trees waving their fronds in a gentle breeze. I could hear the sound of waves breaking on the deserted shore and I tried to match my breathing to their rhythm. A figure appeared in the distance on that shore and began sauntering towards me, kicking the water playfully every other step or so. As he came closer, I saw it was Victor Lloyd. Just like my dog, I'm obsessive—I can't let go of something once I commit to it.

"Miss Kate?" What was Phoebe Jo doing on my beach?

I lifted my head off the mat. "I better get that, Bobby."

He slid off my back and I went over to the wall phone and pushed the intercom button. "Here I am."

"Paco's sitting here in the kitchen looking hungry. It is close to dinner time—what would you like to eat? I've got chicken."

"Okay. Be right in."

Bobby stood up from the mat, crossed his arms, and frowned at me. "It's not good to hold so much tension in your muscles like that. You should be doing some meditation."

"I can't sit still long enough. Drives me nuts." I picked up a basketball and bounced it a couple of times. "Shooting hoops helps me unwind." I dribbled the ball to the foul line and threw a hook shot. Went right in—nothing but net. Big show-off.

WE DEVOURED PHOEBE JO'S oven-fried chicken, corn pudding, and salad. All of us, that is, except Julie Ann who had gone off, somewhat reluctantly, to a friend's birthday party. Julie Ann was a smart girl. She knew that friendships at the age of fourteen are precarious at best and that if she didn't show up, her friend "would never talk to me again."

Julie Ann would rather have stayed with us and tried to influence the flow of conversation by pumping Bobby and Paco for crazy stories of my past adventures. Instead, in her absence, the dinner conversation ventured into more adult territory.

Later, Bobby, Paco, and I took an after dinner stroll around the farm. Paco found himself with his hands full. Thinking he had bonded with Boo-Kat—slipping him chicken under the table—he'd placed himself in charge of keeping my little terror on the trail. Boo-Kat just saw this as an opportunity to take advantage of a big softy and kept trying to sniff out coyotes under every bush.

I was breaking in my new walking stick. The sun had another two hours before it dipped below the horizon, the temperature was still in the eighties, and the trees were buzzing with cicadas.

As we walked around the pond, I told them about the coyote invading the farm and, again, how dissatisfied I was with catering.

Bobby picked up a stone. "Well, everybody has to find their own way. We're all looking for different things. The same thing is happening to Paco. He was no longer happy in Asia and said it was time to come home."

When I knew Bobby twenty years ago in India, people referred to him as a holy man. He seemed wiser than the rest of us, maybe even possessing powers and insights beyond what a Jewish boy from Brooklyn should have. Now, as he studied me, I knew it didn't take a mind reader to see the emotional turmoil I felt inside.

Bobby skipped the stone across the surface of the pond, creating ripples. "We all come to this point, Kate. Some of us are lucky, I guess. We can choose to try something different. Others get stuck into a life they think they can't change and suffer silently."

"I just know one thing," I said, slamming the tip of my walking stick into the ground for emphasis, "I don't want an ordinary life. I don't want it to be routine or predictable. And with my catering that's what it's become. You said your reason for going to New Mexico was to start a new life. You guys had your own business and were successful. What happened? What are you looking for now?"

Paco answered, "I want to make a lot of money."

"It looked like you were when I was over there." I remembered everyone else buying and selling cheap trinkets and clothing. But Bobby and Paco stood out from the crowd. They had their own little network going, bringing one-of-a-kind pieces of jewelry and artifacts out of Asia and selling them to collectors and wealthy tourists in Europe.

Bobby said, "We made enough to buy comfortable houses in Greece and Nepal. Well . . . *I* thought they were comfortable."

Paco scratched his beard. "You don't need a lot of money to live well in Asia, but I'm more materialistic than my brother. When I say I want to make money, I mean *millions*. I see all these guys my age—entrepreneurs who stayed here and are millionaires now. Asia was fun, but I've been wasting time. I just hope it's not too late for me to carve out my own little niche here." Paco pointed at Bobby. "His holiness can be happy anywhere."

Bobby turned to his brother. "Not exactly—I still need lots of sun and I like being able to go up into the mountains."

I said, "All I know is I have to be around people and if I stop catering, that's the part of it I'd miss. But then sometimes I need to get away from humanity, so I'll never give up Trail's End. I love this place—it's my sanctuary."

I dug at the soft earth by the side of the pond with my stick. A little frog leapt out of some hidden burrow and dove into the pond. Boo-Kat saw it and lunged, straining at his leash, almost pulling Paco off-balance.

Choosing to break out of routines means you have to travel on a road that is unpredictable. But that's what I'd just said I wanted. Investigating crime is certainly unpredictable.

At that moment, Charlotte Oakley popped into my head.

"I have to make a phone call. Do you guys want to stay out here by yourselves or go back to the house with me?"

Bobby took my arm. "Can I use your gym? My body's stiff and crying out for its yoga workout."

"Of course."

WE SPLIT UP JUST inside the front door. I went right, into the library, Bobby went left, down the corridor towards the gym, and Paco and Boo-Kat headed for the Great Room with its wide-screen TV and comfy couch.

I plopped down into the leather chair behind my desk and studied the elephant head on the end of my walking stick. What a wonderful gift, I thought, rubbing the ridges that had been carved so meticulously on the elephant's trunk.

My mind had cleared as we stood by the pond. It was as if all this talk about making changes and looking in new directions had opened a channel for fresh thoughts. I had a plan. Sort of. It was more of a next step.

If Victor Lloyd really was killed by someone on board his riverboat, I couldn't just go bumbling around, interrogating the hundreds of guests who had been there that night. It was smarter to be methodical. I decided to work my way outwards from Victor and find out, first, who he really was. What was behind that flashy, overconfident showman?

Murder is usually personal, so I needed to find out what was happening in Victor's private life. The most interesting place to start would be his funeral—it would be a gathering place for people his death had affected. Some would come to cry. Others to sing and dance for joy—secretly, of course. Those singers and dancers were the ones I needed to identify.

I punched in Charlotte Oakley's number.

"Hi. It's Kate," I said, when she picked up at the other end.

"Oh, Kate! What great timing. I was just thinking of calling you. Have you found out something new? Does Victor have underworld connections?" Charlotte's voice was strained with tension.

"Well . . . I did find out he came from Las Vegas—"

"I told you so—"

"That doesn't prove anything. Be patient. I figured you'd know about his funeral—"

"Yes, that's what I was going to call you about. It's on Monday. Melissa says she has to be at Eric's side and is insisting that, since we are almost part of that family, I must attend. I certainly don't like the idea of being considered almost family, but it's my first opportunity to get into that house and see for myself what they live like. You know that

Tammy Lloyd never invited anyone over. It's kind of strange she's throwing her doors open at this time. You've got to come with me, Kate. I'm sure that house has something to say."

A bonus! I was thinking there'd just be a funeral, but a reception in his home was my chance to get up close and personal.

"Charlotte, I can't do both the service and the reception, but I'm anxious to see inside his house, too. What time's the reception?"

"Two o'clock." She gave me the address, though it wasn't necessary. Everybody in Clairmont knew where "that Lloyd family" lived.

I went and joined Paco on the comfy couch and fixed my eyes on the TV screen, and watched the images of some gritty-looking police procedural, but didn't listen to the dialogue. A half hour later, Bobby came in looking all yoga-ized, weightless and blissed out. He sat down in front of the sofa and crossed his legs in one fluid motion that made me hyper-aware of all the kinks and locked joints in my own body.

We'd all had enough of the day. The guys were in the Twilight Zone of jet lag, and I could see them struggling to gear themselves into Eastern Standard Time. Paco was starting to nod off.

I slapped him on his knee and rubbed Bobby's shiny head. "I don't know about you two, but it's time for me to turn in. The house is yours."

They followed Boo-Kat and me up the stairs. We said very short "good nights" and disappeared into our bedrooms. Robert and Phoebe Jo had already retired to their living quarters at the opposite end of the house. The usual night time quiet had descended, but Trail's End Farm couldn't quite shut down yet—there was still a watchful energy coming from the Boone's side of the house. Boo-Kat settled into his bed, and I undressed and put on a nightshirt.

I'd finished washing my face and was brushing my teeth

when I heard a car come up the laneway and stop in front of the house. Julie Ann's voice, just below my bedroom window, said, "Thanks for the ride. Had a great time." The car door slammed, the front door slammed, and Julie Ann ran up the stairs. More like pounded up the stairs with her heavy, clunky-heeled shoes. Once the door at the far end of the corridor slammed, order returned and everyone was in their rightful place. I climbed into bed.

I switched on the radio, expecting to be lulled to sleep by the WAVE's traditional jazz show.

Instead, my eardrums were accosted by, "——*so come for a special Getaway Weekend to Northern Kentucky—the EXCITING side of Cincinnati!*"

Immediately following that, an even more irritating, but recognizable, voice disturbed the peace. *"It's The Big Wow! 707 W-O-W! Dick Rottingham here!"*

What? The radio should have been on the FM band. Phoebe Jo must have been dusting and accidentally switched it to AM. The two stations were at the same spots on their respective bands.

"It is a terrible, terrible tragedy that has befallen the Lloyd family and every citizen in the Cincinnati Tristate area."

I was going to change stations, but decided to listen to what Dick had to say.

"Not only has the Lloyd family been deprived of the love of a wonderful husband and father, whose life was cut oh so very short, but our fair city has been robbed of the potential fruits of an incredibly talented man of vision. It goes without saying that I, myself, am having great difficulty dealing with the shock of losing such a close and wonderful friend. This is compounded by the coincidence that I was on board last night attending that fateful cruise. If I knew, as the rumors say, that Victor was unsteady on his feet, I'd have kept an eagle eye on him and would have literally clung to him like a second skin, ready in an instant to fling my arms around him should he totter too closely to the boat's railing."

Boy! Dick was really milking this one.

"But there's something strange about this accident. I have a feeling deep down in my gut that he didn't fall overboard. I saw him no more than a half hour earlier in the arms of his dear wife Tammy. He did not look slightly tipsy—never mind like a staggering drunk—and, for the life of me, I can't imagine a man of Victor's superb mental and physical constitution imbibing enough alcohol in that half hour before his death to create such a transformation."

I could see what Dick was leading up to. Master Radio Talk Show Host, he was quick to exploit the dramatics of any situation.

"There are people in this town who didn't want Victor's type of high energetic enthusiasm! They didn't care for his visionary plans! They were afraid that Victor's challenge to the status quo would rock too many boats! They just want to eat their bratwursts and chili and go to bed, thank you very much! Someone or an agent of some group tossed Victor to his death before the waves he was threatening to make washed over their own castles of—"

I clicked off the radio. Basically I agreed with Dick, but his conspiracy theory, which was a running thread through almost half of all the topics he dealt with, was a little too over-the-top for me.

Exhausted, I laid my head on the pillow and closed my eyes . . . .

I WAS WALKING in a very dark place.

Something was behind me.

I turned.

Peering at me through the darkness was a pair of squinty, close-set eyes. I'd seen them before. They were Alan Casey's, but I couldn't see the rest of Alan's face—just his eyes. I picked up my pace and began jogging, wanting to get away from him. Over my shoulder, I could see him keeping pace with me and then begin to catch up.

I broke into a run and exited what I now realized was a

tunnel. Suddenly, the sun was blazing and the landscape had a flat, one dimensional quality to it. It was like a colorfully painted backdrop—all yellows and oranges and reds. There were huge boulders teetering on the pointy tips of strangely shaped mountain peaks. The sky was dotted with what appeared to be the outlines of clouds—as though they'd been scrawled with white chalk.

I looked again over my shoulder and into the tunnel. Alan Casey's pinchy eyes were still following me, but as they emerged from the darkness I discovered they were really the eyes of Wile E. Coyote.

I started to laugh and before I could say, *"beepbeep!"* he'd lassoed me with his Handy Dandy Acme Cowboy Lariat Gun and strapped me to a railroad track that just happened to have been laid out on the other side of a row of boulders. As if that wasn't enough, Coyote shoved a lit stick of dynamite into my mouth. Try as I might, I couldn't spit it out.

I heard the rhythmic swishing sound of a paddle wheel churning through water. But there was no water. Even so, turning my head to one side and looking down the tracks, I saw the *Queen of Newport* backing up towards me.

The riverboat's huge red paddles were slicing through the air sending out a spray of red paint. Or so I thought. As it got closer and the spray started hitting my face, I said, "This ain't paint." It was blood. The blades were dripping with it.

Standing at the railing of the upper deck and waving at me was Victor Lloyd, dressed in his gambler's outfit. He was shouting at me. I couldn't make out what he was saying over the din of the churning wheel, but his body language said, "Get out of the way!"

Someone came up behind him—I couldn't tell who it was. All I saw were two arms swinging a giant pink and green neon palm tree. It caught Victor in the back of his neck and sent him over the railing, into the bloody wheel.

The churning turned to crunching.

Sunday, August 22

16

I WOKE UP IN A COLD SWEAT, my nightshirt twisted around
my body like a wet rag. I sat up in bed and groaned. As I tried
to pull the shirt over my head, the muscles in my back and
shoulders complained. Though I'd slept through the night, the
dream I'd had did nothing to relieve the tension of the day
before.

It was almost seven in the morning. Lying in bed wasn't
going to make me feel any better, so I decided to get up and
go stand under a hot shower. I padded into the adjoining
bathroom and switched on the light, startling Boo-Kat who
had obviously been in a deep sleep, his body wrapped around

the base of the toilet. That's his favorite spot on hot summer nights. We passed each other without a greeting. Head down, he trudged out of the bathroom to crawl under my bed, and I stepped into the shower stall, turned on the water and set the dial on the shower head to maximum pulse.

Twenty minutes later, dressed in bicycle shorts and my Cincinnati Reds T-shirt, I was ready for breakfast—I'm always ready for breakfast. I left Boo-Kat stretched out on the floor in front of the guest bedroom Paco was using. He had his nose pressed to the crack of the closed door. I don't know if he was trying to smell through it, see through it, or push it open.

Down in the family kitchen, the Boones were dressed for church and just finishing up their breakfast.

Julie Ann said, "'Morning, Kate. Did I miss any good stories last night?"

"Nope. How was your party?"

"Oh . . . it was okay, I guess."

"You folks are getting started pretty early. Something special at church today?"

Robert pulled on his ear. "Yup. It's our turn to look through the pews for loose change."

"Robert!" Phoebe Jo snapped a dish towel at him. "I can see we're going to have a respectful elders meeting this morning."

Boo-Kat's loud barking echoed in the foyer. Seconds later, he came bounding into the kitchen, followed by Bobby and a yawning, bleary-eyed Paco.

"Hi, guys. Ready for breakfast?" I said, joining the chorus of "good mornings."

Bobby answered, "Sure. Can I help?"

Paco grunted. "Wasn't ready to get up. But I heard this sad whimpering outside my door. It was pitiful. No decent human being could ignore that."

I handed Boo-Kat a biscuit. To the guys I said, "Sit down, I'll toast us up some bagels."

Robert looked at the clock on the microwave, then at Phoebe Jo. "Better get going, Ma. Julie Ann, don't forget your tambourine." He got up, grabbed the guitar and mandolin cases sitting by the back door, and went out to his car.

"Why do I have to play that stupid tambourine, anyway?" Julie Ann said, stomping out of the kitchen. "I don't even know where it is."

Phoebe Jo followed behind. "I'll find it. Just go upstairs and put your shoes on—and not those awful clunky ones."

Bobby and Paco, seated at the kitchen table, watched the goings on.

I poured out orange juice for them. "Are you suffering from culture shock with all this Midwestern family stuff?"

Bobby said, "This is probably the most foreign place we've ever traveled to. But I kinda like it. Don't you, Paco?"

Paco rubbed his baggy eyes. "Yeah. Makes me feel all warm and fuzzy inside. Hey, there's my pal." Boo-Kat was seated at his feet, staring up at him.

"Well, Kate, you can tell it's Sunday morning," Robert said, coming into the kitchen. "Your mother's coming down the drive. She doesn't give up easy, does she?"

Oh, dear.

"Give up on what?" Bobby asked.

"She's always trying to get me to go to church with her."

I could hear the front door open and close, then the sound of Mother's high heels clicking on the hardwood floor of the foyer. I poured myself a glass of orange juice and set the pitcher down on the table.

"Kathleen?" Mother's voice echoed in the hallway.

"In the kitchen."

"Don't worry," she called out, "I'm not here to coerce you into something you don't want to do. I just stopped by to—oh!" Mother stood frozen at the entrance to the kitchen.

"'Morning, Mrs. Cavanaugh," said Robert.

Bobby and Paco offered polite "hellos."

"You look lovely this morning, Mother."

She blinked, coming out of her temporary state of shock, and redirected her gaze towards me. "Why, thank you, dear." After brushing at the skirt of her periwinkle blue linen suit and twisting her gold bracelet around to some preferable arrangement, she said, "Good morning, Robert," and nodded, without expression to my friends.

"Can I get you something, Mother?"

"No. Thank you, dear. I just have a few minutes. I'd like to speak to you in the library."

I pointed to the bagels in front of the toaster and said to my guests, "Go ahead and start—there's peanut butter, cream cheese, and all sorts of jams in the refrigerator. I'll join you later."

Picking up my glass of orange juice, I said to Mother, "Okay, lead on."

Once I'd settled into my swivel chair, I asked, "What's up?" I took a sip of juice and peered over the rim of the glass and across the desk at Mother, who was seated on the sofa.

"Well . . . I was getting ready to go to church and, since it was early, I figured I'd have time to stop by here and tell you about something that happened yesterday. Something you'll probably find interesting."

She could've just called me, but I went along with the game. "Oh? What's that?"

"I was visiting my friend Dorothy at Bethesda North Hospital yesterday morning—you know she had a stroke."

I nodded. "How is she?"

"Well, she can't talk yet, which is actually a blessing, but they say she'll get that back soon. Anyway, I went in through the Emergency entrance so that I wouldn't have to walk so far. There was hardly anyone in there. If you ever have an emergency, Kathleen, I hope you have it on Saturday morning. So I noticed the two people sitting in the waiting area. It was that Gloria Sims and her daughter—you know, those people we helped at Victor Lloyd's party."

I sat up straight—a little more interested. "Oh?"

"I guess they really do have their problems. Gloria looked quite haggard and you could tell Janie was also worried, but she had that impressive take-charge attitude that must be part of her Marine training."

120

"Cut to the chase, Mother."

She pressed her lips together and then said, "I'm coming to that, dear—you're so impatient." She took a breath. "Donald Sims attempted to commit suicide early Saturday morning."

Huh, that *was* interesting. Aloud, I said, "Donald seemed very agitated all evening. At one point, he looked like he was about to have a heart attack."

"Well, according to Gloria—she was very talkative—Donald's been extremely upset about what will probably happen to him when the bank he works for is taken over. I think he has quite a responsible job there—she said he's been with them for twenty years—but I guess he's not important enough to be kept on when the two home offices are merged."

"That's something to be worried about. A middle management type who looks to be closing in on his sixties is not exactly at the top of everyone's hiring list."

"Well, according to Gloria, Donald had been taking sedatives for a few weeks, but in the last week he'd been getting worse and nothing seemed to help. Gloria said she'd tried to lift his spirits and be encouraging, but Donald would just brush her off and say she didn't understand what he was dealing with."

Mother grew strangely quiet and seemed to look inward for a moment. Very softly, she said, "I understand how helpless she must be feeling." A pause. I waited for her to continue. She pulled herself up straight in her chair and stared blankly back at me, then said, "Donald Sims swallowed all his pills."

"Is he going to be all right?"

"Yes, she'd already been told he was going to survive. I think Gloria wanted to talk more, but it's obvious Janie's the one in control right now. She told her mother, 'I think that's enough. Mrs. Cavanaugh probably has something important to do.'"

"In other words, she told her to shut up?"

121

"Well . . . yes . . . I suppose so." Mother looked out the window.

This reflective mood of Mother's was unusual. I asked, "What did you mean when you said earlier you understood how helpless Gloria Sims felt?"

Mother turned back slowly and looked at me. Her eyes were steely and the corners of her lips were pressed down with bitterness. "They're all the same—men. Can't communicate what they're feeling to their own wives. You ask what's wrong and all you get is a grunt for an answer. You say 'talk to me' and they act as if they've been assaulted."

Whoa! Where did *that* come from?

"Your dear father, Kathleen, left me out of so many things. I loved him. I always will. But I believe if he had just opened up to me and told me what kind of worries he had, he'd still be alive. And I worry about you."

"You think I'm going to have a heart attack?"

"You're just the same."

"I am not."

"If I was to believe what you tell me, then I'd think you were perfectly happy and hadn't a care in the world. But I don't believe it for a moment. Something's changed in you these last few months and I don't think you're as happy as you used to be. But will you open up to me? No."

"Mother, I've tried to open up to you, but all I get in return is criticism or pat answers that don't apply."

She shook her head. "You misunderstand everything I try to say to you. If we'd talk more and got to know each other better, we wouldn't have these miscommunications, but you never call me. I always have to call you. If I didn't come over here every once in a while, I'd never see you. And then, when I do come over, I find you have two strange men sitting in your kitchen having breakfast at eight-thirty on a Sunday morning. But I'm sure you're not going to tell me what's going on here. What must the Boones think of you?"

"Oh for crying out loud, Mother, they're friends. They need a place to stay. I have a big house." I could feel my blood starting to boil.

"But they're men! What do you think that looks like? You have an image to keep up!"

"I don't care what that looks like."

"You never have! Oh, what's the sense—" She popped out of her chair. "I'm late."

Mother started to stomp out of the library, but turned at the door. "So? No church for you, today?" Her hands shot up and she waved her fingers as if to erase what she'd just said. "No! Never mind! I didn't say that!"

A few seconds later, I heard gravel flying as Mother floored the gas petal of her Mercedes and zoomed down the laneway on her mission to ask God to save my soul.

17

LOUNGE WAS THE WORD for the day. Bobby and Paco had been running on adrenalin since Thursday, and now, halfway round the world from their starting point in India, they'd run out of fuel. We took a short walk around the farm and sat by the pond for a half hour, watching the water bugs skate across the surface. Bobby practiced skipping stones until Paco said, "Hey, look. The little buggers are surfing."

Bobby stopped. I guess it was against his religion to upset the natural order.

All was quiet, except for the croakings and buzzings in the tall grasses growing by the edge of the pond. The hot sun hitting my head made me feel sleepy. Paco was lying on his back with his eyes closed and I heard a faint snore. Bobby's eyes were at half-mast, so I said, "Let's go back and you guys can crash if you want—I have to be a little more active than this."

Inside the house, Paco headed up the stairs to his bed.

Bobby asked if he could look for something to read in my library.

"Help yourself." I grabbed my straw hat from a hook in the laundry room. "If you want to stay outside, you can set up one of the chaise longues under a tree out back and read there. I'm going to play in the garden."

Bobby waved that he understood and made his way towards the library.

I'd been neglecting the flower beds and they were full of weeds. The mint was taking over the herb garden and there were hours of deadheading to do. It had been so hot, neither Phoebe Jo nor I had been interested in gardening. I figured I'd start with one of the flower beds where I was trying to get white alyssum and purple nierembergia to fill in around the front edge. It just looked like a mass of weeds in between the plants, but I knew that some of those tiny green leaves were reseeds and I didn't want to yank those out by mistake. Here and there you could identify a dandelion or some other obvious candidate for removal, but I decided to wait and tackle that job some other day after the little shoots had grown more. It would be easier to distinguish what to keep and what to pull.

It wasn't much different from a murder investigation where information shoots up from different sources and you can't be sure which is good material and what eventually should be tossed out because it's meaningless. I needed someone to explain what I was looking at, and I also wanted more information about the corpse around which these shoots were growing. I decided to call Uncle Cliff for advice. Being a criminal lawyer, maybe he'd be able to steer me in a more productive direction.

I went back inside to make the call—it was late enough on a Sunday morning even for Uncle Cliff.

"Hi, K.C.," he answered, "heard I missed a killer of a party Friday night."

"Uncle Cliff! That's tasteless."

"Yeah, I know—tried that line on your mother when we

spoke yesterday, and she bit my head off. Guess I'll never be forgiven for talking her into going. I want to hear your take on the evening."

"Yeah, I was hoping to come over and talk about that. This afternoon okay?"

"Sure, you can lounge around the pool with me—that's all I'm going to do."

"Good. Thanks. Be there at two o'clock."

There. That felt better. I was moving forward again, but if I was going to be at Uncle Cliff's by two o'clock I figured I'd better start prepping lunch. I went into the kitchen and mixed up some of my favorite chicken salad with mangoes, oranges, and a curried sour cream and yogurt dressing. I washed enough lettuce leaves for an army and pulled a couple of loaves of sourdough bread out of the freezer.

It was a good thing Bobby and Paco weren't feeling too energetic that day. I didn't want them playing detective and accompanying me to Uncle Cliff's—they were too distracting. Just like Eleanor, Uncle Cliff was a sociable guy and wouldn't want to talk business with me for very long with Bobby and Paco around. He'd be more interested in hearing accounts of their adventures.

I WAS IN MY JEEP, driving south into the old monied section of Clairmont, where Uncle Cliff had his seventy-five acre estate—or "ranch" as he liked to call it. The radio was tuned to WOW for the Reds game, which was the only reason I liked listening to that station. I hooted with excitement as I wheeled right onto Shawnee Run Road—the Reds were beating the poop out of the Atlanta Braves.

A couple of minutes later, I drove between a pair of large stone pillars joined together by a black, wrought iron arch with the initials CTV in the center. I followed the paved driveway through manicured grounds that looked more like a golf course and past the front of Uncle Cliff's house. It was a contemporary design with soaring, multi-level roofs, skylights, and dramatic expanses of window. I circled around to the side and zipped into the spot beside his Harley Davidson. Mother's brother was nothing like Mother.

After two messy divorces, Uncle Cliff's romantic antics with very young women have supplied Clairmont's gossipers with many enjoyable hours of *tsk-tsking,* and it's apparent to me that I inherited my ability to embarrass Mother from him. Even so, she still solicits his advice on legal and business matters. 'Course, she doesn't always follow it.

As I stepped out of the jeep, I was greeted by a pair of waggy-tailed, wet nosed golden retrievers who turned and led me down a stone walkway to the swimming pool at the back of the house. The Reds game was blasting from a boom box. Uncle Cliff was in the water, splashing furiously as he windmilled his way up and down the length of the pool.

I picked up a beach ball and threw it in his path. That got his attention real fast. He stopped, blew water out his mustache like an old walrus, and squinted up at me.

"K.C! Hi! Got two more laps to go," he said, treading water and puffing.

I parked myself on the end of a lounge chair next to the blasting boom box. I turned it down a notch and waited. It wasn't long before Uncle Cliff joined me, toweling himself off.

He sat down and said, "So, the police say Victor's death was an accident. Knowing you, I bet you have your own theories about what happened Friday night. I'm anxious to hear them." He reached down and switched off the radio.

"More like suspicions. I'm working on the theories, but I need more information."

"Okay, first tell me what you saw."

I gave Uncle Cliff a capsule summary of the evening from my point of view, including meeting Peepo Giuliani.

"Peepo Giuliani?" he said, eyebrows raised. "Now *that's* interesting. Very interesting."

"You know him? Who is he?"

126

"I know *of* him—his reputation. Did any of the other guests seem to know who he was?"

"I don't know, he didn't seem to attract any attention. I didn't see him talk to anyone else except to his bodyguard—I think that's who he was—and to Victor. But then at the end, after Victor was found dead, Peepo took charge, ordering everyone around."

Uncle Cliff pulled on one end of his mustache. "Hmm . . . a lot of the guests were probably too young to know who he was or just didn't recognize him. He must be in his seventies by now."

"What do *you* know about him?"

"Peepo Giuliani," he said, shaking his head slowly. "Now there's a name I haven't heard in a long time. Back in the late forties and throughout the fifties, he went under the name Joey Jules or was it Joey Peep? Something like that. Anyway, this is really interesting. His parents were the big news back in the old Newport casino days. They owned The Oasis."

Sproing! Suddenly, a sturdy green stem shot up out of my weed patch, showing great promise. This was definitely a keeper.

Uncle Cliff continued on. "Your Mother was already hysterical about Victor's plans for the new Oasis. Wait 'til she finds out Joey Peep's back in town." He quickly looked at me. "I take it she wasn't introduced to him Friday night."

"Nope. Didn't tell her I'd met him, either. Did his parents own The Oasis right up to the end when it shut down in the seventies?"

"No—and there's a story there. Back in the forties, his father, Carl, was always having battles with the other casino owners in the area and was gunned down. His wife, Pearlie Mae, took over running The Oasis. She and Joey kept the place hopping even though the church ministers in Newport protested about all the gambling going on in Northern Kentucky. Then in the early sixties, Robert Kennedy, who was Attorney General at that time, launched his investigation into organized crime and it got too hot for them. The

Giulianis disappeared. The Oasis was taken over by a more conservative businessman who ran the place as a nightclub minus the gambling. The Oasis was a real swinging hot spot until the mid-seventies when tastes in entertainment changed and the place couldn't draw big enough crowds to stay afloat."

Uncle Cliff stood up and rubbed his head vigorously with the towel to dry his hair. "So, I wonder how Victor Lloyd got linked up to Peepo Giuliani?"

"He told me. Peepo said he was Victor's uncle."

My uncle froze and stared at me from underneath his towel.

I asked, "So it's a good bet Peepo will go ahead and build The Oasis?"

He shrugged. "Anything's possible. I wonder what kind of involvement Victor thought Crown Chili would be interested in?"

I told him about the idea for Crown Chili Mystery Cruises. "Basically, Victor presented it to me as his family values project."

Uncle Cliff laughed. "Well, now that I know who he was connected with—I hate to admit this—but for once, maybe, your mother's paranoia was justified. But Tink has always dragged her heels when it came to pursuing new ideas. Odds were, eventually she'd be right. God help us, we're never going to hear the end of it."

ON MY WAY HOME, I went through my memory bank of old gangster movies and came up with a possible scenario for Victor's death. He came to Cincinnati, thinking he could run away from some situation in Las Vegas—gangster business gone bad? Peepo Giuliani tracks him down. Bodyguard Sammy is the hit man—Peepo wouldn't want to dirty those elegant hands of his. They see their opportunity when Victor's alone and Sammy tosses him overboard.

What about Alan Casey? Peepo threatens to unleash Sammy on him if he talks. Peepo's anger and concern over

Victor's death was just a cover-up. Made sense to me.

Not only were Mother's suspicions looking like they might be well-grounded, but so were Charlotte Oakley's.

Old fashioned vendettas!

Getting married to the mob!

This stuff had me pumped!

18

I WALKED IN MY FRONT DOOR and stood for a moment in the foyer listening for sounds of life. All I heard was the ticking of the grandfather clock.

"Hello?" I shouted. No answer. Maybe they all went out somewhere. I tramped down the hallway and into the family kitchen, where I found a note weighted down by a sugar bowl in the middle of the table. I read: "We're being spontaneous and have gone to the zoo with church friends. Back later this evening. Sure you won't miss us. Heat up the goulash (in the fridge) for dinner. —PJ"

Looking out the bay window, across the backyard, I saw Bobby and Paco lounging under the big maple tree, drinking beer. Boo-Kat was lying in the grass between them and probably begging for a sip. Alarmed at first, I was immediately relieved to see he was tied up to Paco's chair.

My mouth was dry, so I pulled open the fridge door and grabbed a beer for myself. Normally, by this time on a Sunday afternoon, I'd be preparing for the week's work ahead. I really didn't feel like doing that, but Tony would be standing in front of the cork board the next day, waiting for orders. "Hey, Boss," he'd say, "what's the plan?"

I decided to start with the most interesting project—the Casablanca party—and went upstairs to get my journal with the Moroccan recipes in it. I could sit outside under the tree, drink beer with my friends, and pull together a menu at the same time.

Upstairs in my bedroom, at the back of my walk-in closet, is an old, beaten-up cardboard box. I pulled out the box of memories, opened it up, and rummaged around until I found the red notebook that documented my travels to Morocco and Egypt. There are five of these notebooks, each one a different color representing a different part of the world I'd traveled to. On an impulse, I pulled out the orange notebook—India and Nepal. I'd never shown my journals to anyone, but the orange book was bulging with photos and postcards that Bobby and Paco would probably enjoy seeing, so I took that one, too.

"HOW DOES CHICKEN Stuffed with Couscous, with Spiced Honey Sauce sound to you?" I waited for an answer, watching Bobby and Paco leafing through the orange notebook.

Silence. "Hey, c'mon you guys! I said you could look at the pictures. No reading allowed."

I paused and turned the page in the red notebook. "Okay, how about Pigeon Pie?"

Paco looked up with a disgusted look on his face. "Blah! You'd eat those dirty birds?"

"Okay," I said, flipping to the next page, "this is it. Chicken with Prunes, Honey, and Cinnamon." I took a deep swig of my beer.

"Hey, Kate." Bobby held out the notebook and pointed excitedly at a photograph. "Here I am with hair. Who's that skinny dork standing next to me?"

Paco looked over Bobby's shoulder. "Ha. Ha. Very funny." And cuffed him on the back of his head.

Bobby brushed him off as if he were nothing more than an irritating fly. "I have something upstairs in my pack to show you, Kate. Something very interesting."

"Really? Well don't make me wait. Go get it."

Bobby jogged across the grass to the back door and

130

disappeared into the house. He returned a couple of minutes later with a well-worn leather sketchbook under his arm. Plopping down beside me, he flipped it open, found the page he was looking for and placed it in my lap.

It was a pencil sketch of me. A very young me leaning back on my elbows and looking directly at the artist.

Bobby said, "Do you remember that? You haven't changed much."

"I was a little skinnier."

"This drawing is one of my favorites because I think I captured an attitude you had back then. There's a very challenging look in those eyes."

"Yeah. I had attitude." It looked like the cocky young woman was just about to say, "So there!"

"I see something different in your eyes now."

I stared back at him for a brief moment, then down at the picture. I looked at the way Bobby had drawn my bare breasts. They were firm and healthy and sat high on my chest.

"Yeah, I've changed." I looked back up at him. "What do *you* see?"

"There's a softer look in your eyes—not as aggressive." He pointed at the picture. "There you're ready to take on the world and do battle. Now you have an older, wiser look. Like you've survived a few battles."

I didn't really want to say anything to that.

Bobby added, "I'd like to do another sketch of you. An update. Maybe tonight?"

I wasn't ready to give him a complete update. "Yeah. Older and wiser is right. I don't sit around without my clothes on, anymore."

"Why not?" Paco asked. "I still do."

Bobby and I left that comment hanging in the air.

"So?" Bobby looked at me with raised eyebrows.

"Yeah. Okay," I answered, "but I'll decide what pose."

I pointed to my journal. "Did you come to the pictures of Cherry and Jaz in there yet?"

131

* * * * * * * * * * *

FOR THE REST OF that afternoon and all through dinner, my head was filled with a debate.

The first voice I'd heard in my head shouted, "No way!" Nobody had seen me naked in the last seven years, except for all those doctors and medical technicians. Sometimes, when I work in the commercial kitchen and it gets hot, I go without my plastic boob. But that's different—I'm still covered up and Tony doesn't notice anymore.

You would think this was a small matter, letting a friend do a sketch of you, but this "small matter" gave rise to some pretty deep and usually ignored emotions. I was already aware of the poisonous mixture of rage, loneliness, and pity that bubbles up inside of me sometimes. But I was shocked at how intensely those feelings flared up at this situation. I never thought I'd get away with living the rest of my life without confronting this issue. I mean, I didn't *want* to—that would be a very sad life.

Then, just as that toxic brew was threatening to boil over, a second voice cut in and said, "What's the matter with you? How can you be ashamed of the way your body looks. You're alive and you're a stronger person since going through breast cancer."

I agreed. I liked the person I'd become. Besides, anyone who would be repulsed by the sight of my body would not be someone I wanted to know. Of all people, Bobby was sure to react in a mature and respectful way. So what's the big deal? I almost blurted out at the dinner table.

I liked Bobby—a lot. I made my decision.

"TURN A LITTLE to the left, Kate—I'm getting weird shadows under your eyes."

I was sitting in a straight-backed chair in front of the library's west window. The early evening light was still bright but soft. I felt comfortable knowing we weren't going to be disturbed, since the Boones were still out and Paco had happily wandered off to watch TV. But I still had my clothes on.

Bobby was fussing, to an extent I didn't understand, about angles of light coming through the window and where he was going to sit. It went on and on.

Finally he said, "Okay, that's good, I'm happy. You comfortable with that position?"

Nothing had been said about the clothes. "Yeah." That sounded a little tentative.

Bobby studied me for a moment, then said, "A nude pose would be much more dynamic than a drawing of you in your Reds T-shirt."

"Well, I think I should warn you. My body's a little different from the last time you saw it."

"Okay." He waited for me to explain.

"I had cancer seven years ago, and the doctor had to cut off one of my breasts."

Instead of flinging his sketchpad and pencils up into the air and running screaming out of the room, Bobby leaned forward in his chair and looked at me with concern. "I'm sorry. Are you alright now?"

I nodded.

"That's what showing in your eyes. So I guess you're uncomfortable taking your shirt off?"

"No." I pulled the T-shirt over my head, still feeling a slight twinge of anxiety. Aware that Bobby was watching me, my fingers fumbled with the hooks on my bra. I managed to get it off, but not with the one smooth sensual motion that I'd hoped for whenever I fantasized about this inevitable situation. I folded up the bra with my plastic boob still secure in its lacy cup, rolled it in my Reds T-shirt, and stuffed it under the chair. Then I sat up and took a deep breath.

Bobby studied me again for a brief instant, a small frown puckering his forehead. "Raise your hands up behind your head, like you're fixing your braid."

I obeyed.

"That looks good, Kate. Now look straight at me."

I did.

Bobby smiled. "Beautiful—I hope I can do you justice." He began to draw.

I was a little surprised at how relaxed and safe I felt. Bobby hadn't overreacted and made any big noise about my revelation, nor did he seem uncomfortable. I watched his eyes as he studied every part of me and carefully transferred what he saw through his pencil onto the sketchpad. Every once in a while, he'd catch my gaze and smile at me.

I felt wrapped in his warmth and acceptance.

Monday, August 23
8:30 AM

19

I WAVED BACK AS Bobby and Paco made the last turn at the end of the laneway onto the road. My insides were all twisted up and my mind a jumble. Life for the two brothers was pretty light and breezy, but I was caught up in a tornado. It was probably a good thing they'd gone off to gamble in Indiana for the next couple of days, giving me the chance to settle down and sort out the mix of emotions that kept me awake until four o'clock in the morning.

Our sketching session had gone on quietly and successfully for a little over half an hour. At the end, Bobby presented me with a beautiful drawing. Even though I thought the drawing of the younger me was good, he'd developed over the years and I was amazed at how he'd managed to capture what I'd been feeling all through the session. I'd studied his line work, wondering how he got those tiny pencil scratches to express that feeling of trust.

When it was over, I put my clothes back on and we hugged. I stored the sketch temporarily for safe keeping in my desk drawer, and we went back out into the Great Room to join Paco and Boo-Kat. They were both stretched out on the floor in front of the TV, Boo-Kat on his back, his left hind leg frantically pawing the air as Paco rubbed his belly.

Bobby and I sat on the sofa. We watched TV—that is, I pretended to watch. I was vaguely aware of black and white images dancing on the TV screen, but I couldn't tell you what movie it was.

The thing that was hard to come to terms with was that this whole sketching session didn't seem to mean the same to Bobby as it did to me. Drawing nude women was something he did all the time and it was natural that he would want to do a sketch of an old friend. But for me, it took on enormous importance. What I didn't understand at first were the confusing issues of acceptance, self-esteem, and sexuality.

In my fantasies, I'd always seen myself baring my post-mastectomized chest for the first time to some lover and for this bravery I'd be rewarded with a night of passionate love-making, surrounded by flickering candles, a soft jazzy sax playing in the background. Pretty much your cliche romance novel scene.

The way my unveiling actually happened had never entered my mind as a possibility.

I realized I'd been expecting something else to happen—something more than just an I'm-your-friend type of hug to tell me everything was okay. I felt kind of let down and deflated, but at the same time I also realized it was an inappropriate reaction. How could I expect Bobby to react differently?

Nevertheless, that inappropriate reaction had kept me

awake practically all night, and I'd finally gone downstairs to shoot hoops and work off my frustrations.

THERE ARE TIMES I'm happy throwing myself into kitchen work—it has a mind-numbing meditative effect on your brain, especially when you're prepping for large parties and there's lots of chopping, slicing, and dicing to do. I'd seen Tony arrive and go into the commercial kitchen entrance a half hour earlier. It was time for me to clock in.

"Hey, Boss," Tony greeted me. He was standing at the counter in front of the stove, trimming the fat off a huge pile of boneless chicken breasts. "Your love life seems to have gone from one extreme to the other. Just last week there was nothing and now I see you kissing two guys on the front step. Good for you, girl!"

I put my hand on my hip. "First off, we're just friends—" Tony smirked at that, "—and second, my love life is none of your business."

"Okay! Okay!" Tony dropped his knife and flung his hands up to protect his face. "Touchy, touchy!"

I looked at the pan of water boiling on the stove and asked, "What're you working on?"

"I'm poaching chicken breasts for that ad agency luncheon, then I'm gonna make the pesto."

"Okay, that sounds good." I went over to the corkboard to check the schedule. "Phew! We've got a busy day today and I've got to take a couple of hours off this afternoon to go to a funeral reception. Maybe I can get Phoebe Jo to help you while I'm gone, but I think this is going to be happening more often." I turned to Tony. "I don't like dumping all this work on you, so I think it's time you had an assistant."

His eyes widened.

I continued. "Got any buddies who might be interested?"

Tony started to open his mouth.

"*Qualified* buddies," I quickly added.

137

* * * * * * * * * * *

AT TWO O'CLOCK, I pulled up in front of Victor Lloyd's house. I was dressed for the occasion in a sleeveless black rayon knit dress. Expecting the usual goosebump-producing air-conditioning, I threw on the matching cardigan.

There were already a dozen cars parked alongside the driveway, with Charlotte Oakley's Jaguar convertible at the head of the line. I wedged my Jeep into a tight space between a Cadillac and a Lincoln Continental.

I was feeling almost cheerful as a result of my conversation with Tony. It was decided Tony would call a friend of his who was tired of kitchen work in one of the large downtown hotels and see if he wanted to interview for the job. This friend had frequently voiced the opinion that Tony had the best job in town, so it sounded like we had already found an assistant.

Of course, now I was going to have to keep the calendar full of jobs so I could afford the extra salary. No matter, it felt good to be taking another step forward in my new five year plan.

The Lloyd manor was a sprawling, gray brick, three-story affair with a large two-story wing to one side, the bottom level of which was a five-car garage. There were lots of white wood-framed windows, green shutters, peaks and dormers, and even a white-railed balcony on the second level over the entrance.

It was a grand place, one of the finer homes in Clairmont. It made for a beautiful picture. Except for one thing. The lawns weren't up to golf course standards and the flower beds were almost empty. Here and there a few scraggly shrubs were trying to survive despite obvious neglect. This was not the norm in Clairmont.

I walked under a stone archway and rang the front doorbell, expecting some kind of funereal-faced butler-type to welcome me inside. Instead, the door was opened by Sammy, Peepo Giuliani's hulking hawk-nosed shadow, who immediately readjusted his line of vision upwards in order to greet me.

"Hi," I said.

He nodded silently, stepped aside, and allowed me to walk past.

I stepped into a bare hallway and followed the sounds of muted conversation into what I assumed was the sitting room. Except there was nothing to sit on. The only piece of furniture was a table against one wall set up with a temporary bar and a couple of trays of nibbles. There were only about fourteen or fifteen people mingling around—and that included Tammy the Widow in Black, and her son Eric. I knew half the rest, including Dick Rottingham who was off in one corner chatting up some young, gorgeous thing.

Peepo Giuliani saw me and came over. "So very nice of you to come, Ms. Cavanaugh."

"I'm sorry I couldn't make it to the service."

"We're honored you would take the time to come here."

"I wanted to express my condolences." I felt like a two-faced skunk as he took my arm and led me to Tammy.

Melissa Oakley, looking dignified with her blond hair pulled back into a smooth roll, was hanging on to Eric's arm. He looked quite handsome in his black mourning suit, especially with that serious head-of-the-household expression on his face. Wherever the Lloyd family stock came from, they certainly had good genes in the looks department.

Charlotte was hovering close by.

Peepo reminded Tammy who I was, saying, "This is Kate Cavanaugh of the Crown Chili family. You met her Friday night on the riverboat."

She ignored him, focusing her stony gaze on me, instead.

I spoke a few well-chosen words to Tammy. She probably wanted to ask me why I—the "blond bimbo"—was there, but was too polite. And sober. Cold sober. Our conversation consisted of a couple of unremarkable over-used phrases.

As I started to move away, Charlotte stepped up beside me, grabbed my elbow and whispered, "Let's talk in the

139

kitchen."

She steered me out of the no-sitting room, back across the bare hallway and into another almost empty room. This one had a fireplace, a couch, a side table and lamp, and a TV set. It must have been the family room.

I said, "This isn't the kitchen."

"Well that's obvious." Charlotte rolled her eyes. "I'm taking you the long way around, I want you to see this place. Isn't it weird?"

"Sure is. Have the Lloyds stored their furniture or something?"

Charlotte shrugged. "Now I know why Melissa never told me what it was like in this house. I bet it's always been empty. I don't think they own much of anything."

From behind us, a little bird-like voice chirped, "I think you're right about that, dear."

Charlotte and I turned around to find a tiny, gray-haired lady with a face as wrinkled as a raisin smiling sweetly up at us. "I'm Minnie. The next door neighbor." She indicated which direction with a jerk of her tiny head.

"I haven't been in here since the Lloyds first moved in. I came over that day with my special banana bourbon loaf to welcome them to the neighborhood. I was here in this room and it looked just the same back then. Oh!" Minnie put a hand to her mouth. "It's gone!"

"What's gone?" I asked.

Minnie was looking just to the right of Charlotte. She pointed to the wall above the fireplace. There was a large rectangular area where the wall paint was a shade brighter. "They had a lovely wedding portrait hanging there."

"A picture of Tammy and Victor?"

"Oh, yes. They were a beautiful couple. And it had a heavy gold frame. I remember it well because it was the only decoration I saw. It looks like it's just been taken down recently." Minnie clucked her tongue and shook her head. "That marriage was no picnic in the park."

I put on my Heiress Detective hat and asked, "Why do

140

you say that?"

"They always seemed to be shouting at each other about something. But one night in particular, a few months ago, they were making a terrible racket—woke me up. Victor was shouting, 'Tammy, let me in,' over and over."

Charlotte frowned at her. "You heard them? These houses are not close together at all."

Minnie pursed her lips. "Well, maybe you're not up at two o'clock in the morning, but it's very quiet and every little sound travels. Anyway," she looked back up at me, "I got up and looked out my window—I have a view of this house from my bedroom. Well, really just of the balcony because there's this space between the poplars. So, I watch and the balcony light clicks on. Tammy comes out in this beautiful white negligee—"

I asked, "How could you tell what she was wearing?"

Minnie blushed. "I'm a birder. There are lots of trees outside my bedroom window, so I have a nice pair of binoculars my grandson gave me for my birthday." She put a hand up to her cheek. "Oh, dear, I didn't mean to get this far into the story. Well, anyway, Tammy screamed back at him. Called him some awful names and said, 'Go back to your little—' " Minnie leaned towards us and whispered, " 'whore!' There, now I've really said too much. Well, I better go back to the other room. It was nice talking to you." She left.

Charlotte rubbed her forehead. "It just keeps getting worse."

She grabbed me by the hand and led me through what looked like an empty dining room, and into the kitchen. It was a large room with beautiful marble countertops, carved wood cupboards, a cooking island, and a large eating area with a bay window. In front of the window was a cheap wood dining set—your basic bottom of the line World of Dinette's special. There were no personal decorative items.

I said to Charlotte, "You'd think Tammy would be embarrassed to have everyone see how they'd been living. Why did she have the funeral reception here? Blows the whole illusion."

Charlotte shook her head violently. "I don't know and I don't care, Kate. That's not important. Now that I finally have you alone I want to know who those two scary men are out there."

I frowned.

"The big guy with the nose and that shifty little old man with him."

"Oh, them." I would have preferred reporting to Charlotte once I'd gathered all the information and had a chance to put the pieces in place. But she was paying me and had the right to know what I knew.

I said, "The big guy's named Sammy. The little man is Peppino Giuliani, who says he's Victor Lloyd's uncle."

Charlotte gasped.

"I just learned from a reliable source that Mr. Giuliani was one of the owners of the original Oasis when it was a gambling casino back in the forties and fifties."

"Good," Charlotte said, her expression hardening. "That's all I need to know."

She spun on her heel and marched out of the kitchen. I followed her to the front room and saw her stomp up to Melissa and grab her by the arm.

"Melissa," she said loudly, "we're leaving."

"Mom! What are you doing?"

"We have to go home."

All conversation in the room came to an abrupt halt. Everyone watched Charlotte pull her daughter out of the room and push past a startled Eric and an amused Dick Rottingham, who was just walking in.

Melissa called back over her shoulder, "Sorry, Eric. I'll talk to you later."

I was suddenly overwhelmed by the hot, stuffy atmosphere in the room and figured it was either the hostility from the Oakleys and the Lloyds that had jacked up the temperature or I was having a hot flash. But when I saw Peepo pressing a folded handkerchief against his brow, and noticed the trails of sweat rolling down the back of Dick Rottingham's neck, I realized the air-conditioning was minimal.

I peeled off my cardigan and wondered if the Lloyds had enough in their checking account to pay for the electricity.

So, Victor's success was all a facade, nothing more than numbers on paper. The showman had been performing a balancing act on a financial tightrope, juggling cash between accounts. The guy was living way beyond his means, and couldn't even afford to rent the right type of mask Clairmonters demanded you wear to be a player in their game. That explained why no one had every been invited over. But now that Victor was dead, it seemed Tammy wanted people to know the truth. I guess sympathy held some value for the poor *poor* widow.

BACK HOME IN the commercial kitchen, as I helped Tony put together some dessert trays, I mused about what had happened at the end of my visit. After the Oakleys' dramatic departure, I mingled around for a little while in case there were any more bits of interesting gossip to pick up. Everyone settled back into polite conversation. Even Dick Rottingham was boring, though I guess he was saving his opinions for his radio show. I was going to have to start listening on a regular basis.

But one interesting thing did happen as I was getting ready to leave. Peepo told me he'd walk me to my car. As we strolled down the driveway, his hand on my elbow, he asked if he could call me later on in the week.

I'd let him pull open the car door for me. "Would this be a social call or a business call?" I asked, folding myself into the driver's seat.

He smiled. "Maybe a little of both."

"Sure," I'd replied.

The more I thought about it, as I sprinkled powder sugar over a tray of sliced chocolate pound cake, the more intrigued I was by Peepo's request. But there was no sense in trying to second guess what his intentions were—I think Peepo always holds his cards close, now matter what game he's playing.

Before Tony left that evening, I presented him with the recipes for the Casablanca party.

"I won't let you down, Boss."

I was happy that load was off my shoulders.

THAT EVENING, JULIE ANN and I were lolling around in front of the TV set, surfing the channels and looking for some movie that didn't involve rapists, slashers, or stalkers. We landed on one of those classic movie channels just as the black and white image of a paddle wheeler chugging down a river appeared on the screen.

"Stop here, Julie Ann. What's this?"

The title appeared, as if in answer, and Julie Ann read aloud, "*The Adventures of Mark Twain.* That sounds dumb."

"Oh, c'mon, there's nothing else. Let's just see what it's like."

As we watched the opening scenes of the steamboat rolling lazily down the Mississippi River, it struck me as odd how once you're on a certain track everything you encounter seems to relate back to that. In all my years of old black and white movie-watching, I'd never encountered this one before. I amused myself briefly with the notion that someone was going to send me messages through the TV. Maybe Victor Lloyd was trying to contact me from the great beyond and his medium of choice was cable.

Tuesday, August 24

20

I DIDN'T RECEIVE any ghostly messages through the TV screen that night. Despite my imagination, there was no evidence of a spiritual presence emanating from the boob tube. However, the next morning, I did receive physical signs of an evil presence invading my sanctuary.

Boo-Kat and I were making our usual morning trek on the trail running alongside the creek bed when we came upon Robert squatting down next to a carcass. He pointed to the freshly killed and half-eaten rabbit.

"Kate, this coyote's starting to get to me. The trap I set up for him is only fifteen feet away from here, but I don't think he even sniffed at the meat. It's like he's done this just to get my dander up."

Boo-Kat growled at me as I yanked on his leash to keep him from getting at the rabbit.

"I better move on. This is really stirring up his wolf-side."

Robert waved his bony hand. "Yeah, you get outta here. I'll take care of Bugs Bunny."

Deciding to take a shortcut to another trail, I dug my walking stick into the soft ground and started pulling myself up a small embankment. I stabbed the stick in a second time and heard a sudden rustling in the underbrush. Boo-Kat lunged forward, almost tearing the leash out of my hand and throwing me off balance.

"Stop!" I shouted to no avail.

Boo-Kat threw his head back triumphantly, whipping a brownish-green snake in the air.

Before I could even think of what to do next, Robert shouted from below, "Leave him be, Kate. He'll kill it in a few minutes."

So I just stood there, watching my not-so-lovable pet maintain his death grip just behind the head of the snake and shake it so its tail end snapped back and forth, until it went limp and he dropped it on the ground.

I seized that opportunity to pull my dog away from the motionless snake, at the same time using my walking stick to fling it into the brush. Boo-Kat snarled at me. I snarled back and dragged him to the upper trail.

"See you back at the house, Robert," I yelled and broke into a jog. Boo-Kat had no choice but to follow. I wasn't going to let him lick my face for the next few days.

We were just coming up to the back door when I heard a car barreling down the laneway. I went around the side of the house to see who was driving up. It was a sport-utility vehicle. I didn't think anyone I knew drove one of those, so I watched, a little suspicious, until I recognized Eric Lloyd behind the wheel. He didn't look happy as he brought the car to a halt a foot away from my big toe. Boo-Kat started barking.

Eric leaped out of the driver's seat and shouted, "What the hell you think you're doing?"

"What? No 'good morning'? No 'how are you doing'? What's the problem, Eric?"

"You're the problem." He came around to the front of the car and planted himself in front of me.

There are times when being six-foot-three definitely has its advantages and I confess to liking it that way. I stared down at Eric with my Don't-mess-with-me-cause-I'm-bigger-than-you look.

"How so?" I asked, and waited for him to talk himself out.

"You're messing with my life. Mine and Melissa's. She told me all about you investigating my family for Mrs. Oakley. It's tough enough dealing with the arrogant attitude her mother has towards my family without you adding to rumors. Do you think it's been easy living in this town? You have no idea what it's like being an outsider. Mrs. Oakley thinks we aren't good enough to breathe the same air she does. And any rumors about my father you dig up will be just that, rumors. He never did anything illegal, but people always want to believe the worst about someone else—it makes them feel superior. This town's full of two-faced, holier-than-thou bastards. *And tell your mutt to stop his damn yapping!*"

"This is his property, not yours. He can bark as loud as he wants." And Boo-Kat kept at it. However, it was annoying me, too.

Eric took a breath and clenched his fists. "Look, I'm not going to let you snobs run us out of town. I'm going to take care of my mother and protect my murdered father's vision. I'm going to carry on with his plans. The Oasis will be built."

I raised my hand. "Take it easy, Eric. Hold on. Initially, I may have been asked to look into your family's background because Mrs. Oakley was nervous about rumors, but now I'm personally interested in finding out who murdered your father. And I'm sure you are, too."

"Well, if you're so goddamn interested, leave us alone and

go poke your nose into Ted Mueller's business—he's hated my dad since we came to this area. Ted's like a dog that's always been head of the pack. He didn't like it when my dad started competing with him and beating him at his own game. Dad always had great ideas and he's never had any trouble in attracting investors away from that dumb jock's half-assed projects. When Ted saw The Oasis, he recognized the genius in my dad and realized he couldn't compete, so he killed him and somehow got that photographer to cover for him."

Eric moved back to the driver's side of the car and climbed in. "So if you need to play private eye, go sniff around Ted Mueller—" He slammed the door. "Leave me and Melissa alone."

Prince Charming gunned his chariot and took off, leaving me and my barking dog in a cloud of dust.

I couldn't blame the young stud for feeling and acting the way he did. But it irked me to be lumped in with "you snobs." That really pushed a button in me.

LATER, THAT AFTERNOON, I was interviewing Tony's friend, Rick, for our new kitchen assistant position, though it was difficult for me to concentrate on kitchen business. My mind kept going back to the notion of Eric building The Oasis. He made it sound like he was going to do it all by himself, but I figured Peepo Giuliani would be manipulating everything from backstage.

Keeping the family's past a secret was going to be impossible. If *I* didn't reveal who he was, the media was bound to dig it up and blast this information across the airwaves. After all, the public's right to know supersedes a person's right to privacy. So they say.

Tony's pal passed the first interview and I told him I'd be checking his references and would get back to him in a few days.

I was just shaking his hand and saying goodbye at the back

door of the kitchen, when an ear-splitting screech pierced the air, shocking even the cicadas into silence.

We all ran outside. Around in the front of the house, we met up with Phoebe Jo and Julie Ann, who were looking across the lawn towards the trees.

I said, "What the hell was that? We at war?"

"Robert's trying something new," Phoebe Jo answered, "he's gonna scare the coyote away."

"Shit! Scared me!" Tony said, poking his finger in his ear and shaking it.

We heard a siren scream again, but from a different direction. And then a third from yet another part of the farm. We were surrounded.

"Sure is noisy, Miss Kate," Phoebe Jo said.

"Yeah, but if that's what it takes, I'm all for it." We were certainly at war. It was either us or the coyote.

THAT EVENING after dinner, I was at my desk in the library. I was reviewing a printout of my 'Round the World Catering accounts and figuring in the additional salary I would soon be paying, when the phone rang and Phoebe Jo announced, "It's Bobby in Indiana."

I picked up the receiver. "Hey, there. Are you rich yet?"

"Working on it. We're going to stay on for a couple more days—Paco says he's on a streak. That makes me nervous. Hope it lasts, you know what happens when things don't go his way. Remember that tantrum he threw that got us tossed overboard when we were on the Countess' yacht in Greece?"

Of course I remembered. "Well, at least it won't be as long a swim to get back to shore."

Bobby laughed. "Actually, it's kind of fun here. Too bad you're not with us."

"That's okay, I've got my hands full here."

"Yeah, kind of figured that." I heard a mumbling in the background on Bobby's end. He came back with, "Paco wants

149

to know how the investigation's going."

"It's going. Last night I was on a stakeout for four hours. When the suspect showed up I chased him through the streets of downtown Cincinnati at a hundred miles an hour and finally wound up across the river, shooting it out on the mean streets of Newport with said suspect and his three desperado pals. Then I came home in time to eat a Crown Chili three-way before flopping into bed."

"Alone?"

"Alone? What do you mean? Of course I was alone? I'm just kidding around."

"Yeah, yeah, I know that, but I was wondering why you ended it by going to bed all by yourself. That's no fun. If you're going to have a fantasy you might as well go all the way."

That comment immediately plunked Bobby right into the middle of my fantasy and I felt a surprising twinge of disappointment that he wouldn't be back for two more days.

I said, "You coming back in time to party with Eleanor? She'll be real disappointed if you don't."

"Yeah, we'll be back Friday morning."

Just then, one of Robert's sirens went off, and the loud wail could be easily heard through the open window.

"What's that, Kate?"

"Robert's latest tactic in our battle against the coyote."

"How often does that go off?"

"Well, there's three of them all timed differently—I guess I've heard them go off five or six times today."

"That's awful."

"You get used to it after a while."

I later ate those words for a midnight snack. The wailing kept waking me up all night long.

Wednesday, August 25

21

THE RESIDENTS OF Trail's End Farm were a grumpy bunch that morning. I stumbled and staggered my way down to the kitchen at sunup to get a glass of orange juice and take Boo-Kat out to do his business. I couldn't let him out to do even that without putting him on the leash.

Phoebe Jo and Julie Ann were already down there at the kitchen table and, when I walked in, they both started complaining about their sleepless night.

I said, "Me, too. Where's the guy responsible for the bags under our eyes?"

"We sent him out to the woods to tear down his noise

makers," Julie Ann said.

Boo-Kat was running around in circles in front of the back door, so I clipped on his leash and accompanied him to the little doggies' room. Once he'd accomplished his blessing of the lawn, I decided to go for a little jaunt into the woods to see what Robert was up to. But first, I put Boo-Kat back into the house.

I found Robert at the beginning of one of the trails right at the edge of the woods. He was more than a little grumpy, and I heard some rare and colorful words come out of him.

"I know, Kate," he said as I got closer, "you didn't sleep last night, either. But what am I supposed to do? Look!"

I did and saw a fresh rabbit carcass on the ground.

Robert threw up his hands. "Now he's getting closer to the house. The sirens didn't work—just made all the women mad at me."

"I'm not mad, just tired. And I'm tired of this coyote. What else can we do?"

"Well . . . I got one more idea. But you're not gonna like it."

"I don't care what it is. I'm almost at the point of taking your shotgun and camping out here to wait for him. Then I could at least have the satisfaction of blowing his head off myself. What's your idea?"

"Exploders. Just as noisy, but maybe more effective. It'll sound like we're shooting at him."

"That'll just scare him away. I liked your other idea better. Get the Rozzis to come over and wire the whole damn farm and blow him to kingdom come."

Robert was a little taken aback. "Getting pretty aggressive there, aren't you, Kate?"

"I like fireworks!" I stomped back to the house, loaded a bagel with crunchy peanut butter and cherry jam, grabbed a cup of coffee, and went back to bed.

By eight-thirty, I was feeling semi-human and commuted down the stairs to work in my commercial kitchen. Tony was raring to go with his plans for the Casablanca party. He pulled me into the walk-in and started going over what food items we'd need and what he'd already ordered. I guess I was supposed to nod my head and say "okay" to everything he'd done or was planning to do, but it was difficult to keep my mind on even *that* simple task.

I was more concerned about catching two killers. One was lurking around my farm. The other one was getting away scot-free with the murder of Victor Lloyd. And I didn't know what to do about nabbing either one of them.

As far as I knew, the only people who said they didn't believe Victor's death was an accident were Eric Lloyd, Peepo Giuliani, and Dick Rottingham.

Dick liked to sensationalize everything, so I couldn't be sure *what* he believed.

Eric seemed more interested in keeping his marriage to Melissa Oakley on track than in trying to find out who killed his father. At least, that's the impression he gave me yesterday when he told me to leave Melissa and him alone and to go poke around in Ted Mueller's life.

Even so, I was thinking maybe Eric would join Peepo Giuliani in the search for Victor's killer. But then I remembered how angry Eric got when Peepo questioned Tammy that night on the riverboat.

I wondered where Peepo's investigation was taking him. And why did he want to talk to me? On Monday, he said he was going to call me. I still hadn't heard from him.

With all this detective stuff running through my head, you could understand why I couldn't focus on "how many pounds of chicken should we order for Friday night?"

"Hey Boss, you there?"

"Huh?"

"Kate, I was asking you a question, but I guess you really meant it when you gave me this party to handle by myself."

I nodded. "You're capable. What was the question?"

For Tony's sake, I applied myself to the task and we completed the walk-in tour.

But I was still wondering when Peepo Giuliani was going to

call me. When I saw Phoebe Jo in the doorway of the commercial kitchen, I was hoping she'd come to announce that he was on the phone.

"Miss Kate, I just got a call from Kentucky. Momma's fallen. Broke her hip, and you know my Pop—he's helpless without her."

"That's awful. You go," I said, waving my hand, "don't worry about me."

"Well, Robert won't let me drive all that way by myself and I won't leave you with the responsibility for Julie Ann, so that means we'll all be going and leaving you alone here."

"That's okay. I've slept in this house by myself before."

"What about the party on Friday? I was going to help you, but I think we'll have to stay at least over the weekend."

"Don't worry about any of that. We'll manage, you just go take care of your folks. Where's Robert? I need to talk to him."

"He was having coffee in the other kitchen. He's probably on his way upstairs to start packing."

I followed Phoebe Jo down the hallway and into the foyer. Robert was on his way upstairs.

"So what do I do about this coyote while you're gone? You got some kind of bombs you want me to set off?"

"Sorry, Kate." Robert pulled on his ear. "War's on hold until I get back. The Feed 'n' Seed didn't have any exploders in stock—said they'd order 'em for me, but not to expect them until next week some time. You're just gonna have to keep Boo-Kat on his leash."

The front door swung open.

"Now what?" I said, turning. "Oh. Hi, Mother."

Uh-oh. She had that bullish look on her face, like she was about to snort out puffs of smoke.

"Don't 'hi, Mother' me, Kathleen. You have *got* to start communicating with me. I only find out things by accident, through your Uncle Cliff, or when they talk about you in the newspaper. What kind of relationship is that for a mother to have with her only daughter?"

154

Robert and Phoebe Jo scurried up the stairs to safety.

I said, "There's something in the newspaper about me?"

"No, thankfully, not today. But I just got off the phone with your Uncle Cliff. He told me all about this Joey Jules, Joey Peep, Peppino Giuliani—whatever alias that gangster is going by nowadays. I was the one who warned you about that Lloyd family. Then, when you find out I'm right—what's the matter? You can't come to me? Include me in on the discussion?"

I sunk down onto the stairs, propping my chin with my hand. I sighed. "Sorry, you're right. But things are so hectic around here, lately, I—"

"You use that excuse *every* time."

"Well, it's true." I shrugged. "What can I say? I have a hectic life. I'm trying to change that. Maybe in a few years things'll slow down."

Mother stared back at me, looking puzzled. Or maybe she was irritated, I wasn't sure which. Either way, she was speechless—but not for long.

"Kathleen, I don't know what's going to happen to that Oasis project now that Victor Lloyd is dead. But I heard you were at the funeral reception." She jabbed her finger at me. "I'm warning you again. Stay away from the Lloyds and that—" her head shook violently, "—that PEEP!"

"Mother? I think your blood pressure's going up. Your face is turning quite red."

She lowered her accusing finger and took a few breaths to calm herself. "Alright. Enough said about the matter." She patted her hair. "What are your plans for Labor Day Weekend? You're going to watch the fireworks with us on Clifford's boat."

"Well, no. Not this year. How would you like to do something different?"

"But we *always* watch the show from Clifford's boat."

"Well . . . I've been invited to see the Rozzis' fireworks from a different angle this year and was told I could bring my family."

Mother cocked one perfectly drawn eyebrow. She looked hopeful—like maybe her spinster daughter had finally scored a date.

"Dick Rottingham has invited us to spend the evening with him at his sports bar down on the riverfront."

Red flared up again in her cheeks and once-hopeful eyebrows scrunched together in a fierce scowl. Her finger slashed the air in front of my nose. "That's *another* person you should stay away from."

The telephone in my library rang. "See, Mom? Hectic."

Mother followed me into the library. I picked up on the third ring. "Cavanaugh residence."

"May I speak with Ms. Kate Cavanaugh? This is Peppino Giuliani."

"Peepo. Hi, this is Kate." Mother's eyes bulged.

"Hello, again. I know you're a busy woman, so I won't take up your time, but I'm hoping you will accept my invitation to lunch tomorrow."

"Lunch? Tomorrow?" I turned away from Mother. "Yes. That looks alright. What's the occasion?"

"I have a business proposal to make to you."

"You mean Crown Chili?" Mother's high heels had been clicking back and forth on the hardwood floor in front of the window. They stopped.

"No," Peepo said, "I'm much more interested in 'Round the World Catering."

"Oh?" That grabbed my interest and he knew it.

"Good. Let's meet downtown—I'm using Victor's office. Do you know where that is?"

"You better give me the address. What time?" I sat down and wrote the instructions on the pad in front of me, then said goodbye.

Mother marched up to me and peered into my face. "Kathleen?" She rapped her knuckles on the desktop, accenting each word. "What . . are . . you . . doing?"

"I'm going to have lunch with—"

"He's a gangster! You weren't listening—you *never* listen to me."

"I'm just going to—"

"Never mind! I don't want to hear—*oh phwua!*" Mother sputtered, fluttered, and stormed out of the room.

Thursday, August 26

22

WHAT DO YOU WEAR to lunch with a gangster? I stared at my all-too-familiar wardrobe. Nothing seemed suitable, though I couldn't tell you what would. I finally decided on a long, purple dress with tiny buttons all down the front and a kimono-style jacket with a purple and green batik print.

I switched on B-105, turning it up good and loud so I wouldn't be aware of how empty the house was. I felt like a little bean rolling around in a great big box. Tony was working in the commercial kitchen as usual, but the absence of the Boones was not so usual and I didn't like it.

I hardly ever take the time to wear makeup, but there was

something about Peepo's elegant, gentlemanly manner that made me want to play up my feminine side a bit more. Still, I felt stupid trying to get the mascara to go on without clumping, and ended up wiping it all off.

I threw on my dress and stood in front of the mirror, brushing out my hair. As I redid my braid and hummed along with Trisha Yearwood, who was singing a very sad song about being all alone, I tried to imagine what it would be like if the Boones never came back.

Last night had been a real trial. I wasn't expecting it to be so difficult. It wasn't the silence that got to me, it was the *lack* of silence—hearing all those sounds you don't usually notice unless you're in a state somewhere between hyperawareness and anxiety. Guess it was all this coyote-lurking-around-in-the-woods business that had me spooked. I just about shot straight out of bed when I heard him howl for the first time.

But then it made me so mad, I threw open the window and shouted, "Get your ass out of here, you mangy sonofabitch!"

I didn't hear him the rest of the night. Hey, you never know, it might've been as simple as that.

Now I was on my way to a lunch date with a different type of predator.

I painted on some lipstick, kissed at my reflection in the mirror, switched off Trisha, and ran downstairs.

I PARKED MY Jeep in the Tower Place parking lot and went out to the street to find the building where Victor Lloyd's office was. It was just a short walk through the lunchtime crowds that were starting to spill out onto the sidewalks. I rode up to the fifteenth floor in a musty smelling elevator, feeling somewhat energized just by the fact that someone thought my talents were worth discussing over a business lunch. But I still wanted to get out of the kitchen. Even without knowing what Peepo's offer was, I had no intentions of accepting it. Meeting him for lunch was a case of looking for ego strokes. More importantly, it was a chance to study him—I still wasn't sure whether he was one of the good guys or the bad guy himself.

It was easy to tell which suite belonged to Victor Lloyd. When I got off the elevator and looked down to the end of the corridor, I saw two massive wooden doors with gold tone lettering announcing that behind these impressive doors where the equally impressive offices of *Lloyd & Associates Commercial Development, Inc.*

Judging by the conservative exterior of *Lloyd & Associates,* I was expecting to enter a tastefully decorated suite of offices, similar to Uncle Cliff's lawyer's lair.

But that wasn't what greeted me when I pushed open the doors.

Talk about visual overload! Bright lights! Garish colors! Every inch of floor and wall space was filled, used, and taken up—by what? As my eyes refocused, I recognized an eight by ten color photo of the *Queen of Newport*—and I don't mean eight by ten inches. It filled the wall behind the front desk, giving the odd impression that the young bored receptionist was perched on the lower deck. The other walls were covered with huge blow-up photos of Victor's past successes and sketches of future dreams. I recognized Le Galleria and an artist's rendering of his ill-fated Luxury Landing at Newport riverfront condominiums.

The waiting area was jammed with leather sofas and chairs and a gigantic coffee table holding the biggest collection of magazines I'd ever seen. A fierce-looking, life-size replica of an American bald eagle stared down at the seating from his six-foot high pedestal. In the center of the room was Victor's crowning glory—the illuminated model of The Oasis I'd seen on the riverboat. Beams of hot white light, shooting out from spots mounted on the ceiling, crisscrossed the room and highlighted each photo and sketch.

"Can I help you?" a sleepy voice drawled. I recognized the receptionist as the sweet young thing Dick Rottingham had been chatting up at Victor's funeral reception. She'd been very busy, struggling with a crossword puzzle and I could see the boxes were filled with the smudgy remains of letters that didn't work. There were little piles of eraser shavings all over the page.

"I'm Kate Cavanaugh. Mr. Giuliani is expecting me."

She punched a button on the telephone console with the worn away eraser end of her pencil. "Ms. Cavanaugh is here." She smiled at me, not a line creasing her sweet young face.

Sammy appeared in the doorway at one end of the receptionist's desk. He nodded and beckoned to me with a crook of his finger. "This way, Ms. Cavanaugh."

"Hi, Sammy."

I think a smile flickered at the corners of his lips as he turned and led the way down the corridor.

We passed a number of offices, most of them with their doors shut. A few were open and I peeked inside as we walked by. The rooms were furnished, but the desks and drawing tables had been cleaned off and seemed to be just sitting there in the dark, waiting.

When we reached the half-open door at the end of the hallway, Sammy pushed it all the way open and nodded for me to go past him and into the room. Peepo Giuliani, dressed in a perfectly-fitted gray suit and pale yellow silk tie, rose from the tufted leather executive chair. The sun shining through the bank of corner windows behind him caught the silver in his hair and gave him a luminous quality. He came out from behind the desk and walked towards me, holding out both hands and smiled broadly, as if greeting his favorite niece.

I was so mesmerized, all I could do was give him my hands, which he clasped in his.

"Kate, you look lovely. So good of you to come. I hope you like Italian."

"Yes, of course," I said, recovering enough to start taking in my surroundings. Victor's office was subdued in comparison to his reception area—more the dark wood, leather-chaired, old boy's club decor I expected. The only personal effect I

162

noticed was a plaque on his desk that stated, *To Victor Belongs The Spoils.*

"Where are we going?" I asked, already figuring I knew the answer. There was only one Italian restaurant in the area that was elegant enough for someone like Peepo.

"La Cucina."

I was right.

PEOPLE STARED AT US as we walked the few blocks to the restaurant. I couldn't blame them, we were an unusual sight—I towered over everybody, Peepo glowed, and Sammy hulked behind us.

When we reached La Cucina, we were immediately ushered to a couple of tables in the far corner. Peepo pulled out a chair for me at one of them, and sat down beside me. Sammy stationed himself behind me at the second table.

The other diners were trying their hardest to not look at us, but here and there I would see someone grabbing a quick peek.

Peepo leaned forward and smiled at me. "It is a pleasure to be seen in public with you."

I was a little miffed when he waved the menus away and ordered for me. I have very definite ideas about what I want to eat and drink, but I decided to be tactful and let him lead in this particular dance. Just wanted to see where he was going, and didn't want to put him off with any unintentional missteps on my part.

We talked over plates of garlicky shrimp and angel hair pasta. Rather, Peepo talked and I listened. I was surprised at how much he knew about my catering career and lapped up the compliments like a kitten having her first bowl of cream. Halfway through the meal, he came to the point of our meeting.

"I've learned over the years that one of the secrets of success is to surround yourself with people of exceptional ability. Take Sammy over there. He was with Special Forces—served several tours in Vietnam. He's a man with many, many talents and all I have to do is ask him to take care of a problem and it's done—I don't have to worry about it again. I'm in the process of putting together a team of multi-talented people to make sure The Oasis is a success.

"Kate, I want people from all over the world to be drawn to The Oasis for its first-class cuisine. And I am absolutely confident that you are the one to make that happen. I'm offering you the opportunity to not only be head chef at The Oasis but also to expand your 'Round the World Catering, operating it out of my facility. You call the shots—however many assistants you need is totally up to you. It's your baby."

Talk about your ego strokes. A world-class operation with *me* at the helm? I was floating ten feet off the ground and could see myself steering The Oasis towards international gastronomic stardom. Watch out Maisonette, your days as Cincinnati's only five star culinary experience are coming to an end. *Wait, wait!* Grab a hold of yourself, girl! I jumped back down to earth. There were two problems with this picture. First, I had just spent weeks agonizing over the fact that I was tired of being in the kitchen and needed to find a new direction for my life. Second, I doubted Peepo Giuliani was the kind of man who'd truly let a woman run things, judging by the fact that he'd automatically ordered lunch for me without asking what I'd like.

I've never had a good poker face and I'm sure Peepo must have seen my ambivalence, because he turned on the hard sell. He was starting to sound like a commercial for Northern Kentucky tourism.

Complicating my mixed feelings was the fact I knew little about Peepo's past. Once a gangster always a gangster? Hmm, that was starting to sound like Mother. But I certainly didn't want to get sweet-talked into a situation I'd later regret. I needed to know how Peepo's past was going to affect my future before I'd even consider jumping in and becoming such a visible part of his vision.

I held up my hand and stopped him. "Before you go on, Peepo, I have a few questions."

That startled him, but he quickly regained his cool. "Of course, Kate." He held out his hands in an expansive gesture. "*You* can ask me anything."

"There are lots of rumors flying around about you. What I do know for sure is that at one point Peppino Giuliani, aka Joey Jules, was the owner of the original Oasis gambling casino in Newport, Kentucky."

Peepo leaned back in his chair and studied me with amusement. Finally, he said, "You *are* a good detective. What else do you know about me?"

"Nothing very personal. Only that you and your family disappeared when casino gambling was kicked out of Newport, and that The Oasis carried on without the gambling, I thought, under new ownership. But I guess you've owned that property and the land down by the river all these years. Why did you hang onto them and why are you back here now?"

Peepo sat forward in his chair and placed both hands palms down on the table. "How would you feel if your family had spent years building up a successful business, even shedding blood over it, only to be run out of town by a bunch of sanctimonious do-gooders? Well, let's just say I hung on to the properties out of spite, and vowed to come back some day. After my family left Newport, we set up our gambling operation in Las Vegas and hired some people here to keep The Oasis running as a nightclub and restaurant. That worked out for a while, but business slowed to the point where it became more trouble than it was worth. So, we finally closed it down and demolished the building. But I knew someday those plots of land would be worth a lot."

I said, "Yeah, now anything on the riverfront is prime real estate. With the surge of gambling on the riverboats in Indiana, I guess you figured it was the right time to come back. What was Victor's role in all this? Was he really your nephew?"

Peepo fingered his napkin. "Victor was my sister's

165

boy—she's dead now. I kind of brought Victor up in the casino business. He worked for me in Las Vegas from the time he was a teenager, but he was too ambitious to just be an employee. He set out on his own to develop some small commercial ventures in Nevada and was successful. But Victor had gambling in his blood and wanted to get in on the riverboat scene in Indiana. When he couldn't find a place for himself there, I told him he could play with the property in Newport, so he came to Cincinnati and established himself as a local developer. The idea was for Victor to be the figurehead in attracting investors—I realized it was best for me with my reputation to stay back in the wings."

A busboy came and silently removed our empty plates.

"So you're behind the condominium project, too?"

"Yes, I own that land. Rather, my corporation does." Peepo shrugged. "I didn't think the timing was right for that—I wasn't really interested in condos anyway. It was just a fun thing to gamble with, maybe another chance for Victor to get more of a foothold in the local development scene and build up his reputation. No matter what happened, I was still going to go ahead with The Oasis, using Victor to try and interest outside investors. Now that he's been murdered, I have *two* goals in my life. One, build The Oasis. And two, find Victor's killer."

Peepo squinted—not at something he saw, but at some private thought. He picked up the teaspoon in front of him and began tapping it lightly on the table. "I kept as low a profile as I could, but maybe I still have enemies in this town to deal with."

"Do you think someone killed Victor to get back at you?"

"Well, I've certainly held my grudge all these years. Maybe someone else did, too."

He focused on me. The corners of his eyes crinkled as if he'd just heard a joke. "If Victor was killed by that 'someone' because they feared he'd be bringing gambling back to Newport, this morning's news must have filled them with dread."

166

"Did I miss something? What's happened?"

Peepo began his answer with a little laugh. "Harrah's Entertainment, one of the world's largest casino operators, has just expanded into thoroughbred racing. That corporation has joined with GTECH, a provider of online Lottery games, and, together, they bought Turfway Park down in Florence, Kentucky. Now, what do you think will be the next logical step those two companies take?"

That was obvious. "Lobby to make casino gambling legal."

"Correct. A sidebar to this morning's story is that Kentucky's State Lottery isn't pulling in as much money as it used to in the counties bordering Indiana where riverboat gambling is flourishing. The lottery commission isn't happy. Something has to be done to stem the flow of money leaving the state of Kentucky."

Peepo was right, the solution was as plain as the nose on Sammy's face.

"Kate, it's inevitable that gambling will be legalized in Kentucky. The people want it, so why shouldn't *I* be in a position to help provide them with that form of entertainment when the state legislature finally sees the light."

Peepo was being extraordinarily candid with me, a total stranger. I asked, "Why are you telling me all this?"

He looked me in the eyes. "You deserve to know who you'd be associated with. You asked a straightforward question and I'm giving you an honest answer."

Peepo paused for a second, as though gathering himself up for a leap. He leapt. "I was your uncle's best pal."

I was thunderstruck. "Uncle Cliff? He didn't say anything about being your friend."

"No." His tone was gentle, measured. "Not the Vasherhann one. Your Dad's older brother. Nick Cavanaugh."

I had no idea who the hell Peepo was talking about.

167

23

"YOU MUST BE MISTAKEN. My father was an only child."

Peepo's eyes widened with surprise. "They never told you about Nick? I'm sorry, I didn't realize his existence was a family secret."

"There are no secrets in my family. Whoever told you he was my father's brother is a liar." This was not something Dad would keep from me.

"No. This man was not lying to me. Not for all those years I knew him." Peepo's look of surprise had changed to one of concern. "I'm not comfortable being the one to spring this on you, Kate. You sure you never saw any old photographs of your father up to around the age of four or five with a tall, fifteen-year-old boy?"

After thinking about it for a minute, I realized I'd never seen any photos of Dad as a very young child. We had plenty of pictures of serious-looking men with big moustaches and scowling women, but the family albums seemed to ignore childhood.

Peepo said, "Nick ran away from home after he turned fifteen. Because he was tall and strong for his age, he looked older and got work on the freighters. I first ran into him in the Navy during World War II. When we were discharged after the war was over, he came back with me to Newport to work in my father's casino."

I waved my hand. "Don't bother telling me anymore. I think you were taken for a ride."

"Okay. I understand your reluctance to believe me." Peepo lowered his gaze and rubbed his chin, as if thinking hard about what to say next.

He looked back up at me. "Okay, I will tell you a personal fact about your family that couldn't be made up—that only a family member would know. Nick told me his father, your grandfather, used to drive him crazy with his obsessive-compulsive habits."

That struck a cord. Grandpa was that way.

Peepo continued. "One of them was the way he stirred his coffee. He'd count while he stirred twenty times. Not eighteen or nineteen or twenty-one. It had to be exactly twenty. Then he'd tap his spoon twice on the side of the cup."

Images of my grandfather doing exactly that came to mind. I said, "But he did that *everywhere* he went. Lots of people might have known that about him—doesn't make them a member of my family."

Peepo rubbed his temple. He stopped. He pointed his finger at me. "Okay, how about this? Have you ever heard the phrase 'a place for everything and everything in its place'?"

I certainly had. Over and over. "Yes? What about it?"

"Nick told me his father insisted that all the contents of the kitchen cupboards in his home be arranged in a very definite way and he was constantly being reminded that the plates had to be stacked just so, and the cups had to be hanging from hooks in a certain order. Even the groceries had to be put away in their own particular spots. Nick would complain that he could never keep track of it and get it right and, as a result, they'd be arguing constantly. He said he heard that phrase so many times growing up that, even as an adult, when someone else said it, it made him sick to his stomach."

That not only struck a chord, it sent chills up and down my spine. I remembered being eight years old and making myself a peanut butter and jam sandwich at my grandparents' house. My grandfather got all upset when he discovered I'd put the jar of peanut butter back in the pantry alongside the cans of soup instead of beside the mustard. Grandpa didn't yell at me, but from that time on he'd call out "a place for everything and everything in its place" whenever I'd make myself a snack in his house.

Suddenly, what Peepo said had the ring of truth. But I didn't want to believe it. And yet, I found myself asking,

"What kind of work did he do in the casino? Was he a card dealer?"

Peepo frowned. "No, not Nick. Sticking him behind a table would've been a waste of his talents. In the Navy, Nick was a member of the military police, so he had a lot of training in how to handle trouble—of all kinds. Nick was head of the casino's security."

Sounded like that meant carrying a gun. I remembered Mother's talk about gangsters shooting it out on the streets of Newport. "Guess that was a dangerous job. Was he a violent man?"

Peepo took a breath as if he was about to answer, then paused a moment. "I think you would have liked Nick. He was a big guy—taller than you." He became very animated, his eyes brightening as he continued. "Nick was a smart man, very loyal to his friends. Told good stories and even got some of them published."

He was not answering my question. "Did this so-called uncle of mine ever kill anyone?" I was still picturing men in snap-brimmed hats pulling machine guns out from under their trench coats.

Peepo nodded once, cautiously. "Yes. But you've got to remember that back then almost all of the cops in Newport were on the take. They were being paid to look the other way. Even the chief of police had his own gambling casino. At times, there'd be feuding going on between the casino operators and the cops didn't care if we killed each other off. So my Pop set up what you might call his own private security department. That was Nick's job."

The conversation had taken such a bizarre turn, I had no appetite for the Tiramisu the waiter placed before me. I was feeling a little claustrophobic and said, "I need some air."

Without hesitation, Peepo stood up and signaled to Sammy.

"Then we shall go," he said, pulling out my chair as I got up.

We stepped out of the air-conditioned restaurant into the

blinding sun, and stood in silence waiting for Sammy to pay the bill. Oven-like heat rose up from the sidewalk. I took off my jacket.

We headed back towards the office building. Sammy kept his required distance behind us and Peepo made small talk about the weather, the architecture of some of the buildings. I kind of half-listened and nodded my head to show I was paying attention, but my thoughts were grappling with each other. Peepo's recounting of Grandpa's obsessiveness was bang-on, and that touched off a feeling of outrage. How could my parents not have told me about this Nick Cavanaugh? But then, why should I believe Peepo Giuliani? He's a gangster—lying was the least of his sins.

When we got back to the office building, we stopped near the entrance. Peepo clasped my hand in both of his. "Thank you for having lunch with me. I'm sorry if I upset you, I didn't mean to. Let me just say that The Oasis is going to be an exciting place and I want you to seriously consider my offer. You're the perfect person to fill this position, but that's not the only reason I approached you. Kate, I believe you are Nick Cavanaugh's niece. He was not only the best friend I ever had, he was like a brother to me. And through him I feel a personal connection to you."

I turned his handclasp into a handshake, thanked him for the lunch, and promised to consider his offer.

Peepo said, "You sure you don't want me to walk you back to your car?"

"No, thank you. I'm fine. It's parked just down the street."

"Well, goodbye then," he said with a little wave of his hand and a smile. "I hope to hear from you soon." He pushed the revolving door and was swept into the foyer of the office building. Sammy nodded at me and glided in behind him.

I started walking towards the Tower Place garage and was standing at the corner waiting for the light to turn green, when Ted Mueller stepped up beside me. That wasn't surprising. Cincinnati's business district covers a small area and it's more than likely you'll bump into someone you know.

"Hello, Ted. How are you?"

"Well, I just enjoyed a good lunch at *La Cucina*. Saw you there with Mr. Giuliani."

How did Ted know who he was? "Yeah. The food there is good, isn't it?" The light changed and we stepped down into the crosswalk.

"Business lunch?" Ted looked at me out of the corner of his eye.

"Yes."

"Hmm. I'd like to have a business lunch with you, too."

We reached the other side of the street. Ted took my elbow and gently guided me out of the stream of pedestrians to stand under a hotel's awning.

He mopped at his brow with a handkerchief. "Gosh, it's hot."

"You were saying?" I really didn't want to know, but my upbringing dictated I be polite.

"I recommend you not do business with Mr. Giuliani. I've been looking into his background and his past is as black as Satan's heart."

"That's a little dramatic."

"Not when you consider his police record."

Forget polite, all at once I was fascinated.

"Kate, when he was a young guy he was known as Joey Jules."

"I know that."

"But did you know he'd been brought up on charges of assault, second degree murder, the list goes on and on."

Didn't surprise me, though Peepo seemed to be more the type to put out contracts than to do the actual trigger-pulling.

Ted continued. "The charges always got dropped. Either crucial pieces of evidence were somehow misplaced or witnesses suddenly disappeared off the face of the earth."

"Where did you get this information? I know you're not old enough to have read it in the newspapers back then."

"I have a few friends in the Cincinnati police department. After Friday night, it became evident to me this Giuliani was taking charge of Victor Lloyd's project. I wanted to know who the hell he was. Amazing what came up when I mentioned the names Giuliani and Oasis."

"And you're telling me all this because you don't want to see a nice girl like me get mixed up with a sleazeball like him."

Ted nodded. "Exactly. Anyway, Kate, you're getting me away from what I wanted to talk to you about. When I saw you with Giuliani, I figured he was pitching you an offer to be a major part of The Oasis. It stands to reason he'd need a person of your abilities to run that joint's kitchen."

Well, thanks a lot, Ted. He made it sound like I was going to be slinging chili in a greasy spoon. "I've got to get back to work. What *did* you want to talk to me about?"

"Before you say 'yes' to that hood, please give me a chance to pitch you my idea. You know I have my own plans and it looks like Cincinnati City Council is finally going to start moving on the riverfront development issue."

He leaned forward. "It's going to be exciting on *this* side of the river, too. Anyway, I've heard through the grapevine that Giuliani's related to Victor Lloyd. If that's true, then I was right in accusing Victor of setting up The Oasis in case gambling is legalized. That whole family's been a blight on this community. Criminal behavior's in their blood."

Ted's voice boomed with righteous indignation, and a few passersby glanced at us.

I said, "This has been a very interesting lunch break, but I've really got to get home."

"Can I call you, Kate?"

"Yeah, sure." I started to walk away.

"Hey, Kate!" Ted shouted after me.

I turned and saw him wagging his finger at me. Everyone else on the street had also stopped to stare at us.

"The guy's a snake. Don't trust him."

I sort of felt like Eve. Peepo's apple sure looked juicy, but was there a worm inside?

24

I BARELY NOTICED the twenty mile drive from downtown Cincinnati to Mother's house—the Cavanaugh castle that Crown Chili built. It wasn't that my head was full of all those exciting job offers and the promise of international culinary stardom. Rather, a blinding fury was building up inside me and I ranted at Mother in absentia.

I tore up the long, winding driveway, careened around the fountain in front of Mother's imposing, stone mansion, and screeched to a halt next to her white Mercedes.

"Mother," I yelled as I pushed through the front door. "Mother?"

The housekeeper poked her head out from the kitchen. "She's in the back, dear."

I stomped through the cavernous gathering room and out the French doors that led onto a multi-level deck. Sitting at a table under a large, flowery umbrella was Mother. She was wearing sunglasses and a redundant wide-brimmed straw hat. At the sound of the door slamming behind me, she stopped in mid-sip and placed her tall glass of iced tea down on the table.

"Kathleen? What a rare surprise. Tell Loretta to bring another glass, there's plenty of tea here in the pitcher."

"No, Mother. I'm sorry, this is not a friendly visit."

She pulled her sunglasses down to the end of her nose and looked up at me, eyebrows raised in a question.

I stood in front of her, one hand on hip, and told myself to keep the lid on. "I just found out I have an Uncle Nick. No one ever told me about him. Why?"

There was a flicker of shock in Mother's eyes. She pushed the sunglasses back up and pinched her lips together, closing up her face so I couldn't read it.

"I don't know what you're talking about, Kathleen."

174

"Oh yes, I think you do. I just spoke to someone who knew a lot about our family and described Grandpa the way he was in his private life at home."

"Obviously, someone's been telling you stories."

"Which seems to be more than what you've been willing to do." Without mentioning Peepo's name, I went on to relate what he'd just told me about my grandfather and Nick Cavanaugh, leaving out the gangster bits—I didn't want to give her reason to deny anything.

Mother was silent for a moment and then shook her head. "You have to be careful, dear. You're a wealthy woman and people might make up stories just to get closer to you."

I'd been aware of that danger all my life. But, in this case, my gut told me Peepo's story was true.

"There *is* a Nick Cavanaugh, isn't there, Mother. I saw it in your eyes before you hid behind your glasses. Why wasn't I told all these years and why are you lying to me now?"

Mother slammed her glass of tea down onto the table. "How dare you! You have no right to talk to me like that!"

"What kind of family is this—keeping secrets from one another?"

"Secrets? Look who's talking. You keep your whole life a secret from me."

"Because," I said, wagging my head from side to side, "anytime I try to tell you what I'm doing, you criticize it. You never accept who I am, so why should I open myself up to you just so you can verbally abuse me?"

"Yes, yes, you're always right! You always have the answer! And you think your father was perfect, too—you've made him into some kind of god. Well, I'm sick of always being cast as the villain in this family."

Mother took off her sunglasses and threw them on the table. "Kathleen, the truth is your father, James Cavanaugh, was not the most perfect man on earth. Nor was he a god. He was just a flawed human being like the rest of us, who couldn't confront some of his own emotional issues with his family. Yes, he had a brother named Nicholas, who ran away at the

175

age of fifteen. Your father was five."

I kicked one of the chairs. Suddenly, I was more furious with him than with Mother. Flinging my arms up in the air, I shouted, "What's the big secret?"

"Why are you getting so upset? You don't need to start kicking the furniture around. Really, Kathleen, that's childish behavior."

That comment made me want to kick the chair *she* was in.

Mother picked up her sunglasses and began fiddling with them. She seemed to be fascinated with the way the plastic arms folded over each other and, without looking up at me, said, "I really didn't think this situation would ever arise. When I accidentally found out about Nick, your father made me promise never to mention his name ever again. *I* don't understand it totally, but I guess your father felt so abandoned and angry, that was the only way he could deal with it. My loyalties were to him, and I don't appreciate you lashing out at me over this."

"Okay, okay," I said, waving my hand, "now that we're in this situation and Dad's not here, you can tell me the story. How did you find out about Nick?"

Mother clamped her lips in an automatic refusal to cooperate. She thought for a moment, then sighed noisily. "Well, when your grandfather died, we inherited all his possessions which included a couple of photo albums. Even though Grandfather Cavanaugh never spoke of Nick, he still kept a few photos of him. I saw them myself. That was before your father went through those albums and destroyed all the pictures that had Nick in them."

"No." I couldn't imagine him doing that.

Mother slowly raised her head and looked at me. "I'm sorry. I can see you've been crushed by the revelation your father would keep something from you."

"Why did Uncle Nick run away?" I was already feeling possessive of my new-found relative.

"Grandfather Cavanaugh was a trial to live with and work

for and Nick found it impossible to bear and he hated working in a greasy spoon chili parlor. He left without warning and never came back, which broke his mother's heart. Grandmother Cavanaugh died a few years after Nick ran off, and your Dad held that against his brother his entire life—never forgave him. Your father was an angry man. He was angry with his brother and his father, and he held it all in. That was a pattern with him. I think a lot of things made him angry, but he kept it to himself, pretended everything was okay until one day, without warning, his heart gave out. That was it. He was gone."

That knocked me speechless. There was a long moment of pained silence.

Mother reached out and took my hand. I wasn't sure whether she was looking for comfort or attempting to comfort me. Whatever, the gesture felt awkward and unfamiliar. I wanted to pull my hand away, but didn't.

She said, "You have both of us in you. You have your father's wonderful brain for business, but you also have his secretive side. And, I hate to tell you, dear, the very characteristics you hate in me are in you. You can be stubborn, critical, and even arrogant. Remember that the next time you get impatient with me."

I sunk down into a chair, leaned forward, elbows on the table, and dropped my head wearily into my hands. It was all too much. My head throbbed. I just wanted to go home, crawl into bed, and pull the covers over my head until all the bad things went away. The coyote, career burnout, dysfunctional families—

"Um, Kathleen? Who was this person who told you about Nick and Grandfather Cavanaugh?"

I was too weary to play any games. "Peppino Giuliani," slipped out of my mouth with an exhausted sigh.

A noise burst out of Mother. I wasn't sure exactly what it was, but it sounded like a shriek, a gasp, and a curse. Safe to say, Mother did not approve of the crowd Uncle Nick had run around with.

* * * * * * * * * * *

THAT NIGHT—home alone again—I realized crawling into bed and pulling the covers over my head didn't make the bad things go away. They slinked in under the sheets after me. I tossed and turned, my thoughts jumping from one worry to another.

First was my career. I'd slaved over the years to build 'Round the World Catering's reputation, but all of a sudden I couldn't give a flying fig if Ruthie Yankovitch's stupid party was a raging success or a total bomb. As soon as I had that thought, my mind flip-flopped and began obsessing over silly details like did Tony order the right number of napkins.

Then there was the confrontation with Mother and the realization that there were aspects of my parents' life I knew absolutely nothing about. All those years, I thought my Dad and I were close. I even looked on Mother as some kind of intruder on our relationship.

Why couldn't he have told me about Uncle Nick? I was in my twenties when Dad had his heart attack and died—wasn't like I was too young to understand.

I found myself digging up old memories of my father and replaying our conversations, straining to recall any evidence of the angry man Mother said was locked up inside of him.

If Uncle Nick ran away when Dad was only five, how did Dad know why his brother left? Grandfather Cavanaugh would never pass on a story that made himself look bad. Maybe Uncle Nick *did* have some kind of contact with Dad after all.

All that exhausting mental self-torture was blown away by the baleful sound of a coyote howling in my woods.

"God damn you!" I whipped the sheets off my body, jumped out of bed, and was at the open window in two steps. "Leave me alone!"

Boo-Kat scrambled out from under the bed, pushed up in front of me at the window, and barked mindlessly out at the night.

The coyote howled again, mocking us.

Shutting a frantic Boo-Kat in the bedroom, I ran downstairs in my nightshirt and bare feet to the family kitchen. I switched on a small neon light over one of the counters, rummaged through a drawer until I found a key, and strode across the half-lit kitchen and into the laundry room.

In one corner was a long box mounted on the wall. I pushed the key into the lock, pulled the door open, and grabbed one of Robert's shotguns and a couple of shells.

I marched outside and around to the front of the house, loaded up and blasted both barrels into the woods.

Friday, August 27

25

I DIDN'T BAG WILE E. COYOTE—for one thing, I couldn't see him, and the other, it wasn't even my intention to hit him. But just shooting off Robert's gun made me feel a whole lot better and I had a good night's sleep. In fact, I slept in.

It was seven-thirty when I finally woke up. That may not sound like sleeping in, but considering I usually am awake at four or five o'clock in the morning, it was downright decadent. My mind was refreshed, alert, and running at full speed. It hummed away like a little computer running through all my to-do lists, reminding me of the mundane details of living that had to be attended to, like:

Remember to turn some lights on in the house before you go out tonight to the Casablanca party.

The dress you want to wear needs ironing.

Don't forget to call the dishwasher repairman.

Write up a bill to send to Charlotte Oakley.

That last item was the thing I needed to think about.

This whole investigation into Victor Lloyd's background had started out with the purpose of answering Charlotte's questions. She got her answers pretty quickly, so I guess I did a good job as her hired investigator. I should have already drawn up some kind of bill to send to her, but that seemed silly. I didn't feel like I'd done very much. I did give her information though, and that was worth something—my first satisfied customer. Now I just needed to figure out how much time to bill her for and get into the habit of keeping track of my hours.

Charlotte may have been satisfied, but *I* wasn't satisfied. There was a long trail ahead of me. I still wanted to find out who killed Victor Lloyd. Now, because of Peepo's revelation about my long lost Uncle Nick, the investigation had been transformed into something personal. Peepo was the only connection I had to my rebellious relative. In a bizarre way, that also made me feel connected to the old Oasis and Victor's plans to resurrect it. Five'll get you ten, he was killed because of those plans. I felt strangely obligated to prove Victor was murdered and figure out who did it.

LATER THAT MORNING, I was in the commercial kitchen with Tony prepping for the Casablanca party, when the sound of Boo-Kat's barking and a car horn beeping at the front of the house told me the boys were back. I hurried out the kitchen's screen door and ran around the side of the house to greet them.

Bobby held up his hand and gave me a big grin. Paco had his head in the trunk and was busy throwing their bags out onto the driveway. When he turned and looked at me, I was greeted with a grumpy, sour-faced "Hullo."

"Hey, Paco! Hey, Bobby! Where's the money?"

"Probably buying someone a solid gold Cadillac in some pokey river town in Indiana," Bobby replied, pointing at his brother. "Mister 'I'm On A Roll' here lost *everything.*"

"You're broke? Busted?"

Bobby waved his fingers. "No, no. I wouldn't let him touch our real money. We just lost all the winnings we made in the first day."

Paco tossed a duffel bag at Bobby, almost hitting him. "Just? What do you mean 'just'? I won six thousand dollars, and that stinkin' little boat they call a casino ripped me off."

"Well," I said, "glad to see you had a good time. Guess you're not in the mood to party tonight." I shook my head. "That'll be a big disappointment to Eleanor."

Paco blew a raspberry out the side of his mouth. "I've disappointed a lot of women in my life. She'll live."

"Hmm . . . It's probably for the best—you'd be bored. Eleanor said there'd be some friendly backgammon games, small stakes—nothing in your league."

Paco raised his head up for the first time and I could see his funk was beginning to lift. "Oh?" He turned to Bobby. "See? I told you. I've got good karma. I knew there'd be a chance to get back my winnings."

I yanked on his sleeve a couple of times. *"Small stakes!"*

"Nah, they always say that. It never stays small." With a burst of new energy, Paco grabbed two overnight bags and led the way up the steps into the house.

Bobby whispered to me, "I hope you don't regret this."

TONY AND I switched roles in the kitchen the rest of the day. I pretended to be his assistant and let him issue the orders. It was good practice for when *his* assistant came on board next week, though I had to keep reminding him the poor guy might not last long if Tony kept calling him "schlemiel".

183

Even though this was going to be Tony's show—he had to hire the servers, set up the room and see that the food was displayed and served properly—I was expected, as always, to mingle and make sure the guests had a good time. After all, it was *my* reputation on the line.

By five-thirty, Tony's show was ready to roll. The four servers hired for the occasion were helping Tony and I load up the van. Bobby and Paco had pulled out a couple of lawn chairs and were sitting on the sidelines, throwing out encouraging remarks. I was amazed at how they managed to dress so appropriately for the party, but then, on second thought, I realized their wardrobes were made up entirely of clothing from places like Morocco. Tony looked like he always did in his baggy neon-colored chef's pants. I wore a long linen skirt and matching tank top. I figured it was a good choice for this party, since the catalog I'd ordered it from described the color of the reddish-brown fabric as "Moroccan clay".

Tony headed out first in the van, followed by the car carrying the four servers. Paco, Bobby, and I brought up the rear in the guys' rental. Since we were following everybody else, Paco was forced to drive only ten miles an hour over the speed limit, but he still had the CD player cranked up and blasting out one of the Gipsy Kings' wilder numbers at full volume. I was getting in the mood for a good party.

Our little caravan pulled up in front of the Yankovitch's French chateau on their eighty acre estate deep in the heart of Clairmont. Walter "King" Yankovitch was the CEO of Yankie Pineapple, Incorporated. He started making his fortune fifty years ago selling fruit, but his love of wheeling and dealing led him to expand his interests. He'd buy small companies with good ideas but on the verge of bankruptcy, turn them around over the period of a few years, then sell out at an enormous profit.

One of the two young men standing at the edge of the stone courtyard leading to the front door came towards the van. Tony leaned out his window and had a short conversation with him.

Paco turned to me. "I can't get over this place, Kate. Valet parking for a little Friday night bash?"

I looked at the two young men in their neatly pressed chinos and green polo shirts. "They must've been hired just for the evening. Looks like he's telling Tony to go around the back."

Paco followed the van and the car with the servers, and pulled up by the back door that led directly into the kitchen.

As I got out of the car, Tony yelled across to me, "Hey, Boss, what're you doing back here? You should've gone in the front door—old habits are hard to break, huh? Go."

Being the boss, I didn't listen to him, and hung around the kitchen for the first few minutes just to make sure he was setting things up properly. Tony looked at me as if to say *am I or am I not in charge*. He crossed his arms in front of his chest. "Get out there and schmooze."

"You mean, 'get lost'?"

"Yeah."

"Go to it, Tony," I said, and linked my arms with Bobby and Paco, and we trooped out of the kitchen.

The party room was a sea of white, but it was amazing how many varying shades you can come up with. I was already familiar with Ruthie Yankovitch's passion for no-color decor. In this particular room, lily-white sofas and armchairs were scattered here and there over the huge, expansive, cream-colored Berber carpeting. The walls, the blinds on the windows, even the ceiling fans were egg shell. In front of a large bay window stood a pure white, glossy grand piano. I almost wished I'd had my sunglasses. Everything was white on white on white on white—except for spots of green here and there where Ruthie had place a potted palm or fern.

When I saw Ruthie Yankovitch coming towards me dressed in a white palazzo-style pants outfit, I actually found myself blinking a few times. With her shiny silver hair pulled back in a sleek chignon, and some kind of large silver amulet hanging around her neck, she reflected the beams of sunlight coming through the oversized windows. It was difficult to look at her, so I focused on her cigar-chomping husband, Walter. Thankfully, he was easier on the eyes in his beige linen suit. The bright red fez he wore on his head stood out like a spot of blood on a snowy landscape.

They both had that brown leathery skin that announces, *I spend a good part of my days on the golf course and on my yacht.*

Walter brushed aside the gold tassel that dangled in front of his eyes and pulled the unlit cigar out from between his teeth. "Hi, Kate," he said, then turned to his wife. "There, look at that, Ruthie. You're always worrying about Katie Cavanaugh, and she shows up at our party with *two* men."

By the time I got through introducing Bobby and Paco to our hosts, and we had a short conversation, a few early arrivals were already mingling around, anxious to party. The Yanks moved on to greet them, leaving me and my two men to wander. I did my best to stay out of the kitchen, but chewed nervously on my fingers until the servers had finished setting up the buffet table and guests were "oohing and aahing" over the lamb kebabs, chicken with prunes, honey, and cinnamon, big bowls of orange and carrot salad, and couscous with dried apricots and almonds. Between the stacks of Moroccan flatbread and a bowl of eggplant dip was a small dish containing a reddish paste and a tiny spoon. I was glad to see Tony had followed my advice and put a card next to it, stating: *Harissa! Put a little in your dip if you like it fiery!!*

I stood off to one side and watched everyone inch along and fill their plates. I got a smile from Bobby and a wink from Paco, as they carried their plates piled high with food to a corner where they could sit and enjoy it.

I was surprised to see Alan Casey at the back of the line. I wouldn't have thought he was part of this crowd, but there he was, cocky as ever, in black jeans, a Hawaiian print shirt, and what looked like a new panama hat. But then I saw Alan talking to one of the Yanks' smirky-faced sons and remembered they'd been school pals.

When Alan got to the eggplant dip, I watched with interest as he ladled dollops of harissa onto his plate. Even though I didn't like the guy, I stepped forward to warn him.

Alan scowled at me. "Yeah, I can read the sign, but I like hot stuff." He used such a brusque tone of voice, I expected him to add, "What's it to you?" but he didn't. Instead, he nodded towards Bobby and Paco. "See you got your friends here. Weren't they supposed to be gone by now?"

"They left for a few days. Now they're back." I smiled my Cavanaugh smile and said, "Nice hat."

He rubbed his finger along its crisp brim. "Thanks. Bought it today just for this. Says 'Casablanca', don't you think?"

"Sure."

We parted company.

An hour into the party, I'd lost my two men to the lure of riches. As part of the evening's Casablanca theme, Walter had converted his game room into a little casino. There was roulette, backgammon, poker, and a lot of cigar smoke. At one point, I strolled in and saw my buddies seated at a poker table. Well, Paco was playing—Bobby was standing in back of him, watching. And everyone at the table was glowering at Alan Casey.

"C'mon, Casey," one of the players called out, "make your move."

Alan just slumped into his chair, pulled his panama hat down over his close set, beady little eyes, and scrutinized his cards even more intently. It was obviously a very serious game. I went back to the white room.

By now, a young man in a tux was seated at the piano, playing earnestly, though nobody seemed to be paying any attention to him. There was such a din, with all the chattering and laughter, you couldn't hear his music, anyway. What a waste of energy.

I snaked my way through the crowd, listening in on conversations, trying to find one I could contribute to. The chit-chat revolved around topics like business, new car designs, how the stock market was doing, and home decor. I listened in on a conversation about which facial cream was the best in reducing wrinkles around the eyes. Couldn't get into that one, either.

There was no place for me. I would've been happier in the kitchen but, obviously, I wasn't needed back there. I reminded myself this decision to delegate responsibility and move away from being a hands-on boss wasn't going to be easy. I'd figured there'd be a transition period, but I wasn't expecting to feel so adrift.

As I watched people revisiting the buffet table and munching away, I realized that during all the years of catering these parties I'd been pretending to be part of a community, but without having to really participate and connect with anyone on more than a superficial level. Being Clairmont's "Queen of Theme" party consultant was a kind of shield I could hide behind. Now, not having all the busy work of serving food and running back and forth between the kitchen and the party left me with no role to play. Or, at least, not a role I was comfortable with. I didn't know where to put myself or what to do. Grabbing a glass of wine from the tray of a server passing by, I headed over to the piano.

Halfway there, Ruthie Yankovitch came up to me and gushed, "What a wonderful buffet you set up, Kate! Everything's delicious! Scrumptious! You're a marvel!"

I thanked Ruthie and told her next time she saw Tony to repeat her compliment to him, since he did most of the work.

Another reason I'd enjoyed these parties for so long was the fact I needed all those ego strokes. Now that I was giving up that source of gratification, where else was I going to find it?

As my long, tall shadow fell across the top of his glossy white piano, the lonely young musician looked up, startled. Guess he wasn't expecting anyone to visit. He gave me a little nod and kept on playing. I think he started adding a few show-offy arpeggios now that he had an audience. I felt like a gangly, dorky wallflower—just like in my high school days.

Looking out across the room brought back all the painful,

isolated feelings I'd had back then. All the guests seemed to be having a good time. Nobody else was standing around looking lonely and lost. Everyone had someone to talk to and laugh with. Why couldn't Bobby have stayed with me, instead of watching a stupid poker game? Yeah, I know I dangled that opportunity in front of him and his brother as a carrot to entice them to come to the party, but I didn't expect to be dumped almost as soon as we walked in the door.

The pianist broke into a tune that was immediately recognizable within the first bar. I squinted at him, wondering if he'd read my thoughts and was playing *As Time Goes By* on purpose. If he was, then the guy was not only cruel, he was damn corny.

I thought, *Oh stop feeling sorry for yourself, you wimp.* The pianist was now attempting to entertain me with a bad impression of Humphrey Bogart singing. *Oh, puh-leeeze!* I wandered away. Maybe I'd be better off watching the guys play poker.

The ceiling fans in the game room had been turned on and all that blue cigar smoke was being pushed around, giving at least the impression the air was fresher. It was just as crowded—even more so now that Eleanor had arrived and squeezed in next to Bobby to watch the very serious poker game. They made for a geometrically interesting couple. Bobby, a short Jack Sprat toothpick, stood in the shadow of Eleanor's enormous triangular bulk which she'd covered with a bright yellow tent. I swear she never wore the same pair of earrings twice. This time she had gold hula hoops hanging from her ears.

"Eleanor, I didn't see you come in."

"I don't know how you missed me, but you looked like you were flirting with the piano player, so I decided to leave you alone."

"I was not!" I said, a little too loudly, stealing Bobby's attention away from the game. He gave me a quick arch of his eyebrow and turned back to the game when Paco shouted, "Where did that card come from?"

189

Eleanor whispered to me, "Alan's having a really good run of luck."

Uh oh. I leaned down towards Eleanor's ear and said, "Is Paco losing badly?"

"He's won a few hands, but the big boy's definitely running second to Alan. It's kind of exciting. I'd like to get in on the action, but it looks like the game's headed for a showdown between those two."

Bobby shook his head. "This could easily go on all night. I've seen Paco play games that lasted a couple of days."

"Well, if that's the case, then I'd be happy just dealing the cards for them."

I watched as a couple of hands of poker were played, everyone raising their bets and calling for cards. Yankovitch Junior, Alan's buddy, decided he'd had enough and cashed in his chips. It was getting pretty tense, with Paco eying darts at Alan, who returned the stare with his beady pupils.

The party noise in the other room came to an abrupt halt. Then I heard a woman's angry voice.

To Eleanor, I said, "What's going on out there?"

She shrugged as if she didn't care.

I moved over to the door to see what was happening. All the guests had cleared a space in the center of the room. Standing there was a red-faced, slightly disheveled Tammy Lloyd. Her short denim skirt and lime green T-shirt had patches of gray dust on them, as if she'd just fallen on the gravel driveway out in front.

Guess I was the only one who didn't find poker riveting—no one followed me out of the game room to hear what Tammy was shouting about.

Her voice wasn't slurred, but she sounded like she was overcompensating. Her words were measured, enunciated with great care. "I suppose you all expect me to play the role of the grieving widow. That would be the proper thing to do, but then again no one here expects me to be proper."

Tammy listed to one side, then caught herself. "I know what you think of me. None of you ever invited me to one of these intimate little parties. So I've invited myself to this one. 'Cause I'm celebrating."

Shoulders hunched and finger pointed, she slowly turned, aiming at each onlooker. "You're shocked. Ha! *Good!*"

I looked around, studying the reactions. Some guests were open-mouthed, but quite a few were snickering at the spectacle.

Tammy's point stopped at the server still holding his tray of wine glasses. "I'm thirsty. Gimme one of those."

She lunged forward, grabbed a glass off the tray, and downed half of it in one gulp.

Tammy's speech must have broken through the concentration of the poker players, causing a break to be called in the game, because I was abruptly pushed out of my spot in the doorway by Eleanor. She was followed by everyone else in the game room, anxious to see the half-time show.

Tammy lifted her glass in a toast. "To my husband, Victor the Worm. May he be reincarnated as fish bait." She downed the remaining wine, a portion of it missing her mouth and trickling down the side of her chin.

"The man was a louse," she said, accenting her last word with a wave of the empty glass. "He not only screwed every young chippy who'd let him, he also screwed every unsophithic . . ." She repositioned her lips and tried again. "Every unsophisth . . . *oh, shit* . . . he screwed every dumb, ignorant sucker he could find to invest in one of his stupid projects."

Tammy gave the empty glass another wave. The server reached out and took it from her hand. Ruthie and Walter Yankovitch stepped forward, each taking one of Tammy's arms, and tried to usher her out of the room.

Ruthie, always the gracious host, crooned some reassuring words in her ear, but Tammy brushed her away, saying, "I'm not finished celebrating."

Tammy wagged her finger at Walter. "You businessmen. Nothing's more important than—" she whipped around back to Ruthie, "I was living in poverty while Victor put on a big show. Poured every cent we had into keeping up our big Clairmont house! It was just a shell—nothing inside! He sold off all our furniture long ago. Even hocked the gold frame of our wedding picture to pay the electric bill!"

The room was silent. My only thought was she either had to be totally innocent of her husband's death or desperately suicidal to incriminate herself in front of almost a hundred witnesses.

A male voice called out, "Mom. That's enough."

All eyes turned to one end of the room where the ring of onlookers parted, revealing Eric Lloyd. He marched up to his mother. Tammy gave him a surly look. "What're you doing here? How'd you find me?"

Eric ignored his mother and apologized to the Yankovitchs. "I'm deeply sorry for my mother's behavior. She threatened to crash your party, but I didn't take her seriously. When I got home, saw the empty vodka bottle, but didn't find her anywhere in the house, I just knew she was here."

My, my. How polite. Knowing his real feelings for this crowd—he had, after all, called them "two-faced, holier-than-thou bastards"—I wondered how long it had taken him to rehearse that speech.

Tammy's hand flew up and clamped over her mouth. Her eyes bulged, wide and watery. "I'm going to be sick."

Eric apologized again, this time to the guests. As his eyes scanned the room, they stopped and focused on someone standing near me, in the doorway of the game room. Eric frowned. I turned and saw Alan Casey with a sneer creasing one side of his face. Wonder what that was all about?

I turned back and watched Eric give his mother a little guiding push through the crowd. Ruthie took Tammy's other arm and led them both away, I assumed, to a bathroom.

Soon as they left, the guests started discussing and analyzing what they'd just witnessed. Waves of excited chatter and laughter rose up from all the little huddles. For a while, judging from the noise level, I'd say the party had new life. But it didn't last long. Once that topic of discussion was exhausted, the poker players went back to their game, leaving the main party to limp along, totally out of steam. Even though it was only eight-thirty, guests were starting to leave.

I went over to speak to Ruthie Yankovitch, who was standing in a corner, looking very down in the dumps.

She said, "My party's going to be the subject of Clairmont gossip for the next few months. Nobody's going to be talking about your great food, my lovely house, or our generous hospitality. It's all going to be about that poor, sad Tammy Lloyd. Well . . . let's be honest, she's nothing more than a lush."

That was a bit harsh. I expected more sympathetic understanding from Ruthie, but I wasn't going to argue the point. "What did you do with her?"

"I watched her throw up in my toilet, and then her son took her home."

"Maybe I should tell Tony to start cleaning up?"

More people were coming towards us to say their goodbyes to Ruthie. She patted her sleek chignon and sighed. "I suppose so. No one's going to eat anymore."

"I'll get right to it. Sorry, Ruthie."

In the kitchen, I found Tony sitting at the table, munching on a sandwich he'd made of flat bread and lamb kebab.

He'd just taken a huge bite and, seeing me, held up his finger, chewed once or twice, then spoke through the wad of food. "What's the story out there, Boss? Is the party over?"

"Yeah, a lot of the guests are leaving. We can start cleaning up."

Tony slammed his kebabwich down on the plate. "That sucks! The first party I'm in charge of winds up being a dud. Why did that old drunken lady come and spoil it? Why did something like that have to happen at *my* party?"

Wearily, I sat down at the table across from him. "Tony, by now you've been to enough of these parties to know something unexpected *always* happens."

I heard Eleanor's voice calling, "Katie?" The kitchen door opened a crack and I saw a mass of black curls, then Eleanor's triple-chinned, smiling face poke through. "Oh, there you are. We're moving the card game to my place."

"You are?" I stood up. "Bobby and Paco are going with you?"

"Well, the game's pretty hot between Paco and Alan. Neither one of them's ready to let go of that battle. But I don't know about Bobby."

"Figure on Bobby coming, too. He always keeps an eye on his brother."

Eleanor laughed. "*My* eyes've been on Paco all evening. *I'll* gladly watch him." She beckoned me over with her index finger. "Kate, darling, come here."

I stepped to the door and she pulled me out into the next room. Even though there was no one around, she spoke in a low, conspiratorial voice. "Big disadvantage to being so tall is *you* don't always see what's going on down here where the rest of us live. That Bobby's had his eye on you *all* night."

I frowned. "We're just friends."

"Kate, you're blind. *I* noticed it. Every time the two of you were in the same room, he'd steal looks at you, *admiring* looks. Translation? He's got the hots for you."

Well, I'd had the hots for him, but quickly doused those flames after our drawing session Sunday night. He'd had his chance to make a move and didn't. "So you're going to play matchmaker and give me an opportunity to be alone with Bobby?"

Eleanor shook her head vigorously, making all her big curls bounce. "Yeah. You're gettin' it."

"Well, you might be surprised. Bobby'll probably choose to tag along with Paco."

"Oh, Kate! You're something else. If someone doesn't help you with your love life . . ."

"I prefer to let things happen the way they're going to naturally."

Eleanor reached up and patted me on the cheek. "You'll

see. This *is* natural."

We split up. Eleanor went back to the card game. I pushed open the kitchen door and said, "Tony, I'm going to start bringing dishes in from the buffet table."

"Okay. I'll be there in a sec."

I nabbed a couple of the servers along the way and told them to start clearing away the food. I returned to the kitchen and took over stacking dishes in the dishwasher and scrubbing some pots in the sink. It was not my responsibility to be in the kitchen up to my elbows in hot, soapy water, but I had to busy myself with something. I'd like to pretend it didn't matter what Bobby chose to do and, in fact, there was a little voice in my head saying *I don't care if he prefers to watch a stupid card game, we'll still be friends.* But my stomach jumped every time the kitchen door opened and one of the servers walked in with a tray of dirty glasses.

So where was Bobby? I kept expecting him to come looking for me to announce he was going to Eleanor's. Neither one of the guys was the type to take off without telling me. It was getting quieter and quieter in the white room. Where was everybody?

After a while, my anxiety became unbearable. I just had to see what was happening out front.

26

I'D PULLED OFF my rubber gloves and was untying the strings of my apron when Bobby walked in.

"So, Kate, need any help?"

I stared at him. "Aren't you going to Eleanor's?"

"Nah, I've been around enough gambling this past week to last me for a while. But Paco's another story—if I tried to tear him away from that game, he'd never let me hear the end of it."

I wasn't picking up any signals from Bobby one way or the other. Was he really bored and just wanted to go home, or was he pretending nonchalance while busily planning out his move on me? Shit! I'd let Eleanor infect my sense of reality. Why'd I do that? I should know better—her take on life always sounded more like a script from As The World Turns.

I accepted Bobby's offer to help at face value and handed him over to Tony. Half an hour later, we'd paid off the servers and were loaded up, ready to go. I said a quick goodbye to Ruthie and Walter, and joined Tony and Bobby who were waiting for me in the 'Round the World Catering van. Bobby reached behind him to open the sliding door, and I jumped in the back. As Tony maneuvered the van down the dark driveway, I turned sideways to stretch my legs across the back seat and give them a rest.

"Long night?" Bobby asked.

"Well, most of them go a lot longer than this. Right, Tony?"

"Yeah. I'm still mad this one ended so early."

"It wasn't your fault. You still did a great job. Want to fly solo again next week? You'll have your assistant by then."

"*Alright!*" Tony drummed a riff on the steering wheel. He looked in the rearview mirror at me. "But you gotta let me be the boss on that one—he's not gonna take me seriously if you're still hanging around, double-checking everything I do."

"I know. I'm sorry. It just feels weird not having a role to play."

Bobby asked over his shoulder, "You always need everything to be so structured? You've got to learn to cruise, Kate. That's when life gets interesting."

"You and Paco are masters at that—you've been cruising forever. But don't you wish some times you had a little structure in your lives? I don't understand how you can leave everything you had back in Asia and fly off to New Mexico without some plan."

Bobby turned in his seat so he could face me. He feigned

surprise. "You have no faith!"

"Faith? In what? Myself?"

"In the journey. Just flow along, don't look behind you, and don't worry what's up ahead. Sometimes you have to get around some big boulders, but then other times it's all smooth sailing."

"It's not that simple, Bobby. I've got to make some changes in my life. I'm not happy where I am right now."

"I understand, Kate, but sometimes there's a danger in making too many plans. You might disagree with me, but I think you can get so occupied, pouring all your energies into constructing some vision for your future, you wind up not living in the moment."

Tony piped up, "Oh, yeah. I know what you're talkin' about. There was a song like that. Remember, Kate?" He began singing and bobbing his head. "Da de da de da . . . Don't worry . . . be happy—" He turned to Bobby. "She'd scream and turn it off every time it came on the radio in the kitchen."

I groaned. "You guys—"

Bobby reached back between the front seats, grabbed my hand and squeezed it. I took that as a signal and squeezed back. Now to see if we both shared the same code book.

Boo-Kat was barking as we trundled up the laneway to my house. The poor little scruffer wasn't used to being left alone. We pulled around to the side entrance to the commercial kitchen and unloaded the van. All the while, Boo-Kat yapped and scratched at the door to the kitchen like a crazy dog, but health regulations dictated he stay out.

After Tony left and I'd greeted my poor, neglected pet, there was an awkward moment when I wondered *what's next*. Usually after one of these parties I'm starving to death and I sit down and gorge myself on whatever's in the refrigerator—more emotional eating than anything else. Even so, at that moment, my stomach made a loud, grumbling noise.

"I'm going to cook up some food," I called over my

shoulder as I walked down the hall toward the family kitchen. "Want anything, Bobby?"

"Food? Now? We've been eating all night."

"I never eat at my own parties," I said, reaching into a cupboard and pulling out an omelette pan.

"Well, you go right ahead and do what you normally do. I'll just sit here and keep you company." He slid into one of the chairs at the kitchen table and propped his head in his hands.

Bobby looked weary and I felt stupid. I was probably suffering more from a case of nerves and sexual tension than hunger, but I went ahead and cooked my omelette and poured myself a glass of wine. "Would you like some?" I asked, already reaching for another glass.

Bobby waved his hand. "No, thanks. I've had enough." He put on his calm, Buddha smile and waited.

His slightly amused gaze made me feel very self-conscious. In between mouthfuls, I filled the air with chatter about the party. Boo-Kat saved me from making a complete and utter ass of myself when he stood nose to the back door and demanded to be taken out.

Bobby was about to open the door. I reminded him, "The coyote—he's gotta be on the leash."

"Okay, where is it? I'll take care of him, you enjoy your omelette."

"In the laundry room. Thanks, Bobby."

He got the Flexi-leash, struggled a moment as he tried to clip it onto my over-excited terrier, then stepped outside. I took a long swallow of wine. "Kathleen Frances, you're such a jerk," I said aloud.

I quickly finished my meal and threw the plate, the cutlery—even my expensive omelette pan—into the dishwasher. I gulped down the rest of my wine and headed out the door.

There was no need to turn on the porch light, the backyard was illuminated by an almost full moon. I could see Bobby sauntering around at the far end, gazing up at the sky as

Boo-Kat snuffled the grass in search of the perfect spot to bless.

I looked up. It was one of those clear nights when the sky looked like an enormous black canopy pierced with millions of tiny holes, through which shone the cold bright rays of an infinitely huge spotlight aimed directly at me from trillions and trillions of miles away.

At that moment, it seemed as if Bobby and I were the only two people on the planet. I walked across the lawn to join him.

"It's beautiful out here," he said.

"Yeah. Sure is." No more chattering like some nervous fourteen year-old on her first date.

We walked around in silence for a few minutes. There were little cracklings and rustlings in the woods that destroyed the feeling of being alone. Boo-Kat stopped, perked up his ears and sniffed the air. I sensed we were being watched. As I imagined cold eyes somewhere in the woods trained on me, every muscle in my body tensed. I was not going to let that damn coyote chase me indoors.

At that moment, my hand brushed against Bobby's and he grabbed it. I felt a sudden rush of warmth shoot up my arm and through my entire body. "Kate, you okay? Your palm is clammy."

"Let's go sit there," I said, pointing to an old, bent willow garden bench.

He held onto my clammy hand as we made our way over to the bench and sat down. I imagined every move we made was being studied. Bobby tied the end of Boo-Kat's leash around the leg of the bench, stretched his legs out in front of him, crossing his ankles, and leaned back to look up at the stars. I envied his calm and tried to ignore the intruder, concentrating instead on the warmth and softness of the night air.

I took in a deep breath, smelling the grass and the faint scent of sandalwood soap Bobby had bathed with before going to the party. "I'm really glad you came to visit," I said, surprised at how shaky my voice sounded.

Bobby stretched out his arm along the back of the bench, silently inviting me to snuggle up. I slid close and he wrapped his arm around my shoulder.

He said, "I think we were supposed to do this twenty years ago."

I was opening my mouth to respond, but, instead, found myself eagerly accepting the touch of his lips against mine. We kissed like we had only this one moment to make up for all those years. My heart beat wildly and all the tension in my body seemed to drain down my legs and melt into the ground. Bobby made a little groaning sound. The lock I'd used to shut away any feelings of sexual desire shattered, and all that yearning I'd pushed back and denied came rushing out. Even if I wanted to, there was no way to stop. I pressed myself up against him, feeling his heart pound through my breast. We kissed like we were trying to devour each other.

Out of the blackness of the woods, a desolate, bone-chilling howl split the hot, thick air. It slashed between us like the blade of a knife and I fell away from Bobby. Glaring into the woods, I cursed the coyote. Boo-Kat barked angrily and strained at his leash.

Bobby said, "Let's go inside."

I dragged my snarling dog back to the house. Bobby walked along beside me, his hands stuffed in his pockets, eyes focused on the ground in front of him. I wondered if he felt the same way I did. I was so aroused, I was afraid I'd burst the next time his fingers accidentally touched me.

Inside the house, I released Boo-Kat from his leash. Immediately, he ran up to the bay window, pressed his nose against the glass, and continued barking out his death threats to the invader.

I looked at Bobby, and said, "Upstairs?" He nodded. I led the way to my room. Inside, we freed each other from our clothing, though I took over when it came to unhooking my bra and setting aside my prosthesis.

We sat down on the edge of the bed. Bobby began stroking

my hair, kissing my neck and shoulder.

"Can I undo this?" he said, touching my braid. I nodded and he pulled the elastic off the end and ran his fingers through my hair, loosening the tight plait.

My breath was coming in short, quick gasps. Bobby pressed his cheek against mine, his lips brushing my ear. "Slow down," he said. He repeated the words again, making them sound like a mantra. "You don't want this to be over in the first minute."

I laid back, resting my head on the pillow. Bobby knelt beside me on the bed and began caressing me, running his hand over the curve of my hip and down the side of my leg. I let him study me and explore my body with his fingers, stroking up over my belly to the flat side of my chest. He continued his exploration, feeling the hollows and bony ridges that were once covered by a soft breast. If we hadn't already gone through our drawing session the week before, I probably would have tensed up as soon as he touched me there. Instead, to my surprise, it was a sensual experience. When he began tracing the thin white scar that cut across that half of me, it seemed as though his very touch had a palpable energy—the same warm, accepting energy I'd sensed from him as he sketched me. It radiated from his fingertip, through all the barriers I'd put up and into places I'd kept dark and hidden, right down to my core.

Bobby straddled me, bent down and brushed his lips across my breast. I reached up and clutched his hips. As his tongue flicked lightly at my nipple, my back arched and I heard myself moan. I pulled him down on top of me.

IT WAS NOT exactly the way I expected it to be—it was better. Guess I thought, with all his exotic experience, Bobby's sexual repertoire would consist of contorted positions from the Kama Sutra or some kind of Tantric yoga maneuvers—more to do with performance than emotional connection. He probably did know all those techniques, but that night he was tender, playful. In the end, I lay next to him feeling deeply satisfied, connected, and cared about.

We were silent for a while, I with my head on his shoulder. The bright moonlight shone through the window onto the bed. My skin was a pale bluish-white, contrasting with the dark all-over tan of Bobby's skin. I propped myself up on one elbow and examined his sharply featured profile, running my fingers through the tufts of black hair on his chest.

I said, "We sure are opposites."

He turned his head and smiled at me. "How so?"

I took his arm and held it up against my belly. "Look at the difference."

Bobby dropped his gaze, then looked farther down the bed and started rubbing his big toe against my calf. "That's where the biggest difference is."

I followed his gaze and laughed. His leg was stretched as far as it could reach.

He said, "The bed's a great equalizer—I can pretend we're the same height when we lie down. You know, this is the first time I've been able to look you straight in the eyes."

"First time for me, too." I held his gaze and basked in its warmth. As he bent forward to kiss me, the coyote howled outside.

Bobby gave me a quick, soft kiss and then said, "That's the loneliest sound I've ever heard."

Boo-Kat responded downstairs with his high-pitched, manic barking. I sighed and laid my head back down on the pillow. Staring up at the ceiling, I imagined some evil creature stalking through the dark woods, its close-sct yellow eyes focused intently on my house. I found it interesting that when I wanted to conjure up something evil, my brain automatically pulled up Alan Casey's close-set eyes from its clip art file. No, wait. Interesting is too mild a word—it was startling. Did I really think Alan was evil with a capital E. He was certainly *slimy*.

I thought back to that exchange between Alan and Eric

Lloyd at the party and realized it was Eric who was looking predatory. Why? Whatever the case, my gut was twisting with anxiety.

I said to Bobby, "We better go get Paco."

Bobby jerked his head around on the pillow and frowned at me. "Why? He's got his own car."

"Well, I feel responsible for Paco. He doesn't really know where he is, and he's with strangers he's just met tonight—"

Bobby laughed. "That's the story of his life."

"He might get lost coming home."

"If my big brother can find his way around Bangkok, I'm sure he can get around Cincinnati, Ohio. Paco can take care of himself."

I propped myself up on my elbow. "Bobby, I love lying in bed with you, but I can't enjoy it with this nagging feeling in my gut. Paco's already lost a lot of money and he was losing tonight and he was playing against Alan and I don't like Alan and—"

"And you think there's going to be trouble between those two?"

"Yeah."

"Well then, call you friend Eleanor and find out what's going on. Tell her to kick him out and send him home."

I sat up.

"What're you doing?" Bobby asked.

"Gonna call Eleanor."

"I was just joking."

"Well, I'm not." I picked up the receiver. "Oh, damn. Gotta go downstairs and look up her phone number." I pulled on my kimono and ran downstairs, leaving Bobby staring at the ceiling. Seconds later, I was plopping back in bed, furiously paging through my address book.

"Here it is." I punched in the number.

Eleanor picked up after the first ring.

"Hi, Eleanor. It's Kate. How's the card game going?"

"Party's over, darling."

"What? How long ago?"

203

"Kicked them all out about a half hour ago."

"Half hour ago? Paco should've been home by now."

Bobby sat up.

"The card game got outta hand," Eleanor said, sounding pissed off. "Alan was getting close to wiping Paco out when Paco starts yelling and calling Alan a cheat. That's not the type of behavior I'll stand for under my roof, so I sent them packing. I don't know when you'll see Paco. He said he still wanted to party and asked me where to go. I sent him downtown. Told him there where places around Main Street in Over-the-Rhine, so he might be there somewhere, but I said there are places all over town. 'Fraid I can't be more specific than that."

Oh, great. "I'm very sorry about this, Eleanor. Now I'm really worried about Paco. He was determined to win back his money. Did you get the idea they were going to continue the game someplace else?"

"No way. Alan called him a sore loser and said the game was over."

"Well, I guess we'll just have to work our way through all the bars, one by one."

"If it helps you any, the last thing I yelled to Paco as he tore out of my driveway was to stay away from Gable's. That's where Alan and all his buddies hang out."

I said, "Goodbye," hung up the phone, and relayed to Bobby what Eleanor just told me. "I feel terrible about this."

"It's not your fault, Kate. Paco's my responsibility—well, he's old enough to be responsible for himself, but he's used to me always being there to patch things up. I had more enjoyable things on my mind," Bobby said, combing his fingers through a lock of my hair and sweeping it behind my shoulder.

"We better go look for him. Right?"

"Probably a wise thing to do," Bobby said, wearily.

We pulled on our clothes—Bobby wearing the same outfit he'd worn to the party, while I left my party dress in a heap on the floor and put on a pair of jeans and a T-shirt.

As we climbed into the Jeep, Bobby asked, "You're leaving the house unlocked?"

"Paco might show up while we're gone."

We headed out into the night on our rescue mission.

27

EVEN WITH A BRIGHT MOON, nighttime makes the narrow road from my farm treacherous. It winds through the dark woods with no shoulders, no lights, and no warnings of sudden hairpin turns. But I was used to it and barreled along at forty-five mph, which was turning Bobby's brown knuckles white.

"It's not an emergency, Kate."

"This is the way I always drive down here. Besides, there's nobody else on the road."

Even as we made our way down Loveland-Madeira Road to the I-275, we didn't encounter any other vehicles. From the I-275, I connected to I-71 and announced, "We'll be landing in downtown Cincinnati in ten minutes."

The landscape of empty, black, rolling hills quickly gave way to the rusty metal, crumbling brick, and broken glass of the city's outskirts.

Bobby broke the silence with, "They're really serious with these signs, aren't they."

He was referring to the Department of Transportation's rash of new road signs with their warnings of long delays, closed exits, and size limitations. We'd flown past five already and were just coming up to a sixth one. They seemed to get progressively bigger, with the letters now screaming, "ALL VEHICLES OVER SEVEN FEET WIDE PROHIBITED BEYOND 471." Then another one said, "DOWNTOWN RIVERFRONT USE EXIT 2." I half-expected the next sign to say, "YOU CAN'T GET THERE FROM HERE!"

I turned off at Reading Road/Gilbert Avenue, and explained to Bobby, "They've practically shut the whole place down with their road construction."

"So, what if Paco didn't follow the signs? Would he just drive off into the river?"

"Worse. He'd get lost in Covington, Kentucky."

We drove through a run-down section of Cincinnati, past rows of red, yellow, green, and blue brick buildings, and dreary storefronts. The sidewalks were desolate. The orange glow from the streetlights seemed to spot the occasional empty beer bottle, loose newspaper, fast food container, and other miscellaneous bits of garbage that littered the ground.

Bobby was staring out his window. "I don't think Paco's going to find much action around here."

I pointed through the windshield. "Just up there is where we're going. We're in Over-the-Rhine. Sections of it are still bad, but new businesses are moving in and fixing up some the buildings. You'll see."

We turned the corner and I parked on the street. "Might as well start here."

We spent the next hour walking up and down the sidewalks, going in and out of very loud, dark places.

Bobby said, "Paco's not going to like these bars. Everyone's too young. Besides, it's the wrong kind of music."

"Let's go back to the car and drive over to the other streets. There are a couple of quieter jazz clubs around there."

I stayed at the wheel while Bobby checked them out. Each time he came back, shaking his head. "Nope. No luck."

After we'd been in and out of every bar I knew of in the neighborhood, I announced, "That's it for this part of town."

"Now what?" Bobby asked, "We just going to cruise the streets, hoping we bump into him at some intersection?"

I was beginning to feel tired and rubbed my eyes. "Let's say he never found his way to this area. He'd probably head for the center of town where the brightest lights are. There's not much going on down there, except for the big hotels . . . they all have bars, so maybe . . ." I shrugged. "Let's call home first, just in case he made it back."

I pulled the cell phone out of my purse and punched in my number. All I got was a recording of Robert Boone's voice saying, "We can't come to the phone, blah, blah, blah."

I waited for the beep and said, "Paco, it's Kate. Pick up if you're there." I waited thirty seconds, but no one answered. I checked for messages. Nothing. Frustrated, I said, "Bobby, how come you guys don't have cell phones?"

Bobby scrunched one corner of his mouth. "We haven't caught up to Western ways yet." He shook his head. "Might never."

I pulled out into the road and continued on through the deserted streets. "There's Gable's—Alan Casey's hangout," I said, pointing out the window. "That's the bar Eleanor warned Paco to stay away from." The place was jumping.

"Stop!"

I slammed on the brakes and pulled over to the curb. "What?"

Bobby said, "It's worth checking out—you tell Paco not to do something, chances are that's exactly what he'll do."

I reversed gears and backed up to a spot right in front of the bar—it was a no parking zone, but I turned off the ignition and started opening my door.

"What're you doing?" Bobby asked. "I'll just run in and out. You don't need to come with me."

"I want to see what kind of place Alan hangs out in."

Inside, the bar was dark and crowded. The All Purpose Rock & Roll Band had just finished a set. Bobby took my hand and started cutting a trail through the huddles of highly-animated twenty-and thirty-somethings. The room was filled with the loud laughter of strangers who were pairing off for the night, and the tight silence of those going home by themselves. I'd bet there was ground in between where a lot of fake phone numbers were exchanged.

After checking out the row of tables along one wall to no avail, we headed over to the crowded bar. Bobby turned and looked up at me. "Do you always get these stares?"

I nodded. "Uh huh. I'm used to it, but sometimes it's a real pain."

The bartender closest to us had the thick neck, enormous torso, and tattooed arms of a World Wrestling Federation villain. He acknowledged me immediately and asked over the heads of other customers, "What can I get you?"

"At least it gets you good service," Bobby said, pulling out the photo he'd been flashing at all the bartenders in town. "Have you seen the guy on the right with the big head of hair in here tonight?"

The wrestler took the photo, studied it for half a minute, then shook his head. "Sorry." He shrugged one shoulder. "But I don't see everybody."

Eyes squinting, he turned his attention back to me. "Don't I know you?" His eyes widened. "Yeah! You're that Amazon Detective—the chili gal. You on a case or somethin'?"

All the heads within earshot swiveled in my direction. Bobby chuckled.

I played the game. "We're trying to track this guy down."

The bartender showed the picture to his partner, who said, "Nope." Then he called out, "Hey, Sally!" A young woman with three nose rings and carrying a tray of drinks came over. "Show this to the other gals and ask if anyone saw the fat hairy guy tonight." She went off on her mission.

I was surveying the crowd when I noticed two men getting into an argument in a far corner of the room. I said to Bobby, "I'd be less worried about Paco if I knew he wasn't with Alan."

To the bartender, I asked, "Do you know Alan Casey? He's supposed to be a regular in here."

"Yeah, sure. He was in tonight."

"He was?"

Bobby added, "When?"

"Might have been around eleven. Sat right there in front of me." The wrestler pointed to one of the stools. "Within five minutes, he had some blonde coming on to him. She was a knockout . . . tiny black dress barely covering the goods, if you know what I mean. She was a real nervous type though." He shook his head. "Alan's not usually so lucky—they had a couple of drinks and left together. Guess every dog has his day."

I felt a lot better, knowing that Alan seemed to be occupied for the evening. Good luck to the blonde.

Sally Nose Ring came back with the photo, shaking her head. "Sorry, no one's seen him—Oops!" As she handed it back to me, the picture slipped out of her fingers and fluttered to the floor. I bent down to get it and noticed the place needed a good sweeping. There were cigarette butts, chewing gum wrappers, used stirrers, a plastic straw tied up in a bow, a balled-up cocktail napkin, and a couple of rejected business cards. The plastic straw bow looked familiar. Oh, yeah. At Victor's riverboat party. I straightened up, handed the photo to Bobby and held out the tied up straw in front of the bartender's face.

Before I could ask him anything about it, he said, "That's what I mean by nervous—the blonde was constantly playing with those things. Left a couple more of them in the ashtray."

To Bobby, I said, "I've seen these before. I don't think Alan got lucky—he was meeting someone he already knew. C'mon. Let's go."

I tossed the straw in an ashtray and thanked the bartender for his time. Outside, we jumped back into the Jeep and headed down Walnut Street. We turned right on Fourth and went down a few blocks and turned back up to Fifth Street, where I parked. There were two hotels right next to each other, and a third one right across the street.

"Let's start at the Hyatt," I said.

We went into the lobby and headed for the lounge. It was obviously all closed up for the night. A young man was running a broom over the tile floor. Behind the bar, a woman dressed in a crisp white tuxedo shirt, black bow tie, and black slacks was printing out her cash receipts and balancing the evening's accounts.

Bobby and I entered the lounge and walked up to the bar. The bartender said, "Sorry, we're closed."

"That's okay," Bobby answered, "we just want to ask a question." He showed her the photo.

"Oh, him." A smile broke out immediately on her face. "Yeah, sure. He's a great gabber. I kept the place opened as long as I could for him."

I said, "You mean he was just here?"

"Well, until about fifteen minutes ago when I had to kick him out and close up."

Bobby and I exchanged looks that said "Oh, shit."

She waved her hand. "Oh, but he's still here—"

"He is?" We shouted. The news gave me a badly-needed shot of adrenaline.

"Yeah, he checked in. Said he was in no condition to drive anywhere. He must've been boozing it up someplace else, because I only served him one drink."

We thanked her and headed for the front desk. Two young men in black suits greeted us—they were so alert and chipper, it almost made me forget it was past 2 AM. Bobby explained the situation to the one acting like he was in charge.

The desk clerk listened carefully, then called up to Paco's room. "Hello, this is the front desk. Sorry to disturb you, sir, but there's a gentleman here who says he's your brother." He listened for a moment, then looked at Bobby and said into the receiver, "A little guy, tanned, real short hair, dressed in a—yes, she's extremely tall . . . yes sir, good-looking, too . . . Very good. I'll tell them." He hung up. "Your brother will be down in a minute."

Five minutes later, Paco burst out of the elevator like a bear who'd been roused out of his beauty sleep. His mass of gray-black curly hair was sticking out at all angles. He scratched his cheek through the bush of his beard. "Can't a guy get some rest and how the hell did you get here so fast? I just talked to your machine ten minutes ago." Paco's voice reverberated in the empty, high-ceilinged lobby.

"We were concerned about you," I said. "Eleanor told us

you got into an argument with Alan Casey—"

Paco swatted the air at the mention of the name. "That asshole is a goddamn cheat. I'd like to get my hands on his—"

"Why don't we talk about this on the way home," Bobby suggested.

"Right. Let's get the hell outta here." Paco went over to the desk and had a brief conversation with the clerks, then rejoined us. "Okay, we're outta here."

I said, "Bobby, you'd better—"

"Yeah. I'll drive."

I went back to the Jeep and waited until I saw the rental car come out of the hotel's parking garage and pull up alongside me. All I could see at first was Paco in the front passenger seat, waving his arms around as he ranted. The window lowered, letting Paco's cursing escape out into the warm night air.

I heard him shout, "But I didn't believe the signs. The next thing I knew, I was driving over some damn bridge into Kentucky. Got lost for I don't know how long—"

Bobby pushed his brother back against the seat and peered over at me.

I told him to follow.

Bobby gave me a lopsided smile. "Just don't go too fast."

And that's how my first romantic evening in years ended—all screwed up.

Saturday, August 28

28

I SLEPT FOR THREE HOURS. Boo-Kat woke me up at seven with a series of loud, squeaking yawns that said, "I need to go out." I lifted the sheet and slid out of bed as quietly as I could, so as not to wake Bobby from the deep sleep he was obviously enjoying. I put on my kimono and padded down the hall, past the three guest rooms. The doors of the first two stood open. From behind the closed door of the third room, I heard Paco's thunderous snores. What a night.

Downstairs in the family kitchen, I turned on the coffee maker, hooked up my pet to his lifeline and accompanied him out the back door. I didn't want to walk around on the dew-soaked grass in my bare feet, so I sat on the back step and played out his Flexi-leash as he wandered about, stretching the line taut to its limit. When Boo-Kat had finished kicking up chunks of sod behind him, I started trying to reel him in, but he resisted. His whole body stiffened as he tilted his head and sniffed at the air, analyzing some interesting scent. He jerked his head and targeted a spot on the edge of the woods with his eyes. His tail quivered as he strained on the leash. I yanked it. All I got was a growl in response. After a couple more hard yanks, Boo-Kat dutifully returned.

Back inside, I gave him his morning biscuit, and went about the business of feeding myself—toasting up a bagel and slathering it with some peanut butter and cherry jam. Coffee cup in one hand and bagel in the other, I stood at the bay window and surveyed my kingdom.

I went back in my mind to that part of last night's activities that had been so unbelievably enjoyable. All the crazy running around Bobby and I did after our love-making gave the whole experience an unreal, dream-like quality. I fantasized about how the rest of the night might have been spent if I hadn't felt so damn responsible for Paco. But what *did* take place between Bobby and me was real and I played it over and over again in my mind in an effort to relive it. I wanted to experience again the taste of his lips, the feel of his skin against mine, the fragrance of sandalwood soap, every word he whispered to me. I committed it all to memory and stamped it "FRAGILE—STORE IN A SAFE PLACE".

I poured myself another cup of coffee and curled up on the loveseat across from the kitchen table. The sun was streaming in through the window. It was going to be a picture postcard day, perfect for touring Cincinnati, so I started thinking of the major attractions, drew up an itinerary, and waited for my two guests to get up.

By noon, we were picnicking in Eden Park. Later, we wandered around the narrow, winding streets of Mount Adams, then took a lovely riverboat ride on the Ohio River. I added my own points of interest to the riverboat captain's running commentary—like "this was where we were when I first saw Victor Lloyd mangled up on the paddle wheel." Paco took us on a tour of the Kentucky side of the river, showing us where he got lost the night before. He pointed out the Irish pub in Covington, where he'd stopped for "an hour or so to get my bearings."

We ended our perfect day at one of the riverboat restaurants in Newport, watching a Boone County Search and Rescue team fish a body out of the river.

* * * * * * * * * *

LATER THAT NIGHT, we turned on the 11 o'clock news. Even with our bird's-eye view of the tragic scene on the river and all the excited talk amongst the restaurant patrons, we had been unable to find out what was going on right before our eyes. But my antenna was up—two dead bodies on the river within the span of a week was highly unusual.

It was the lead news story with plenty of video footage, taken from the river's edge, of Search and Rescue personnel hauling the body out of the water. The first surprise was the reporter's description of the condition of the body and what it was wearing.

The male reporter's voice-over said, "The horribly slashed body of a white male was found by Mr. Charles Brannigan who was enjoying an evening ride on his motorboat. It appears the body was weighed down by a backpack filled with rocks. According to Mr. Brannigan, the rocks weren't heavy enough to keep the body totally submerged."

The picture cut to a shot of Mr. Brannigan, a jolly-looking fat man in a Cincinnati Reds baseball cap. "It was the foot sticking up outta the water that caught my eye. Haven't heard of anything like this happening around here since the hey days of the casinos. But a knapsack full of rocks is a poor imitation of a Newport nightgown."

The next shot was of a high-ranking Newport police

officer. From offscreen, the reporter asked the man, "We've heard reference to Newport nightgowns. Does this killing appear to have the markings of organized crime activity?"

The officer deadpanned into the camera, "We have no information of such activities at this time."

Paco turned to me and asked, "What's a Newport nightgown?"

Two weeks ago, I would've just shrugged, but since Uncle Cliff had enlightened me, I started to explain, "It's made out of concrete—" I was cut short by the second surprise.

The news anchor announced, "The victim has been identified as Alan Casey, a noted photographer and the owner of a photography gallery in Montgomery."

We were stunned for a moment. Then Bobby and I both turned and stared at Paco, who shouted, "What?"

Bobby said, "I hope you're not the only one who had a fight with him last night."

"It was an argument—verbal—I never laid a hand on him."

I said, "We didn't say you did it, but you may have to answer some questions about what you were doing last night. Someone's bound to tell the police about the card game."

Paco shrugged. "And I'll tell the cops Alan was cheating. I kept playing 'cause I wanted to figure out what he was doing—catch him in the act and show everyone else what a rotten cheat he was. I'm not worried. That guy's such a jerk, he probably made people want to kill him everywhere he went."

I was willing to bet Alan's violent death was directly related to Victor Lloyd's so-called accident. Peepo Giuliani probably had Alan fitted with a make-shift Newport nightgown with Sammy as his emergency seamstress.

Bobby looked at me and said, "Well, we know Alan went to Gable's and left with some good-looking blonde."

Hmm. A blond hit woman? No. I could imagine a woman slashing at someone with a knife . . . but weighing him down with rocks and hauling him into the river? More likely,

Sammy used a blonde to lure Alan out of the bar. I filled the guys in on who Peepo Giuliani was, how he was connected to Victor Lloyd, and then told them my theory.

Bobby held up his hand to stop me. "Wait a minute, Kate. The bartender told us she was a real nervous type. That doesn't sound like a pro to me."

I said, "Okay. Here's another scenario." I told them who Melissa Oakley was and about her engagement to Eric Lloyd. Then I explained the looks exchanged at the party between Eric and Alan when Eric came to pick up his drunken mother.

Paco said, "So?"

"Well, let's say Eric doesn't believe Alan's story that Victor accidentally fell overboard and, instead, thinks Alan pushed his father into the paddle wheel." I shrugged. "Maybe they were arguing over money. Over women. I don't know. Whatever the case, Eric blames Alan and uses Melissa to lure Alan out of Gable's. Melissa fits the bartender's description. She's blond, good-looking, and probably nervous as hell, knowing what Eric's planning to do to Alan. But I do remember her saying she'd do *anything* for Eric."

I said to Bobby, "Remember that plastic straw I found on the floor at Gable's and showed to the bartender?"

"Yeah. It was all tied up in a bow."

"I saw the same thing on Victor Lloyd's riverboat the night he died. There were a few of them. Someone left them in ashtrays in the area around the bar. The same blonde was at both bars."

Sunday, August 29

29

IT WAS ANOTHER GROGGY MORNING. For some of us. Bobby and I had spent half the night sitting up in bed trying to poke holes in my theories to see if they held water, discussing why people murder each other, and, in general, contemplating the vagaries of human nature. Not a very romantic way to spend our second night together. Though I felt certain I was on the right track, my theories were based on the assumption that Alan had killed Victor Lloyd. And that was the big hole—why would he do that?

We marveled at how Paco was taking everything in stride—his loud snoring evidence he wasn't worried in the least. He had also taken in stride the new sleeping arrangements. After saying our "good nights" at the top of the stairs, he'd called out over his shoulder, "My little brother gets all the lucky breaks."

It was 11 AM and I was squeezing oranges when the doorbell rang. My first thought was, "Mother's here." But she never rings the doorbell and it was too late for one of her grand Sunday morning entrances—at this hour she should be sitting in church.

Actually, the realization she hadn't come to pester me about going to church that morning was a little unsettling. We hadn't talked since our confrontation and a vague sense of guilt was growing inside me. For some reason—I hadn't stopped to work it out yet—I felt it was my responsibility to make the next move.

The doorbell rang again. "Who is that?" I said aloud to myself. I wiped my hands and went to find out.

I opened the door to three men. I knew the one who stood two inches taller than me. Looking up, I flashed my Cavanaugh smile. "Good morning Officer Skinner."

Clairmont Ranger Matt Skinner, poster boy minus his horse, touched the brim of his Smokey Bear hat in a one-fingered salute. "'Morning, Ms. Cavanaugh. This is Detective Robinson." He indicated the blond, middle-aged man next to him, then pointed to the young black man who looked like a body-builder. "And this is Detective Reese."

In a perfectly synchronized movement, Detectives Robinson and Reese pulled out their badges and held them out for me to inspect.

Robinson said, "We're from the Newport Police Department. We're conducting an investigation into the death of Alan Casey. We would like to speak to a gentleman named 'Paco'. We've been informed that he's staying with you."

Boy, that was fast. "Please come in." I didn't bother pretending to be surprised.

Matt Skinner gave me a surreptitious once-over, then

frowned as he and the other two men entered the house. Guess he didn't approve of my slightly offbeat outfit and bare feet. To someone who was a member of what had just been voted the "Best Dressed Police Department" in the country, my black bicycle shorts and black T-shirt I'd borrowed from Bobby, with its OM symbol in gold embroidery on the front, probably did not fit into his concept of proper attire.

I directed Mr. Fashion Policeman and the two synchronized detectives into the library, saying, "I'll go get Paco."

Bobby was at the top of the stairs—a quizzical look on his face. I said, "Do you think Paco's awake yet? The police are paying a friendly visit and want to meet him."

Bobby was about to rap on Paco's bedroom door, when it swung open. Paco stepped out, hair still wet from a shower, and grumped, "Yeah, I heard."

We traipsed downstairs and into the library. I made all the introductions, watching with interest as one team sized up the other.

Paco was used to being questioned by policemen in all parts of the world. Even so, as he launched into his answer to "what were you doing Friday night after the card game broke up at the home of Ms. Eleanor Sloane?" he couldn't keep the antagonistic attitude out of his voice. I wanted to kick him and tell him "be nice." But all I could do was look at Bobby and smile weakly. Bobby put his arm around my waist, gave me a quick squeeze and kept it there. One of Skinner's eyebrows shot up—he wasn't keeping his reactions a secret that day. Then I caught a little pucker of a frown on his face before he quickly turned away and focused his attention back on Paco. Did I see a hint of jealousy in those brown eyes I used think of as pools of chocolate pudding?

Once Paco finished his story, Detective Robinson asked, "Is there anyone who can verify you were at this Irish pub in Covington when you say you were?"

Paco held up his hands, baffled. "I don't know. I talked to a bunch of strangers. Real chummy, but we didn't exactly trade calling cards. Maybe some of the waitresses remember me—I mean, I was there an hour and a half."

Detective Robinson glanced at his cohorts, then back at Paco and said, "Thank you for your cooperation. We'll be in touch."

I knew they hadn't come here to ask my opinion, but I was determined to voice it anyway. I suggested to the officers, "You may want to look at the link between Alan being the sole witness to Victor Lloyd's tragic accident and Victor's alleged gangster background. Perhaps someone held Alan responsible for Victor's death and decided to pay him back."

Skinner stifled a smile and informed the detectives, "Ms. Cavanaugh puts a lot of thought into cases like this."

Detective Reese nodded, then asked me, "Do you have any suspicions?"

Ignoring Skinner's amused expression, I said, "I've no proof of *who* did it, but I can give you a possible scenario." Then, without naming any names, I gave them my blond hit woman theory, using the twisted straws as my link between Gable's bar and Victor's riverboat party. "Find that woman and you'll probably find the last person to see Alan Casey before he was killed."

Detective Reese wrote down what appeared to be two words—probably "screw ball."

AFTER THE POLICE left, *I* was the one who had to be calmed down.

"I HATE BEING LAUGHED AT!"

Paco shook his head. "They're just cops, Kate. Who cares what they think? It's not worth getting upset about."

"Well, I've been here before—*a couple of times*. That Skinner should know by now to take me seriously. I've come up with good hard evidence for him before. But he still has the nerve to stand here in my library, in my house, and snicker at me. I can't let that go."

Paco said, "Kate, it's not worth—"

"Yes, it is! I'll find out for myself who tied up those straws."

The boys let me rant on for a few minutes, but even I got tired of hearing myself mouth off about Skinner. I said, "I wish I'd seen who twisted up those straws. There were other women on board that night who fit the bartender's description. But those two things just don't match up in my brain."

Bobby said, "Sometimes we see things that get recorded in our memory, but we're not conscious of it. It might have just been a tiny action off in the background somewhere. If you want, I can do a kind of guided meditation with you that might bring out more of what you saw on board the riverboat that night."

I shook my head. "Meditation doesn't work for me—I don't have the patience."

"But I'll be guiding you. It's a very active form of meditation. If you want answers, this might lead you to some." Bobby shrugged. "It's up to you."

I wanted those answers, but at that moment searching my memory was like banging my head against a brick wall. My skepticism towards Bobby's suggestion wasn't helping any—it just added more bricks. Normally, I'd sort out problems like this by shooting hoops in my gym, but sleep deprivation had left me physically exhausted, and I couldn't muster up the energy for that. I sighed. "Okay, Bobby. I'll try."

Paco scratched his beard. "While you two go floating around some astral plane, I'm gonna get me some breakfast." He headed for the kitchen.

Bobby took a pillow off the sofa and placed it on the floor. "Lie down."

I stretched myself out, he sat cross-legged beside me. First, he took me through some guided imagery to calm me down, which sort of worked. I felt a little better. Then he had me watching my breath go in and out. It seemed like it was quiet for a long while. I couldn't feel the floor beneath me, instead, I felt like I was floating. I lost track of time.

Bobby said, "You're boarding the riverboat." He had me walk around the decks, reporting everything I saw.

"Focus on the straw," Bobby said. "Where are you?"

"On the middle deck. It's in an ashtray."

"Examine how it's tied up. Is one end longer than the other?"

"No. It's tied very carefully. The ends are even."

"What's around the ashtray?"

"It's just an empty table."

"Is there anything else inside the ashtray?"

"A chewing gum wrapper. Blue lettering—Trident."

"Is anyone around you?"

"No. I'm by myself."

"Okay. Take me to the next place you see the twisted straw."

"I'm talking to Victor Lloyd. We're at a table next to the bar."

"Where's the straw?"

"In an ashtray."

"Okay. Focus on the straw. Is there anything else with it in the ashtray?"

"Cigarette butts. Someone's shouting, 'There's a fire!' There's another straw in an ashtray on the bar. It's on fire. Someone pours a bottle of water on it."

"Who's there?"

"I see Donald Sims and some other people."

"Look at all the faces. How many men? How many women?"

"I . . . I don't know. All I can see is Donald Sims pouring his bottle of mineral water into the ashtray."

I sat up. "Maybe Donald Sims saw her."

30

I RUSHED OVER TO MY DESK and pulled the telephone book out of one of the drawers, and began leafing through it.

"What the hell are you doing?" Bobby asked.

"I'm looking up Donald Sims' phone number."

"God! You *are* impatient." He got up off the floor and shook his head. "You haven't given it a chance, Kate."

"But I wasn't going to remember any more faces."

"How do you know? You're not trusting the process."

"Well, this is my way of doing things." I was in the "U's" and had to start flipping back the other way. "I have to run around and talk to people—I can't just sit in a room and meditate on it."

Bobby threw up his hands and turned to walk out the door. "I'm going to get some breakfast."

Guess there were more differences between us than just height and skin tone.

I didn't have any trouble finding Donald Sims' number. But I wondered how appropriate it was to call someone who was just recovering from a suicide attempt to ask questions. Where was Miss Manners when you needed her? On the other hand, I figured I'd *better* ask Donald in case he . . . well, I could start with his wife. Gloria would probably be the one to answer the phone. Telling her the complete truth—that I was looking for a possible killer—was definitely not the best tactic. However, it wouldn't be lying to tell her I was just trying to locate someone who'd been at the riverboat party and thought Donald might be able to help me. That story couldn't possibly upset either one of them.

After working all that out and convincing myself that I was doing no harm, I punched in Sims' phone number. Yep. Gloria answered. She was very surprised I called. We engaged in some polite preamble in which she told me that Donald was suddenly doing much better and thanked me for my concern. I felt like a heel. But I couldn't stop now and boldly made my request.

Gloria said, "Oh. I'll go ask him."

I heard her speak to someone in the same room. A few seconds later, she was back on the line, saying, "Sure. Would you like to come over this afternoon?"

"Um . . . yes. Great."

We set up a time and Gloria gave me directions. I thanked her and hung up. That was almost too easy—I was expecting at least *some* hemming and hawing.

Another tricky question for Miss Manners: how do I tell my houseguests their company is not wanted while I go out for an afternoon of detecting?

Thankfully, that problem solved itself. When I went back to the kitchen, Paco announced his own plan to assist the police investigation.

"Might be a good idea for me to go back to that pub in Covington," he said. "Remind the waitresses who I am, maybe even see the same guys I was talking to Friday night. I think they were regulars."

I agreed. "Good idea."

"Little brother's coming along with me," Paco said, nodding his head towards Bobby, who added, "He needs witnesses for every minute of his life."

Bobby smiled at me. Wrong. It wasn't a smile. It was an automatic muscle contraction, not an expression of any real feeling.

I said, "You really did help me, Bobby, and I'm grateful for that."

"Good."

"Sorry I am the way I am. But—"

Bobby held up his hand, stopping my apology. "Don't worry, it's not a problem."

* * * * * * * * * *

BY TEN PAST TWO, I was off to Donald Sims' house in Montgomery. I pushed a CD into the player and sang along with Bonnie Raitt:

*"They're not forever, they're just for today
One part be my lover, one part go away."*

I switched tracks to another song.

The Sims family lived in an attractive, older neighborhood of split-level and two-story houses with small yards and large trees—your average, middle-class, Ozzie and Harriet home.

I found the park on Zig-Zag Road Gloria told me about on the phone. It was full of people and balloons. Seemed to be some kind of special event going on and I had to stop and wait for a couple of mini-vans in front of me to make their left turns into the parking lot before I could turn right into the cul-de-sac where the Sims lived. A dark blue Lincoln Town Car with tinted windows looked a little out of place in the lot full of mini-vans and bicycles.

I made my turn, found their house near the end, and parked on the street. Gloria was already holding open the screen door and waving at me. "Welcome, Kate. Come in, come in. Oh, please watch your step there."

I almost twisted my ankle on the uneven concrete walkway, but shifted my weight and did a little bounce step.

"Are you alright, Kate?" Gloria asked.

"Fine."

"I'm very sorry about that. We haven't had a chance to fix it yet."

"I'm okay," I said. "Thanks for letting me come over." I stepped into the vestibule and was directed to the living room which was small and neat, but the furniture was a little worn around the edges.

On a glass coffee table, Gloria had set out a tray of biscuits and what were probably her best china coffee cups. Donald got up from his recliner and shook my hand. I was shocked at his appearance. I remembered him being dumpy and red-faced just a little over a week ago. In that short span of time, it seemed he'd lost at least twenty pounds—his pallid skin hung loosely from his cheek bones. This was no ordinary case of mid-life crisis. Donald looked like someone who was totally ruined. His attempt at suicide may have failed, but his fear of being downsized out of a job was going to eventually kill him anyway.

Janie came into the room, said, "Hello," shook hands with me, and sat down on the end of a sofa next to her father's chair. Looked like this was going to be a real party.

As I remarked on the family pictures hanging on the walls around me, Gloria poured coffee, and sat down next to Janie. I felt really big and dumb and awkward. Maybe I should've stayed on the floor in my library and worked things out, using Bobby's method.

I opened the conversation with, "Well, Donald, I'm glad to hear you're feeling better." Shit, what else do you say to a stranger who's just tried to commit suicide—glad to see you're alive?

Donald motioned for me to sit on a chintz-covered armchair. He sat back down. "Gloria says you're looking for someone who was on board the riverboat last week. How can I help you?"

"I'm looking for a blond-haired woman. She has a nervous habit of tying plastic straws into bows. I saw you dousing one that was on fire in an ash tray, so I was wondering if you noticed who left it there."

He shifted around in his La-Z-Boy. "I remember seeing the plastic straw on fire and emptying my bottle of water on it, but I don't remember any blond women standing around."

"Well, did you see anyone twisting straws like that anywhere on board?"

Donald frowned and thought for a minute. "No . . . can't say that I did."

I turned to Gloria and then to Janie, asking them both, "Did either of you?"

They both shook their heads in the same manner at the same time.

Donald asked, "Is there something else about this blonde that might spark my memory? Why are you looking for her, anyway?" He caught a sharp glance from Gloria, then quickly dismissed the question with a wave of his hand. "No, no, never mind. That's none of my business. I'm just one of those real curious types. Sorry."

I debated how open I should be with him. It really wasn't necessary for me to tell him anything more, but sometimes a little conversation can bring out unexpected information. I figured it was safe to tell Donald, "I think she was a friend of Alan Casey—"

"Oh, yeah." Donald grabbed the arms of his chair and pulled himself up straighter. "I saw the report about him on TV. Are you helping the police on that case?"

"No," I said quickly.

Janie piped up for the first time. "Who's Alan Casey?"

Gloria answered, "Oh, you know, dear. That's the man they pulled out of the river yesterday. You met him on Victor Lloyd's riverboat. He's the photographer who took our picture as we boarded the boat."

"Oh, yeah. The guy with the panama hat."

Gloria frowned at her daughter, half-distracted. "I guess." She turned to Donald. "Do you think we'll ever get our photo?"

I don't know what was so horrible about Gloria's question but, at that moment, she got a look from both Donald and Janie that seemed to say, "How dare you ask such a thoughtless question?"

Gloria reacted to those looks with a nervous, "I guess things got a little complicated at the end of that evening. Oh, never mind."

It was a puzzling moment, but I didn't linger over it. I munched on a biscuit, drank some coffee—it was good—and asked Janie, "How long are you home for? Do you have to go back soon?"

"Yes, ma'am. I have to report back on base by oh-eight-hundred hours on Thursday." Janie reached over and patted Donald's arm. "I'm worried about Dad, but he says not to."

Donald winked back at her.

We chit-chatted a few more minutes, then I looked at my watch and made a graceful exit.

The family-friendly event in the park was still going strong. More mini-vans had jammed in around the dark blue Lincoln.

On the way home, I stopped off at the grocery store and picked up three tubs of ice cream—Rocky Road, Cherry Garcia, and French Vanilla—and a package of waffle cones.

Trail's End was quiet, save for Boo-Kat who, of course, was yapping and whining at the door as I drove up. I put away the ice cream and hooked him up to his leash to take him out for a poop. But first, I listened to the messages on the answering machine. The only one of importance was from Phoebe Jo saying, "Mama's mending and Pop's learned how to cook a pot roast. We should be back home tomorrow around lunchtime. Hope everything's okay."

It was one of those late summer afternoons I love so much—the sun bathes the farm in a warm gold light. Without the smoggy haze that usually stifles Clairmont, everything seemed to stand out in sharp focus. The air wasn't as sticky and, for a change, it was actually quite pleasant outside. I decided to take Boo-Kat for a walk in our woods. We had to reclaim our stomping grounds—but I left the responsibility of marking the territory to Boo.

It was tempting to free him from his leash. I didn't feel any eyes on us or hear the crackling sound of a stalker skulking around in the dry underbrush—but my antenna was still up, sweeping the area.

Even though I've complained about being lonely, being alone is very important to me, and I reveled in this hour of rambling around my farm with my dog. Bobby and Paco wouldn't be back until six.

My normal life had been pushed aside by the events of the past two weeks and I felt the need to reconnect with it, if only briefly. Tony would be back at work in the kitchen tomorrow with his new assistant, so I figured I'd better spend some time that evening organizing the catering schedule for the week ahead.

Then there was Mother.

Maybe I'd better call her, our relationship was certainly on the rocks. Her disapproval of the fact I had two single men staying with me in my house was probably one reason she was staying away. She didn't even know what was actually going on here, but that didn't matter as much as what it looked like to the neighbors.

I laughed to myself. My farm is at the end of a private lane and totally surrounded by woods, so even if the neighbors got out their birding binoculars like the sweet, little old lady living next door to Tammy Lloyd, none of them would be able to see us running around naked on my front lawn in broad daylight. So it's not what the neighbors see, it's their imaginations Mother's afraid of.

I was avoiding the major reason for our falling out. Dad.

Seeing Janie Sims and her father that afternoon, sitting side-by-side, acknowledging each other with a touch to the arm and a wink, made me flash back to my relationship with Dad. That's the way I wanted to remember us, and that's why I was so angry at Mother. She was trying to show me the human side of Dad and I didn't want to see it. She was right to call me arrogant. I like to think of myself as a seeker of truth, but when Mother tried to show it to me that afternoon, all I could do was scream and kick like Daddy's little six-year-old princess.

With a sudden feeling of shame, I remembered her statement, "I'm sick of being cast as the villain in this family."

It was time to try and patch things up.

After bringing Boo-Kat back in, I tried reaching Mother, but had to leave a message with Loretta. "Just tell her I called," I said.

All this family angst crap was making me hungry. Bobby and Paco were bound to be hungry, too, so I started marinating some chicken breasts for the grill, made a huge salad, and husked some corn. But all I really wanted was my

231

tub of Rocky Road ice cream.

They came home in high spirits—not because they were drunk, but because one of the waitresses remembered getting hit on by Paco Friday night. We enjoyed our celebratory meal and spent the evening drinking lots of wine and laughing at Paco. He kept trying to impress me with his card tricks, but the cards weren't cooperating. The capper to the evening was Paco asking Boo-Kat to "pick a card—any card." He did, and immediately chewed it up into a soggy wad.

I fell asleep that night, curled up next to Bobby, blissfully unaware that the newspaper deliverer was tossing a bomb onto my driveway.

Monday, August 30

31

THE ENQUIRER'S FRONT PAGE exploded in front of my eyes:
KNOWN GANGSTER
KEEPS OASIS ALIVE
IN NEWPORT!
Under those inch-high headlines was a picture of
"Peppino Giuliani, new CEO of Lloyd & Associates
Commercial Development, Inc.", an artist's sketch of The
Oasis complex, and four columns of copy. Then the real bomb
hit. I screamed. There in the bottom right hand corner was
my picture. The sidebar headline read: *Chili Heiress Chosen As
Oasis Head Chef.*

I didn't learn anything new from the article about Peepo. In fact, I was surprised the media hadn't latched onto him earlier. But the story about me was a different matter altogether—I hadn't even thrown my chef's hat into the ring to be considered for the position.

It was seven-thirty in the morning and, even though I knew Mother wouldn't be up yet, I left my coffee and bagel cooling on the breakfast table and called the Cavanaugh Castle. Her housekeeper's perky voice greeted me.

"I know my mother's not up yet, Loretta, but please do me a big favor. You know those pink post-it notes she's always using? Stick one on the front page of the newspaper, right next to my picture, and in big letters write: *THEY'RE WRONG! CALL KATE!*"

Loretta promised to do it right away.

I hung up, knowing Mother was going to blame me anyway.

It was too early to call Peepo at his office, he probably wouldn't be in until—oh, damn! Tony was going to be driving up the laneway at eight-thirty on the dot, hopefully followed by our new employee, and I'd forgotten to print out the job schedule for the week.

With a sigh, I picked up my bagel and mug and dragged myself into the commercial kitchen. I clicked on the computer and stared into the screen. Oh, what to serve all these hungry people. I constructed my menus with the standard repertoire—didn't have the time to be exotic. But these were regular clients and I didn't want to serve them the *same old, same old*, so I checked their job histories, juggled menu items around and made sure I wasn't repeating myself. But then again, maybe I was wasting mental energy 'cause they'd all be canceling once they read the article.

I printed out the schedule, tacked it on the bulletin board, and made my way to the library. The grandfather clock in the foyer said eight-twenty-five. Time to call Peepo.

As soon as I announced my name to his receptionist, she quickly said, "Oh, yes, of course! Just a moment!"

I was on hold for maybe ten seconds, listening to Mozart, when she came back with, "Mr. Giuliani will be right with you."

I went back to more Mozart. They say listening to his music can make you smarter and think clearer. Well I decided right then and there, since Peepo owed me an explanation, I'd take advantage of my temporary position of power and get his reaction to Alan's death. I knew Peepo's answer would make me either more suspicious of him or less. But only time would tell whether or not it was a smart thing to do.

I'd just conceived my bright idea when my train of thought was abruptly interrupted by Peepo's voice. "Kate? I know why you're calling."

"Peepo, I don't like having my picture in the paper even when the story *is* true."

"I hope you believe me when I say I was misquoted. It's entirely the reporter's mistake."

"Wonderful. I'll tell that to the Board of Crown Chili. How did my name come up at all?"

"The reporter asked if anyone in the local area was going to be involved with The Oasis, and I told him, 'Of course. We are committed to using local talent.' I said we were approaching certain people in the community and you were one of them. I admit I dropped your name, but I certainly didn't say a deal with you was signed, sealed and delivered. I'm sorry, Kate. I don't blame you for being angry. Maybe I can get that reporter fired."

"Yeah, well, I'd settle for a retraction from him in tomorrow's paper."

"Fine."

It sounded like Peepo was ready to ring off, so I just plunged in with, "That was strange news about Alan Casey."

I let that comment hang in the air for a beat and could almost hear Peepo thinking about it.

Finally, he said, "Yes. That was most unfortunate. It's going to make finding Victor's killer a little more difficult. But, as I told you, I surround myself with talented people.

Sorry, Kate, the phones are going crazy around here and I really must go. I'll be talking to you soon."

That didn't clarify anything. So much for my smart idea. I turned Peepo's cryptic comment around in my head, studying it from every angle. All I got was a headache.

I heard the crunch of car tires on the gravel drive outside. Tony was arriving for work, on time as usual. I left the library and headed back to the commercial kitchen.

Bobby was just coming downstairs. "Morning, Kate. Are we going to see anything of you today? Or is it a full day of cooking?"

"I'm sorry, Bobby. You might catch glimpses of me here or there, but it's going to be kind of busy."

He bounded down the stairs and gave me a quick hug. "No problem, I can amuse myself. Paco's pretty well adjusted to the time zone now—he'll stay in bed 'til eleven."

I caught up with Tony at the bulletin board in the kitchen. He raised his eyebrows at me. "Hey, Boss. Saw your high school picture on the front page today. So that's why you've hired me an assistant. You're going off to work for the mob."

"Wrong. Grab a cup of coffee and I'll fill you in."

For the next five minutes, I gave him the condensed version of the story of my connection with Peepo and my newly discovered Uncle Nick. Tony kept pressing me for all the details of my family's dysfunctional relationships. I glossed over most of them, but gave him enough information to prompt him to say, "Shit, Boss, that sounds almost Italian."

I *hmphed*. "Wouldn't know about that, but now, out of the blue, the Cavanaughs have a blood relative that connects us to the glory days of Newport casinos. Mother is not very happy."

Tony took a sip of his coffee, then said, "As my Pop always says, 'you can pick your nose, but you can't pick your relatives.'"

The phone rang and I jumped up to answer it. Caught it in mid-ring. Before I got the receiver to my ear, I heard,

"Kathleen?"

"Good morning, Mother. Hope you got my message."

"Yes, but it doesn't help me feel any better. Just think how this looks to everybody. The damage is done. I tried to call Clifford, but he's in court today. The three of us need to get together and discuss what to do about this."

"About what? We'll get the paper to retract the statement. I mean it's wrong and that's that."

Mother sputtered. "I left a message with Clifford's secretary and as soon as he gets back to me, I'll call you. I want us all to meet here tonight, but I'll call you."

"Okay. 'Bye, Mother."

I heard a car pull up and park outside the kitchen door. "Sounds like your assistant, Tony."

He looked out the door. "Yep. It's Rick. Now get lost, Boss."

I didn't "get lost" right away. Instead, I hung around a few minutes, gave my new employee an official welcome, then pretended to look up something on the computer in order to eavesdrop on Tony's supervisory techniques. I could feel his vibes trying to push me out of the kitchen. Finally, after dawdling in front of the bulletin board, studying the printout of the week's work schedule, I said, "I'll be in the library," and left the kitchen.

Bobby had the TV on in the family kitchen. I shut the library door behind me, so I could have some quiet. After arranging a couple of pillows on the floor, I stretched out and tried to give Bobby's method a second chance.

Watching my breath go in and out soon got boring, and, before long, I was totally engrossed in the details of my telephone conversation with Mother. After a couple of minutes of that, I was totally engrossed in what to serve at the Opera Guild's fund-raising luncheon next month. Then I found myself analyzing the biscuits I had eaten at the Sims' on Sunday afternoon. My brain was brimming with junk.

I went back to concentrating on my breathing. I envisioned the straws. "Talk to me, straws. Tell me how you got so twisted." The straw bows danced around in my head and began to look like plastic pretzels. I imagined a bowlful on the bar at Gable's. I took in a deep breath and followed it back out. So who was the blonde? I squeezed my eyes tight and saw Melissa Oakley tossing the straws into the bowl. My mind stalled and refused to budge. I was pretty sure she wasn't the one, but it seemed I wasn't going to be able to move on until I eliminated her as a suspect.

I popped up off the floor, went to the telephone, and punched in Charlotte Oakley's number. The question I had could have been asked over the phone, but then I wouldn't be able to see the expression on Charlotte's face. I was going to invite myself over. She answered on the third ring.

"Charlotte? Oh good, you're home. I have to talk to you right now."

"Now?" she asked. "What about?"

"The case."

"But I thought that was finished."

"Maybe not. I'll be over in a few minutes."

"Well . . . I was just going to . . ." Charlotte clicked her tongue, "Oh . . . alright."

"Thanks. Be there soon."

I looked down at myself to check my clothing. Yeah, I was clean—no food spots on my shorts or 'Round the World Catering polo shirt. I punched the intercom button on the phone and announced to Tony in the commercial kitchen, "Going out. Be back in about half an hour."

I then poked my head in the family kitchen where Bobby was sitting at the table eating breakfast and watching Jerry Springer—catching up on American culture, I guess.

"I have to go out. Everything alright in here?"

Bobby nodded silently, his mouth full of cereal.

"Be back in half an hour."

CHARLOTTE AND MELISSA LIVED IN a Country French Manor on five lushly wooded acres. It was a low, sprawling, one-and-a-half story with a white-washed stone front and inlaid brick designs over the green-shuttered windows. A pair of wrought iron benches and potted topiaries flanked the brick steps leading up to the front double glass doors.

I pushed the doorbell and heard its *bing bong* bounce around the cavernous foyer with its slate floor and large stone urns. Through the glass panes of the door, I saw Charlotte come out of her living room and primp herself in the hallway mirror before opening the door.

"What's the problem, Kate?"

"Can I come in?"

"Oh, yes, yes, please."

She led me into a living room that did not carry through with a Country French sense of decor. It was just as cold and hard as the foyer. Marble pillars marked the entrance to the room. Everything inside seemed to be made of glass and wrought iron—even the few upholstered pieces still managed to have sharp edges. The main color scheme was gray and cold blue. I suppressed a shiver and sat down on the pointy edge of a sofa.

Not wanting to waste time with too much introductory explanation, but also not wanting to sound blunt or impolite, I said, "Charlotte, I know, as far as you're concerned, my investigation into the Lloyd family was completed. But there have been new developments that have raised more questions in my mind and they concern Eric."

Charlotte's eyes widened. "Oh?"

"But first, I need to know if Melissa has a nervous habit of twisting things, like plastic straws."

"Twisting? What do you mean 'twisting'?"

"Tying them into bows and leaving them sitting around—like in ashtrays."

Charlotte screwed up her face. "Not here at home. I don't know what she does out—she's not a nervous young woman. I brought her up to very sure of herself."

I didn't prod, 'cause I didn't get the chance. At that moment, Melissa herself stormed into the room, aiming her mouth at me. "Who do you think you are, sticking your nose into Eric's life and asking questions about me?" Her angry voice echoed off all the hard surfaces in the room. "Don't you think you've done enough harm with your snooping?"

"*Melissa!*" Charlotte glared at her daughter, then turned to me. "Sorry, Kate. I didn't bring her up to be rude."

"You are not going to destroy my plans to marry Eric Lloyd."

"I asked Kate for her help so I could save you from making that terrible mistake. But you're too obstinate to see the truth of what Kate has uncovered. You're still running around with that sonofagangster, and you never tell me what you're doing. All I can do is imagine the worst and I'm worried sick every minute you're out. Last Friday, I sat up in bed, frantic until I heard you come in. It was three o'clock in the morning—"

"I *told* you. Eric's mother got sick at that party and we had to pick her up and take her home. But then she got sicker, said she couldn't breath, so we took her to the hospital. I was sitting in the Emergency Room with Eric until after two o'clock in the morning."

That took Melissa and Eric off the hook. That also left the blonde's face a blank.

32

I WAS HELPING Tony and Rick carve whales and killer sharks out of cucumbers and zucchini, when Robert Boone stuck his head in the doorway. "I'm back," he said.

"Just you? By yourself?"

"Yep. Phoebe Jo's Pop had a little accident in the kitchen—made her nervous, so she decided she'd better stay.

But I had to get back here to see what was going on with that coyote. Phoebe Jo said she'd call when I was to come and fetch her and Julie Ann."

"I'm glad to have you back. I missed y'all."

I brought him up to date with the critter problem, even admitting I'd blasted his shotgun—he'd find out soon enough.

After lunch, Robert was anxious to get back to the Coyote War and took Paco and Bobby to the Feed 'n Seed to pick up the exploders he'd ordered. Mother finally called back and informed me that the emergency Crown Chili Board meeting was taking place at eight-thirty that evening. I spent the afternoon in the commercial kitchen working on a table centerpiece—making a fruit salad-filled watermelon boat for our sharks and whales to swim around.

Bobby and Paco were really hitting it off with Robert and spent the rest of their afternoon helping him rig up his anti-coyote system.

When they finally came back to the house, I asked Robert, "So when do sections of my woods start blowing up?"

"I'm not going to blow up anything. Not yet. I explained this to you before," he said, calmly. "They work just like the sirens did—on a timer—only these sound like gunshots. They'll start going off tonight after dark. But they're all set at varied times so they should scare him away before he notices a pattern."

"I hope so."

AT EIGHT-FIFTEEN, I climbed into my Jeep Cherokee, bound for Mother's. I didn't bother changing into any kind of business-like attire because this "emergency meeting" was going to be a dressing-down for me anyway. As I pulled out of my laneway, I pushed in Bonnie Raitt's CD. Her music was what I needed to get into my don't-mess-with-me-I'm-a-big-girl mode.

On my way down the hill from my farm, I noticed a car

behind me taking the curves very carefully—obviously someone from out of the neighborhood, since the rest of us locals could maneuver the turns at forty-five miles per hour blindfolded. At the bottom of the hill, I had to stop and wait for a line of traffic to pass before I could turn onto the main road. In my rearview mirror, I watched the car behind me creep along the straightaway, as if the driver had pegged me as some reckless maniac and was giving me lots of room. I turned into the traffic, muttering, "Jeez! Talk about your defensive driving."

AT EIGHT-THIRTY on the dot, I walked in the front door of the Cavanaugh Castle. Mother and Uncle Cliff were waiting for me in the hunting lodge-like gathering room, seated in the matching over-sized leather armchairs. It was such a masculine room and I'd often wondered why Mother didn't redecorate it after Dad died, but now it kind of made sense. She was using the imposing stone, leather, and dark wood decor of the room as a prop. I wouldn't put it past her to intentionally hold our meeting in this room, instead of in her flowery English sitting room, for the very purpose of reinforcing her position as Head of the Cavanaugh Clan, Chairwoman of the Board, Queen of the Universe, and Ruler of My Life.

I bent down and kissed both Mother and Uncle Cliff on their cheeks, then sat cross-legged between them on the floor next to the coffee table, and began nibbling on a bonbon from the bottomless bowl of chocolates Mother always kept there.

"So," I asked, "what's up?"

Uncle Cliff began with, "Are you committed to Crown Chili?"

I was a little taken aback by the abrupt opening question. "What do you mean?"

"Exactly that. How important is the family business to you?"

"I'm very proud of what Grandpa Cavanaugh and Dad

were able to do in building the company—if that's what you mean."

"No. We're asking 'What does it mean to you?' Are *you* proud to be part of it?"

"As a family accomplishment? Yeah, sure. But I get more of a sense of personal accomplishment from my own business. What are you two leading up to?"

"We're . . . " Uncle Cliff cleared his throat, "we're concerned about the kind of publicity you've been getting lately. It affects Crown Chili's image, you know."

"I can't help it if the media is getting their facts wrong."

"But it's your behavior that's attracting their attention. You really need to consider the kind of people you're seen with. Remember, every time one of us goes out in public, we're being watched."

I was shocked—those were Mother's words coming out of Uncle Cliff. How dare she use him as her mouthpiece. I turned and glared at Mother, silently accusing her.

Uncle Cliff pulled my attention back to him with, "Any hint of shady business associations can affect the bottom line of a family-oriented business like Crown Chili—"

"But I told Mother I would make sure they printed a retraction. Wait a minute. Uncle Cliff, you were just as insistent we go to Victor Lloyd's unveiling on his riverboat as I was."

"That's not associating with him, that's just being smart and paying attention to what's going on in the city. I didn't go and have lunch with Peppino Giuliani in a popular downtown restaurant, at the very height of the weekday lunch hour."

My blood pressure was rising—it was all I could do to control myself. "I'm glad I did, otherwise I would never have found out my father had a brother. Does *Uncle Nick* come under the heading 'shady associate'? Am I suppose to pretend he never existed—just like you have?"

"Well, that's not all, Kathleen." Mother tilted her chin at her brother as though prodding him to go on.

Uncle Cliff shifted his body around in his chair, suddenly looking very uncomfortable. "We're also concerned about the friends you have coming and staying at your farm."

I frowned at him—I couldn't believe what I was hearing.

"They seem to have a habit of getting into trouble around here, and that also draws unwanted attention to the family."

"What?!" I jumped to my feet and shot my uncle with a fierce stare. "Look who's talking! Two very public, very messy divorces! Running around town showing off female trophies less than half your age! In other words, it's okay for you but not for me. As a man, your escapades can drag Crown Chili's name through the mud and the only reaction is 'boys will be boys.' But God forbid *I* should so much as splatter a little sauce on it, and you're afraid public outrage will rise up like a tidal wave out of the Ohio River and wipe the Cavanaugh Empire off the face of the earth!"

Uncle Cliff's face turned red. He looked past me towards Mother. "She's got a point there, Tink."

"Clifford! This is one of my daughter's favorite ploys. She turns every discussion we have into some melodrama, tries to make me look stupid, then stomps out. Kathleen, please sit down. We have serious matters to discuss here."

"I'm being serious."

"Good. Well, answer this, dear. At some point, you're going to have to run Crown Chili. Are you committed to taking over those responsibilities?"

I felt the sides of a box going up around me. "I'm not ready to answer that question."

"You better get ready. We need an answer soon so that we, Clifford and I, can plan the company's future. Since you're not occupied with raising a family, and it looks like you never will be—"

"Oh, I see. Being occupied with my own business doesn't count. Anyway, the two of you have years before you need to think of stepping down."

Uncle Cliff said, "It's a gradual process, K.C. If you're going to take over, you'll need to start playing a more active role now. This is the time to make your decision. I don't mean this very minute—but soon."

The air was getting stuffy. I felt their expectations pressing in on me—the whole house was pressing in on me. I just stared at Mother and Uncle Cliff. They sure wanted to close the lid on the box, but they'd need my cooperation to nail it shut.

33

THERE WASN'T MUCH MORE to be said, except "Good night."

I didn't drive as fast as I normally do through the dark, quiet streets of Clairmont. Depression had taken hold of me and I felt too weighed down to move very fast. It's not that I wasn't expecting to come to this crossroad—being the only Cavanaugh child, it was always assumed I'd take over Crown Chili. Over the years, I'd given it a lot of thought, but still, I wasn't prepared for this night's confrontation. It didn't help that Mother and Uncle Cliff, of all people, pressured me with obligations to the family name, double standards, and the need to conform in order for the Crown Chili tribal mask to fit snugly. It just repelled me. I wondered if it was that same pressure that drove Uncle Nick away. I really didn't know what to do.

As I began winding my way up the hill towards my farm, Uncle Cliff's statement—"every time one of us goes out in public, we're being watched"—came to mind. I hate that. As a gawky adolescent bean-pole-on-stilts, I was always subjected to stares and hoped that once I became an adult things would change. They didn't. And I just kept getting taller. But now because I'm a single, wealthy woman, they don't just stare, they watch. And it wasn't just the public that was watching my every move—I was constantly being scrutinized and judged by my own family. It was like living my life in a spotlight. I squinted as the reflection of someone's high beams in my rearview mirror hit my eyes. I reached over and flipped up the mirror to cut down the glare.

That's why I built Trail's End Farm—to get away from the glare.

I pulled into my laneway and heard the car behind me continue past.

Now, even the privacy of my sanctuary was not enough to protect me from watching eyes. Damn coyote.

My farmhouse glowed like a welcoming light at the end of the laneway. I parked around the side of the house, got out, and stood in the full moon light for a few moments, listening to the sounds coming from the open windows of the Great Room in the back. Robert, Paco, and Bobby were playing guitars and piano and singing an old tune from The Band. When they got to the chorus, they sang at the tops of their voices:

"the night they drove old Dixie down . . . "

Didn't sound half bad.

They were having fun, but I couldn't join them. I was so filled with a confusing mix of depression and anger that if I'd walked into that room, the vile vibes emanating from me would contaminate the moment for them.

I opened the front door. Boo-Kat was there waiting for me. He licked my hand and sniffed around my ankles, then followed me through the foyer and down the hallway to the gym. It felt like I was sneaking around in my own house—but no one needed to know I was home just yet.

Inside the gym, I flicked on the overhead fluorescent lights. Boo-Kat ran to a basketball that was beside the Soloflex machine and began pushing it with his nose around the parquet floor, playing doggie soccer. I have no idea how he keeps score. The soles of my sneakers squeaked as I walked over to another basketball. I picked it up and dribbled it over to the half-court.

Bobby has his method of dealing with stressful problems, and I have mine. His consists of getting into a relaxed position, controlling the breath, and repeating a mantra to clear the brain of mind clutter. For me, practicing my foul shooting was the way to access that Zone. Get comfortable at the line, focus on the hoop, clear the mind of everything else, get into a rhythm. Bounce the ball several times, focus on the basket, shoot. "Yes! Two points." Bounce. Focus. Shoot. "Yes!" Bounce. Focus. Shoot. "Yes!"

Alright, so basically they're the same methods.

After a few minutes of this activity, Boo-Kat was tuckered out from winning the World Cup of Soccer, and I was deep into the Zone, my brain completely empty of the crap that had been stuffed into it during the previous hour. This blank state of mind was enjoyable while it lasted. But nature abhors a vacuum and the first thing to come rushing back in was The Case of the Carved Photographer, filling up every nook and cranny of my brain with bits of remembered conversation, twisted straws, and shouts of "Man overboard!"

It was as though my mind needed to work out all the problems I was facing and started on the one that seemed most workable.

Beginning with the premise that Alan was killed because he saw who caused Victor Lloyd's death, the question remained: "Why didn't Alan tell the police that night who did it?" None of Victor's family members believed he fell overboard, as Alan claimed, and I knew from past experience not to trust anything that sleazeball said.

The only possible answer was that Alan was benefiting from what he had seen happen. Alan was hired to photograph and document the evening's festivities, and a professional photographer's first instinct is to point a camera and click.

Initially, I thought Alan pushed Victor overboard, but now, I theorized that during that span of time between the first shout I heard and Alan's call for help, Alan could have been photographing the killer and making a split-second decision to become a blackmailer. It would've been very easy for him to pocket that roll of film before handing all the others over to the police as Peepo had ordered him to.

I made a slow circle around the gym, dribbling the basketball as I walked and thought.

The last time I saw Alan alive was at the Yankovitchs' Casablanca party, and the only conversation we'd had was brief and insignificant. I complimented him on his panama hat, to which he said, "Thanks. Bought it today just for this. Says 'Casablanca', don't you think?"

It was brief, but now not so insignificant. If Alan had just bought his hat that day, how could Janie Sims have seen him wearing it on the riverboat a whole week before? It was Victor Lloyd who was wearing a panama hat that night and nobody would get those two confused. So Janie *had* to have seen Alan the night he was murdered.

Okay, now let's try to make sense of why black-haired Janie Sims, a member of the United States Marine Corps, would put on a long blond wig and short black dress, and somehow track Alan to a bar, pick him up, and kill him.

Back up to the riverboat party. Why were the Sims there? Donald had to have had some kind of relationship with Victor to be on the guest list. Was he Victor's banker? I don't think Donald's little suburban bank had the capacity to service Lloyd & Associates Commercial Development, Inc. Was Donald Sims a high-powered businessman with lots of capital to invest? It didn't look like he had money to burn, especially with his bleak, jobless future. No, Donald was acting more like an investor who'd been burned.

Boo-Kat's whimpers interrupted my train of thought. He was circling around in front of the door—his way of saying, "I gotta go!"

"Okay, okay." I took one last shot at the hoop and missed. We hurried out of the gym. As we passed the Great Room, I realized there'd been a break in the music, so I decided to poke my head in and announce I was home.

"Kate!" Everybody said at once.

"Hi, all. Just going to take Boo out. Be back in a few

minutes."

Paco immediately launched into a rowdy Hank Williams song:

> *"Hey, Heeey, good lookin',*
> *whaaaatch'a got cookin'?*
> *Howzabout cookin' somethin' up with*
> *meeee?"*

In the kitchen, I hooked Boo-Kat up to his leash and opened the back door. He shot out with such force, he tore the leash right out of my hand.

"Boo-Kat!" I shouted. "Here!" He played deaf and streaked across the lawn towards the woods, the plastic Flexileash grip bouncing behind him. I hoped it would get him hung up on a bush before he got too far into the woods. He must've smelled the coyote. I grabbed my walking stick and shouted over my shoulder, "Boo's loose!" and chased out after him.

The moon was so bright it was easy to see where he disappeared into the woods. As I ran across the lawn, the music in the Great Room continued just as loud and rowdy as before, so I knew no one had heard my shout. But there was no time to waste, I didn't want to lose track of Boo.

Even though he'd entered the woods where we usually started our walks, he didn't stick to the path. I plunged in after him. The moonlight was still filtering through the trees, but the foliage was so thick it allowed only thin, penlight beams to hit here and there on the ground. I couldn't take the path at full speed but, just like the road coming up to the farm, I knew the turns and twists well enough to maneuver them in the patchy light.

My dog wasn't in my sights anymore.

"Boo-Kat, come here!" I shouted over and over at the top of my lungs. I could hear him charging through the underbrush. He'd been waiting two weeks for this showdown. My attempts to call him away from his prey were a waste of breath.

The closest Boo had gotten to the coyote was down by the creek bed and it seemed he was going in that direction, so I stayed on the path, expecting to meet him there.

In contrast to the woods, the creek bed was bathed in the bluish light of the full moon. At this time of year it's always dry, but the terrain is rough and rocky, making it difficult to move quickly without falling. Boo-Kat had moved so far ahead of me, I could no longer hear the progress of his pathfinding. I stopped at the edge of the creek bed and listened. Maybe without the noise my own feet were making, cracking twigs and scattering stones, I'd be able to hear even a faint, far-off rustling in the woods that would tell me where he was. All I heard was the sound of crickets and frogs calling their mates.

Up until losing him, the sounds of his movements were always to my right, so I headed in that direction, upstream, stopping every now and then to listen. A slight breeze kicked up, making the tops of the trees bend. Their branches made loud swishing sounds and I silently cursed, demanding them to stop. A moment later, the breeze subsided. I tuned my ears again to the dense underbrush. Nothing.

Where the hell was he? I started thinking I'd made the wrong assumption and that Boo-Kat's nose had taken him in a different direction. I was growing panicky with the fear that the longer he was out here trailing the scent of the coyote, the more likely it was he'd run into the invader.

I heard the snapping of a twig in the distance, followed by the rustling of leaves. Was it my dog or the coyote?

Cautiously, I moved towards the sound, holding my walking stick up in front of me, ready to defend, attack—whatever.

About twenty feet ahead, I saw the top of a bush shake. A small creature broke through the foliage, the silver-grey fur on his back almost glowing in the moonlight. He sniffed the ground excitedly.

"Boo-Kat! Here!"

My dog quickly turned and looked at me. He was panting heavily, but smiling, too—his mouth wide open and tongue hanging almost to the ground.

"Come here!" I shouted.

Ignoring me, Boo-Kat went back to sniffing the ground. He froze for an instant. He'd picked up a new scent trail. Recharged, he dashed up the creek bed away from me, wagging his stubby tail like an out of control metronome. He was heading back towards the house. I ran after him as fast as I could, catching myself as I stumbled on the stones. Nose to the ground, Boo-Kat darted to the right, up an embankment and back into the woods.

I got to the spot where he'd been sniffing and started scrambling up the embankment after him. Dry twigs and thorny branches slapped at my bare arms and legs as I pushed through, leaving dozens of scratches that began to bleed. The brush had been trampled by something bigger than a coyote or a dog, and it was this new path that Boo-Kat was following.

We were in the middle of dense woods and his Flexi-leash *still* hadn't caught on anything, but I was closing the distance between us. The rustling sound of Boo-Kat's push through the tangle of underbrush was getting louder. So was the music. We couldn't have been more than two or three hundred yards from the house. I picked up my pace, ready to lunge for his leash as soon as I saw it.

I tripped over a branch and landed on my face. I was picking myself up and spitting out a mouthful of dirt when I heard a growl so vicious and bloodthirsty I couldn't believe it came out of my dog. Maybe it was the coyote.

More growling, followed by a series of barks I recognized as Boo-Kat's threats.

I picked up my walking stick and rushed towards the barking.

The barking switched to a sudden high-pitched yelp of pain.

My weapon at the ready, I broke into a small clearing.

There was the predator crouching in the underbrush.

Cold eyes already claimed me as her next victim.

It wasn't the coyote.

Even in the dark and with her face smudged with black, I

251

knew it was Janie Sims.

Boo-Kat was lying on his side, whimpering. Blood oozed from a gash across his shoulder and back.

I shouted, "What have you done to my dog? What the hell are you doing here?"

As Janie, dressed in dark clothing, straightened up, she moved through a patch of moonlight. I saw the glint of metal. She had a huge hunting knife clenched in her hand. I imagined what she looked like wearing a long, blond wig.

Janie's eyes locked onto me. She raised her blade and took a step forward.

Boo-Kat growled, his fangs bared in a vicious, yellow grin and tried to lunge at her leg. That got Janie's full attention.

I instinctively jabbed my walking stick at her chest—knocking her back—then a quick upwards swing, trying to hit her arm to knock the knife out of her hand. Missed.

Janie recovered, then cocked her head, silently acknowledging the fact I wasn't going to just let her walk up to me and slit my throat. She assumed a fighting position—knees bent, knife out and ready to slash.

Boo-Kat continued growling.

I had to keep Janie away from me—stall for time until I saw a way of escaping. But I couldn't abandon my pet.

I was big and had a long, heavy stick, yet I knew I was no match for a Marine trained in knife combat. The music from the house, sounding so close just a couple of minutes ago, might as well have been on the other side of the world. I asked, "What do you want?"

Janie took a step forward. "I was just going to watch you—didn't expect to get my opportunity tonight."

I stepped backwards. "Opportunity for what?"

"You were getting too close."

We moved around in a circle. I stayed on the balls of my feet to move quickly and had my five-foot-long walking stick extended out at the ready. "Too close for what?"

"Don't play dumb. You were smart enough to pick up on the straws. I screwed up when you came over. Soon as I

252

mentioned that scumbag Alan's hat, I knew you'd be on to me—should've kept my mouth shut."

Janie started to lunge towards me with her knife out.

A sound like a gunshot rang out in the night air, startling both of us into looking in the direction of the noise. Someone was shooting?

Two more sharp, firecracker-like *pop*s.

I remembered Robert's exploders and quickly recovered.

I thrust my walking stick's elephant head deep into Janie's throat and sent her reeling backwards. She slammed against a tree and staggered back towards me, gasping for air, then cursed.

More exploders went off at different points around the farm. *Pop!Pop!Pop!* This time neither one of us was startled.

The Marine let out a primal yell, as she lunged once again at me.

I swung my stick with all my might.

Janie stumbled.

I missed. The elephant head barely grazed the side of her head.

She crumpled to the ground, her knife falling from her hand.

What the hell—? I didn't hit her *that* hard.

Janie had fallen into one of the shafts of moonlight shining through the foliage above and I could see a dark liquid forming a stain on her shirt in the middle of her chest.

I was stunned. Turning quickly, I scanned the dark woods, first in one direction, then in another. Something moved about ten yards to my left. Gliding away from me in the direction of the creek bed was the figure of a large, hulking man. Within seconds, he disappeared into the darkness.

I had to get Boo-Kat back to the house. I ran to where he lay and heard him whimpering. I dropped my stick and gathered him up in my arms. God, he was losing a lot of blood.

I ran to the house, leaving the bitch to fend for herself.

IT MUST HAVE BEEN a shocking sight—me standing in the doorway of the Great Room, scratched and muddy, holding my bleeding dog in my arms. But then everything got real orderly after the initial shock wore off. The police and the vet were called. Wounds were cleaned and bound up. Robert deputized Paco and marched out to the woods with his shotgun to make sure Janie stayed put.

The police showed up immediately and, while Bobby waited with Boo-Kat for the vet, I led Matt Skinner, three other Clairmont Rangers, and the two paramedics to the spot where I'd left Janie Sims. We found a bloody trail and Robert and Paco fifty yards deeper into the woods. The two of them were staring down at the Marine.

Robert said, "She's a tough one, but she's not going anywhere now." He pointed back down the bloody trail. "She dragged herself all the way here, trying to get away."

The paramedics quickly went to work on Janie. Apparently, she still had some life in her.

"Who shot her?" Skinner asked, nodding at the shotgun Robert was holding.

Robert shrugged. "I don't know."

Everyone turned and stared at me.

"Kate?" Skinner said.

In my mind, I watched again the hulking figure of a man slipping into the darkness. "I don't know."

34

JANIE SIMS DIED A few hours later that Monday night without ever regaining consciousness. Boo-Kat fared much better and was stitched up and convalescing at home.

My farm was searched for the gun that was used to shoot Janie, but nothing turned up. They did find a car registered to Gloria Sims parked on the outskirts of the property. It was the same car that crept behind me down the hill, earlier that evening. The Clairmont Ranger Evidence Team descended on it with their dusting powders and vacuum cleaners, looking for fingerprints, threads, hairs, blood samples—anything that might help solve one of the two killings of the past week and a half. They also found another set of fresh tire prints a few hundred feet from the Sims car.

Ranger Matt Skinner and Detectives Reese and Robinson were forced to take me seriously. As a result of my linking Janie to Alan's murder and my theory connecting Alan to Victor's so-called "accident", the Clairmont and Newport police departments got a court order to open Alan's safety deposit box in his bank in Montgomery. In it were photographs and negatives showing Donald Sims pushing Victor Lloyd overboard. Pretty stupid of Janie to kill Alan before getting hold of them.

Donald Sims was arrested within hours of the discovery.

THURSDAY AFTERNOON, Bobby, Paco, and I were lounging in the backyard in a shady spot under the big maple tree. I heard a car coming up the laneway and went out in front to see who it was.

A dark blue Lincoln Town Car with tinted windows, bringing me an unannounced visitor, parked next to my Jeep. I'd seen that car before, too—down the street from the Sims' house.

The driver's side door opened and out stepped Sammy, in dark glasses. He acknowledged me with a nod of his head and opened one of the rear passenger doors. Peepo Giuliani got out carrying a shiny red paper gift bag.

I walked towards him, extending my hand. Peepo took me by the shoulders and surprised me with a kiss on each cheek.

He said, "I'm very happy to see you're well."

I invited both of them in, but Sammy declined, saying he'd stand outside and wait.

In the library, Peepo asked, "Did you happen to read the

255

article on the front page of today's *Enquirer?*"

I assumed he was talking about the news that the Governor of Kentucky had sent a letter to state legislators proposing a discussion about building a dozen or more casinos in Kentucky. I answered, "Yes. I guess that's potentially good news for The Oasis."

"Very much so. I hope you will still consider my offer. But that wasn't my reason for coming here, today. I heard you've been having problems here for a while—predators invading your farm. I trust the situation has been taken care of."

"Well, the *coyote's* still out there, but I think I owe my life to you."

"No you don't."

"Alright. Indirectly then. As you told me once before, you have some very talented people in your employ."

"Yes. Take Sammy for example. He's a very good tracker. He can even follow the trail of a rat from the deck of a riverboat and through the streets of Cincinnati."

I pictured a pair of beady, close-set eyes. "Did that trail lead from a card game, to a bar, and back down to the river?"

Peepo smiled at me. Then he handed me the paper gift bag. "I brought you some things I've been holding onto for years. I want you to have them."

I pulled out an old, twenty-five cent paperback book. Its cover was creased and torn in one corner, its pages yellowed. I read, "*LITTLE MEXICO.*" The colorful artwork under the title showed a tough-looking guy shooting a gun while hanging onto a half-dressed blonde who was screaming her head off. At the bottom of the cover I read the author's name, "Nick Cavanaugh." My heart jumped. I looked at Peepo. "My Uncle Nick wrote this?"

He nodded. "Yes, and a lot of others. He had a series for a while."

"But I've never heard of them."

"They've been out of print for a long time. The books sold reasonably well during the fifties, but he didn't have a big

256

audience." Peepo nodded in the direction of the bag. "There's more."

I reached in and pulled out a dark wood pipe with a chewed mouthpiece. It had a straight stem and cracked bowl that still had a crust of burnt tobacco in it.

Peepo said, "It's one of his rosewoods. He left that one behind when he disappeared."

"Disappeared? You mean you don't know what happened to him—whether he's dead or alive?"

Peepo shook his head. "I tried for years to find him."

Why was I surprised? I already knew my Uncle Nick suffered from the Cavanaugh wanderlust. The last item in the bag was a black and white photograph with a white, scalloped border. Two young men dressed in tuxedos and standing next to a large, winding staircase smiled back at me. One was Peepo with dark hair. The other had lighter colored hair—maybe blond—and was very tall.

On his face, I saw my Dad's lopsided grin.

ON SUNDAY EVENING, Robert, Paco, Bobby, and I were sitting outside on the deck of Dickie's Sports Bar & Grill. It was closed for the night and was jammed with hundreds of Dick Rottingham's "closest friends", all sipping vodka martinis and waiting for the show to begin. Well, Robert wasn't drinking alcohol—but he couldn't get any higher than he was. Since Phoebe Jo and Julie Ann were still takin' care of Mama and Pop, there was nothing keeping him from accepting the controversial radio talk show host's invitation to watch the world famous Rozzi family shoot off their annual WEBN End of Summer Extravaganza from "the best seat in town," as Dick himself boasted.

Over half a million spectators lined both banks of the Ohio River. The river itself was clogged with hundreds of boats of all sizes. Everybody was hooting and hollering and tooting their boat horns, which made it difficult for me to hear what Dick was jabbering on about, even though he was shouting right into my ear.

Dick was really hung up on the Donald Sims story. You'd think he'd have exhausted that topic by now—it was all he'd talked about on his radio show the past four days.

"Kate, mid-life is a dangerous time for men like Donald. You can't be trusted to make good decisions. You make desperate moves. Now, see? Donald left his poor wife destitute, investing everything he had into Victor Lloyd's condo project—thought it was his last chance to make big bucks. But some men just gotta face facts. It just ain't gonna get any better, so you might as well go and buy that red sports car and have an affair with some young babe."

I turned to Dick. "Do you say this stuff just to shock people or do you really believe what you—" Before I could finish my question, a heavily-miked voice boomed out from a barge in the middle of the river, over the racket of crowd noise, and welcomed everyone to the show with, "Are you ready?"

I bet the decibel level of the cheer that answered could have been heard by the man in the moon. The announcer led everyone through the traditional shouting match between the Ohio and Kentucky sides of the river. I think Kentucky won.

The show opened with a classic Led Zeppelin tune at an ear-splitting volume. Everyone screamed as the first shots were fired and the sky lit up with flower-bursts of bright green and red.

The heavens were assaulted by rockets trailing plumes of red, white, and blue smoke. Showers of gold sparkles rained down into the water. As I watched, I was filled with an unexpected anxiety. This was a dangerous time for me, too. I certainly had big decisions to make and they were all intertwined with unresolved emotional issues. Looking down at the river, I tried to pick out Uncle Cliff's boat. I assumed Mother would be on board, but I wasn't sure—we weren't on speaking terms. What was I going to do about her? About Crown Chili? What about my own business?

I envied Bobby and Paco their free and easy lifestyle. But it was rootless—not for me.

I didn't regret anything that had happened between Bobby and me, but his leaving was going to be hard. I was going to miss him, even though I knew we were going down different roads and were too independent to make any kind of life together. Besides, nobody could come between him and his brother—they were paired for life.

I stole a look at Bobby and saw a bright pink burst of light reflected on his upturned face. Everyone around me "oohed!" and "aahed!"

I suddenly realized I was facing a different kind of danger. My preoccupation with worries about the future was killing the time I had in my hand. I was missing the good stuff.

I quickly turned and looked up at the sky just as it erupted into an enormous pyrotechnic mosaic of exploding rockets, flaming spirals, and thousands of gold and silver man-made stars.

It was beautiful.

ABOUT THE AUTHOR

CATHIE JOHN is the wife/husband writing team of Cathie and John Celestri.
They live in Loveland, Ohio with their Welsh Terrier.